Murder

Helen Cox is a Yorkshire-born novelist and poet. After completing her MA in creative writing at the York St John University, Helen wrote for a range of publications, edited her own independent film magazine and penned three non-fiction books. Helen currently lives by the sea in Sunderland, where she writes poetry, romance novellas, the Kitt Hartley Yorkshire Mystery Series and hosts The Poetry-gram podcast.

Helen's *Mastermind* specialism would be *Grease 2* and to this day she adheres to the Pink Lady pledge. More information about Helen can be found on her website: helencoxbooks.com, or on Twitter: @Helenography.

Also by Helen Cox

Murder by the Minster
A Body in the Bookshop
Murder on the Moorland
Death Awaits in Durham
A Witch Hunt in Whitby
A Body by the Lighthouse

HELEN COX

Murder in a Mill Town

QUERCUS

First published in Great Britain in 2022
This paperback edition published in 2023

QUERCUS

Quercus Editions Ltd
Carmelite House
50 Victoria Embankment
London EC4Y 0DZ

An Hachette UK company

A CIP catalogue record for this book is available
from the British Library

PB ISBN 978 1 52942 150 7
EB ISBN 978 1 52942 151 4

10 9 8 7 6 5 4 3 2 1

Typeset by CC Book Production

Printed and bound in Great Britain by Clays Ltd, Elcograf S.p.A.

Papers used by Quercus are from well-managed forests and other responsible sources.

For Janet, who will be lovingly remembered.

CHAPTER ONE

'Did you hear about the murder that happened out towards Hebden Bridge?' Detective Sergeant Charlotte Banks said, to the last person in the world she ever thought she'd be asking for help.

Well, perhaps second to last.

There was a pause before Kitt Hartley responded. She was sitting in an armchair in the third-floor office of the Vale of York University Library in her usual navy skirt suit, drinking a cup of tea. Banks spent very little time in libraries due to her horrendous working hours. But on the few occasions she'd had cause to step inside this particular library, even she, a straight-talking detective sergeant with very little time to get lost in the world of books, had been swept away by the quiet wonder of the place.

Though of course she had visited the odd bookshop or library here and there, Banks was convinced she had never seen quite so many volumes under one roof. Then there were the dreamy murals painted on the ceiling, many of which seemed to depict mythological figures. Banks wasn't too sure which mythological figures exactly; she left that kind of thing to the academics. But there was no doubting that the paintings themselves were entrancing, whether you really understood what you were looking at or not. There were a hundred other tiny little touches to this rather unique building that set it apart from any other venue you might visit. From its ornate architraves to its mosaic floor, the architect had thought very carefully indeed about every surface, lighting fixture and doorknob.

Perhaps it wasn't so surprising then that Kitt, who had taken up private investigation and thus often found herself in alarming situations, quite liked to hide out here two days a week during her part-time shifts.

At Banks's mention of the recent murder in West Yorkshire, Kitt hesitated on the next sip of her drink and offered Banks a little nod. 'Happened last Wednesday, didn't it? In Andaby? Hard to miss a headline like that one. Crushed by a steel yarn tub at an industrial museum. I can barely stand to think about it. The very idea makes me wince. From what I read, the victim was a manager at the museum. That poor woman. Who would even do a thing like that, I ask you?'

Banks, who was standing next to an oak table at the centre of the room, swallowed hard at the thought of someone toppling one of those hefty metal canisters, once used to hold the yarn in the old textiles mill, onto a body.

After almost a decade in the police force, Banks had seen all kinds of physical cruelty but nothing quite so strangely brutal as that. 'It's not exactly your average act of violence, I'll grant you. Whoever found the body will probably have had the shock of their life,' she said.

Kitt placed her teacup on a nearby stack of books. Though this space was for staff only, you'd only guess that by the sign on the door. Besides a couple of beaten-up armchairs that looked like they might have been purchased early in the last century, every surface in the room was stacked with books on all kinds of subjects. Kitt oversaw the Women's Studies section but it seemed this office was a dumping ground for any spare book in the whole library.

Still, at least it smelled better than the staff room back at the nick. According to Banks's superior, Detective Inspector Malcolm Halloran, who was romantically involved with the librarian-turned-sleuth, she was partial to a particular type of tea that kept the atmosphere here laced with citrus. It was certainly better than the smell of overcooked coffee and stale vending machine sandwiches Banks had become accustomed to at her place of work.

'You can say that again,' said Kitt refocusing Banks's attention on the morbid matter she'd come here to discuss. 'Very sinister indeed. I've worked some odd cases in my time but this takes the biscuit . . . Oh, on that note, Custard Cream?'

Kitt waved a biscuit tin in Banks's direction but she declined the offer.

'At first I wondered how the investigating officers had ruled out a terrible accident,' said Kitt, while helping herself to a biscuit to dip in her tea. 'But apparently there were enough questions raised at the scene for the police to classify it as a murder.'

'Yeah,' said Banks, tucking her thumbs into the pockets on her jeans. 'You have to be certain about the evidence in front of you to classify a case as a murder.'

'Oh, I know. From everything Mal's told me about the investigations you run, I know it's not a decision made lightly. Obviously, there wasn't enough information in the papers for me to discern exactly what factors suggested foul play. Something like that happening, well it's bad enough when it's an accident. But the idea that somebody did it deliberately, doesn't bear thinking about really, does it? Are you investigating the incident? I would have thought Andaby was a bit too far west for your team.'

Banks went to answer but, as was sometimes her custom, Kitt didn't pause for breath.

'And besides anything else, aren't you off work soon for the wedding of the year, and the honeymoon of a lifetime? I must admit when you first came to see me at the front desk, I thought you might want to talk about something wedding-related, rather than police business. Especially since you're out of uniform.'

It was then that Kitt paused, offering Banks a way back into the conversation. Now that she had an in however,

Banks found herself wondering precisely what to say. How to talk about that one thing she so often went out of her way not to talk about.

Taking in a long, slow breath she ruminated on the best way to explain herself. Why she was here, in the back offices of the local university library at eight o'clock on a Saturday night. The blind fear she was trying to square up to just now however, scrambled every thought in her head. She wasn't even able to offer a measured smile acknowledging Kitt's reference to the fact that she and Evie were due to get married just two weeks from now.

Banks had agreed an unpaid three-month career break with her superior officer, Chief Superintendent Ricci, so that she and Evie could hit all seven continents on their honeymoon. That's what she should be focusing on right now: marrying the woman she loved beneath the blessing of the May sunshine. The lead up to their wedding was supposed to be amongst the happiest times of her life. Instead, the last forty-eight hours had been a harrowing blur punctuated with sleeplessness and dread. 'We're not officially investigating that case, no,' Banks at last heard herself say. 'And yes, tomorrow's my last day on shift before the wedding.'

Kitt pushed a strand of long red hair out of her face and offered Banks a polite little smile. She was seemingly searching Banks's face for some clue, before speaking again. 'I've always admired your sparing and cogent use of the English language, Charley. And I consider myself a sensitive reader of people as well as books. But if there's something important you want me to take away from this conversation, I'm afraid you're going to have to give me a little bit more of a hint. Is there an element of the murder in Andaby, or the investigation of it, that's troubling you? And if so, might it not be best to talk to Mal about it?'

There was no missing the confusion in Kitt's voice and Banks couldn't blame her for that. People had difficulty reading Banks all the time. Her deep brown eyes were powerful when staring down suspects in the interrogation room but gave little away to those who knew her. Since she and DI Halloran had walked in to this very library some six years ago now, she and Kitt had had very little to do with each other. This might not have been so strange if Kitt and Halloran hadn't started dating. And if Banks wasn't due to marry Kitt's best friend. She and Kitt had, by proxy, shared a good many experiences, from joy right through to despair. But the two had always kept a courteous and respectful distance. In part Banks had deliberately remained aloof. Kitt may have training in private investigation but such skills weren't officially recognized by the force. Consequently, Banks was convinced that at some point the meddling Kitt did in official police cases was going to end in someone getting fired. Keeping a safe distance was merely a simple and prudent measure to make sure that that someone wouldn't be her.

With all this in mind, Kitt must be wondering why, of all

people, Banks was spewing details of a case she wasn't even investigating to a woman she spent little time communicating with? She didn't yet know that Banks's whole world was quite possibly on the brink of crashing down around her ears.

'My brother, Ewan, he lives in Andaby. He has done for almost three months now,' Banks said. Unable to find any other way in to what she had to say. She had been trying to avoid this very situation for as long as she could remember. Yet for all her striving, here she was unable to outrun the shadow cast by her older sibling just over twenty years ago.

'Is that so?' Kitt said with a shake of her head. 'I wasn't aware you had a brother. Sorry I missed that detail. I consider myself quite a good listener but I'm fairly sure Evie has never said anything about him.'

'No, it's not your fault. I never mention him,' Banks could hear the snap in her tone and took a deep breath. She knew that her Glaswegian accent often made her voice sound a little harsher to some folk than she meant it to. Sometimes, being a copper, that worked in her favour and commanded a certain degree of respect from criminals to whom respect didn't come particularly naturally. But this was much more than an edge to her consonants. She could practically hear herself seething.

'And, you're worried for Ewan's safety? You want me and Grace to do security detail on him? Make sure whoever's responsible for the murder isn't for some reason coming after him? He must be quite unnerved after an incident like that happening on his own doorstep. Of course, we'll be very happy to help in any way that we can.'

'I can see why your mind went there,' Banks said, wishing that was why she needed to engage the services of Hartley and Edwards Investigations – as a little sister concerned for her elder brother's welfare. That's what somebody in a normal family would do. Somebody who shared love rather than deep suspicion and distrust with their blood relatives. Banks knew objectively that her brother had loved her and that she had once loved him back. But those days didn't even amount to a solid memory any more. Any admiration for him had completely disintegrated. 'Like I say,' Banks continued, pushing the words past her teeth. 'Ewan's only just moved to Andaby. Supposedly for a fresh start and to reconnect with me.'

'Reconnect? Has he been living abroad?' said Kitt.

'I wish that was where he'd been,' Banks said, steeling herself for the next sentence about to fall out of her mouth. 'You see, he's just been released from prison. For murder.'

CHAPTER TWO

Kitt's jaw fell just a fraction, at these words but she soon corrected her expression. Banks found herself at once grateful that, unlike her giddy assistant Grace, Kitt could be relied upon to respond sensitively and appropriately at all times. The unpredictable antics of Kitt's colleague at Hartley and Edwards investigations, was one of several reasons why Banks had sought Kitt out here, at the library, rather than at their investigative offices on Walmgate. Her bride-to-be, Evie, could be daft as a brush at times, but somehow Banks found her special brand of silliness sweet, alluring even. Where Evie kept her banter within reasonable boundaries however, Grace carried on as though limits were a concept she'd never heard of.

Of course, Banks acknowledged privately that there was much to like about Grace. For one thing, she was an undisputed expert at online research – an invaluable skill when it came to crime-solving. For another she could always be depended on to lighten the mood and, without fail, she wore the most dazzling ensembles at any given social event, often by sporting garments that hinted at her Indian heritage. In spite of all these positive attributes however, the last thing Banks needed at a time like this was the irrepressible repartee of Grace Edwards.

'You're . . . ' Kitt paused, sensible enough to know she was on very rocky ground here. 'You're perhaps worried your brother had a hand in what happened to that woman because of his history? Am I understanding right?'

'It's . . . something I've considered,' Banks said. Doing her best to pretend that she'd been able to view the murder at Andaby in a rational light.

Her brother had seemed remorseful, humble even, on the few exchanges she'd had with him since he'd moved to West Yorkshire and they had agreed to try and repair their relationship. But Banks had no real idea what the impact of his twenty-year prison sentence might have been on him. Or exactly how he felt about his sister joining the police force. What if he had come to see her as the enemy? And if so, what lengths might he go to in order to discredit her? A question she had pondered more than once since she had learned about the murder early on Thursday morning.

'Is this murder the same MO as the murder your brother committed all those years ago . . . ?' Kitt said, snapping Banks out of her thoughts. 'Oh, no, what am I saying? That's ridiculous. How many stray industrial-sized yarn tubs is a man likely to have access to in one lifetime?'

'Actually, though obviously that's the aspect the newspapers have seized on, that wasn't the cause of death in this case. The true cause of death hasn't been released,' Banks said.

Kitt started at Banks's statement. 'Not the cause of death? But how? Those things weigh a ton. I mean, that's probably not even that hyperbolic a description. Surely the weight of one of those is enough to kill anyone?'

This was the point of no return. Banks was about to relay information known only to the police to a civilian. She had to tread very lightly here. Especially if her brother did have any hand in that murder. She didn't want anyone accusing her of trying to help him get away with what he had done by leaking confidential findings.

'I've already been in touch by phone with the officer in Andaby who's leading the investigation. A DS by the name of Jo Robinson. I knew that Ewan would be on their suspect list. He's a recently released parolee and he'd taken a life before. There was no question that they'd be knocking on his door. I wanted to identify myself as an ally to the investigation – rather than an ally to a potential murderer, so I gave DS Robinson a call, pretty much as soon as I heard about what had happened, to explain the situation. She was appreciative, and, although she's understandably keeping case information compartmentalized for obvious reasons, she did tell me that the victim, Siobhan Lange, was already dead by the time her body met with that yarn tub.'

'It seems an odd thing to do,' said Kitt. 'Kill someone using one method and then go to the pains of toppling a heavy object to crush them.'

Banks, unable to stand a minute longer while talking about a murder her brother might have committed, slumped down into the spare armchair and tried to steady herself. 'I agree. It definitely falls into the strange behaviour category. When the killer does something with the body after death it's usually for one of three main reasons. Firstly, it can be performative or ritualistic.'

'Like when certain serial killers arrange bodies in particular formations. Or leave calling card marks on the body,' said Kitt.

'Right,' Banks said with a nod. 'But unless we're about to see a spate of murders across the region in which the victims are all crushed with industrial equipment, I'd say it was one of the other two common rationales: either the killer was enraged with the victim when the murder took place, or it was strategic and the perpetrator was trying to cover their tracks, though I must admit if it is that last one, they chose a very strange method of misdirection.'

Kitt shrugged. 'Perhaps whoever did this was hoping such a bizarre turn of events would be a distraction to the police. Or that it might keep them from finding out the true cause of death . . . Did DS Robinson go so far as to relay that?'

'Aye, she wanted to know if Ewan might have exhibited any behaviour that indicated he would carry out such an act. From what they could tell, before she was crushed by a yarn tub, Siobhan Lange had been strangled.'

Banks watched Kitt's hand involuntarily rise towards her throat, her fingertips tracing the collar of her white shirt. 'So, the industrial museum where the body was found wasn't the murder scene?'

Banks paused. She'd already revealed the cause of death of a murder victim to someone without a badge. Perhaps she should stop there? But then again, it's not like the problem she was facing could be solved through official channels. And if she wanted Kitt's help then keeping her in the dark wasn't going to be an option for long. 'Current thinking is that the murder did happen in the museum but not in the room where the body was found. I don't know which room the crime took place in, however. As I say, there's only so much information available, even to me, given the severity of the crime.'

'Makes sense,' Kitt said, now toying with her necklace. 'And strangulation . . . was that how your brother . . . well, you know?'

Banks shook her head, appreciative that Kitt couldn't bring herself to finish that sentence. That she was trying to make this conversation easy on her. Just now, Banks needed all the support she could get. 'In his case it was a fight gone wrong. Or so he said. He claimed he never meant to kill the guy he was fighting with. That he'd tried to get out of it and de-escalate the situation but his opponent forced the issue. Of course, I'll never know if that was the truth.'

'What was the fight about?' Kitt asked, reaching for her satchel and pulling out a notebook. 'I won't write down anything the police have discovered about the death of Siobhan Lange, and I won't name your brother in my notes,' she clarified. 'But I'm assuming you're telling me all this because you need my help and if I can make a few scribbles about the background, it helps when I'm trying to work things through.'

Banks nodded her approval. Relieved that Kitt had just taken the cue and that she hadn't had to explain herself any more than necessary. There were so many scenarios swarming around in her head right now, she was grateful Kitt hadn't forced her to start speculating on the exact nature of her brother's involvement in this case or to lay out all the reasons why she needed to launch her own clandestine investigation into the events in Andaby.

'The fight our Ewan had was over a woman,' Banks explained. 'He was twenty-four at the time. The dobber had been seeing this lass behind her husband's back. The husband inevitably found out, as they always seem to do, and came after him. Our Ewan's one of them lads that, to look at him, you wouldn't think there was much fight in him. But he can more than fend for himself. And he did that night.'

Kitt looked up from her notebook. 'Terrible as that must have been. It does sound more like an accident than anything else. Besides, what possible motive would he have for killing Siobhan Lange after just three months of living in a new place? It's barely enough time to unpack your belongings, let alone make an enemy you want to kill.'

'That, I don't know,' Banks conceded. 'And I suppose that's the problem. It could be that Ewan has nothing to do with this. That all this concern and overanalysis of the situation is just old ghosts having their way with me. But what if it's not? Can I really take that chance?'

The time her brother had spent in prison had not made answers to such questions any easier. Banks had communicated with him only a handful of times in the twenty years he had been inside. Most of those before she joined the police force. Even though there was a family connection, and she thus would have been able to explain any visits she made, she didn't consider it a wise career move to be in regular contact with a known murderer.

The few times they had spoken, Ewan had been full of remorse over what his actions had cost both him and his family. But Banks had never known how much she could trust the sincerity of those outbursts. Was her brother truly sorry for taking a life that night? Or was he just sorry that it led to such dire consequences for him and the people who had once looked up to him? Over the time she had been in law enforcement, Banks had learned that the answer to that particular question usually determined whether a convict would offend again.

'I understand your fears Charley, really I do,' Kitt said, putting the lid back on her pen and setting her notebook to one side. 'But would your brother really be stupid enough to commit a crime like that straight after getting out of prison? Especially when he must have known the police would knock on his door if anything untoward went on?'

Banks shook her head. 'Our Ewan's a lot of things but he's not stupid. Not *that* stupid, anyway.' All of a sudden a grin rose to Banks's lips. Memories of the way she and Ewan used to gripe at each other over the family dinner table in their teenage years seemed to flood back in an instant. The game was to find the most inventive way of calling the other stupid. Banks's all-time favourite insult to her brother had been: *You're what's known as a double disappointment: an airhead with a face for radio.* She could probably come up with much better now but at sixteen she had thought that statement the height of wit. Just as quickly as the grin surfaced, however, it faded and tears filled her eyes. All that good humour and feeling was gone now. Long gone. And there was no getting it back.

Kitt, who had seemingly noticed the private little moment Banks was having, paused before asking her next question. Giving Banks a bit of time to compose herself again.

'Any idea about whether your brother knew Siobhan Lange?' Kitt asked when she did finally speak.

'He told Robinson that he had flirted with her in the local

16

pub one night about a month after he arrived at Andaby, but nothing came of the interaction. According to Ewan it was just a bit of harmless Friday night fun.' Banks pursed her lips. 'But there's something not quite right about his version of events, I know there isn't.'

'What makes you say that?' said Kitt.

'After I spoke to Robinson on the phone, I went to see Ewan in person. She knew all about my visit. The plan was to see whether his account changed. If it did, Robinson was going to bring him in to the local station for more thorough questioning.'

'And did he tell you the same tale?'

'Yes, he told me the same things he told Robinson. But when he was speaking . . . I don't know, there was this look in his eyes that reminded me of when we were kids and he wasn't telling the whole story.'

Kitt tilted her head. 'Taking the innocent until proven guilty approach, maybe he did get to know her a little better than he's letting on. Slept with her, for example, but doesn't want to admit it because he knows you'd suspect him.'

'Maybe. But the whole chain of events seems like too much of a coincidence to me. Ewan moves to Andaby and three months later they have their first ever recorded murder? And it's not just that. He's been in prison in Scotland for the last twenty years. That's going to change a person. And the people he's been mingling with for those twenty years are hardly the cream of humanity's crop.'

Kitt sighed. 'I do see why you're concerned. What about an alibi? Can someone confirm where he was on the night of the murder?'

'Apparently, yes they can,' Banks replied. 'He says he was with a lass he's been seeing, a local woman called Nancy Murphy. And she's confirmed she was with him in the murder window, which the medical examiner has judged as being sometime between seven and nine last Wednesday evening.'

'Well, he's got an alibi, that's something.'

Banks raised an eyebrow at Kitt. 'Come on, you know better than that. Lovers and partners of suspected criminals aren't necessarily the most reliable source of information.' The ferocity had returned to Banks's voice and she took yet another deep breath to calm herself.

'Not . . . historically,' Kitt conceded. 'But she can't have been seeing him that long?'

'They met when he first moved to Andaby but it took a few weeks for them to make anything official, from what he tells me.'

'So, we're talking just over two months, at most? I'm not sure about you, but I'm not going to go out on a limb and lie to the police for someone I've been dating for so short a time, no matter how much I like them. Should I ever be suspected of conspiracy to murder again, I wouldn't lie on anyone's behalf, and Mal knows it.'

'Noted,' Banks said with a grudging smile, which again soon faded. 'The thing about Ewan is, he can be very convincing. Charismatic, you know? He asked me if the word of his girlfriend would be enough, or if it was too shaky and he'd end up as the prime suspect anyway.'

'On that showing he's clearly more than aware that the sudden appearance of a dead body in Andaby doesn't look good for him. What did you tell him?'

Banks shrugged. 'The only thing I could tell him: the truth. That just like last time he went away, there was a threshold of evidence the officers had to meet and, if his alibi checks out, he's got little to worry about. When he was convicted for murder, he was covered in the victim's blood and was present at the scene when they carted the almost lifeless body off to hospital. The guy he killed was pronounced dead on arrival. So, the evidence was pretty damning to say the least. This time though, well let's just say that if the police had anything at all they could pin on him, he'd already be on his way back to prison.'

There was a silence as Kitt digested all that Banks had said.

'Forgive me for asking this,' she said at last, 'it probably doesn't seem very high on the priority list given all that you're facing, but she is my best friend . . . Does Evie know what's going on here?'

'She knows I've got a brother who's been newly released from prison, that the subject is a deep source of shame for me and that he is not invited to the wedding.

'She doesn't know exactly what crime he committed then,' said Kitt.

'No, she knows it was bad and probably suspects the truth. But she's been good enough not to push me about the particulars.'

'She always was a sensitive soul,' Kitt said, warmly. 'She wouldn't put a person she loved through the wringer unnecessarily. You've got to love her for that.'

'That and much more . . . I always knew though, that if we stayed together, eventually I'd have to tell her everything. And that's what I'm on my way home to do now. So hopefully, there will still be a wedding.' Banks heard her own voice come close to breaking as she said these words and the sound surprised her. She was not one for great shows of emotion in public. But the thought of losing Evie after all they'd been through together was a pain she couldn't even bear to contemplate.

Kitt rose from her seat, walked slowly towards Banks and ran a hand down her arm. It was the first time the two had ever made physical contact, but just then she was grateful that Kitt had abandoned social etiquette to provide a little comfort. 'You know our Evie better than that,' Kitt said. 'She's not going to desert you at the first sign of trouble.'

Banks nodded, hoping if she agreed strongly enough with what Kitt was saying that her words might become prophecy.

'What about Mal?' said Kitt. 'I'm assuming he doesn't know about this, and that's another reason you came to me about it.'

'Halloran, like almost all my other colleagues, doesn't know anything about it. Ricci as my most senior officer is aware. But perhaps for obvious reasons, given my job title, this is a secret I've guarded closely. I won't make you keep a secret from your partner though,' Banks said. 'I'll tell Halloran myself when I see him tomorrow.'

'You don't have to, you know?' said Kitt. 'Mal and I have shared information in the past, when necessary, but neither of us would ever break a confidence we had promised to keep. We both understand and respect that.'

'And I appreciate it,' Banks said. 'But no, it's time. He needs to know the truth. If only so he can vouch for me in case the worst happens.'

'The worst being . . . ?'

Banks looked hard at Kitt before replying. 'You know what a stickler I've been about the rules over the years. This is why. Officers like me, with people in the family who've committed crimes, can't afford to step away from the thin blue line. If Ewan's got something to do with this – anything at all – and I disappear on my honeymoon for three months, suspicion might start to fall on me too.'

'You don't really think things could go that far, do you?'

'It wouldn't be the first time I've been framed, would it?' said Banks, referring to a case Kitt had worked a few years back now. On that occasion, Banks almost faced dismissal due to planted evidence. 'I've worked too hard and too long to let him take my career away from me. The force will never let me officially investigate a personal matter like this, quite rightly. But I can't leave it to chance that my own flesh and blood might get away with murder, and I can't find out the truth working on my own either. That's why I've come to you. I need to know, Kitt. If my brother killed that woman. If he did, if he's been that bold knowing that with his record the police would come knocking, there's every chance he might do it again.'

CHAPTER THREE

The following Monday morning saw Banks's car crest a hill in the valley of Calderdale, below which stood the small market town of Andaby. From her temporary vantage point, Banks caught a glimpse of the thatched roofed cottages built along The Rochdale Canal. The ones that always seemed to feature in postcards sent from this part of the region. These undeniably quaint residences were surrounded by several rows of Victorian terraces on either side of the water, which were in turn broken up by a town green and a small market square. Standing proud above all other structures, however, was Andaby Industrial Museum. An attraction housed in an old textiles mill, complete with a towering chimney and blocky, brutal frontage.

With its rich history in manufacturing, Calderdale was not a region short of old mills to convert. But this particular site had been chosen for the museum because it was situated right next to the railway station and a small, adjoining viaduct. Those stone arches framed rolling hillsides, and the tracks ran straight through the valley. A fact which made the museum more accessible to potential visitors and afforded passengers some of the most atmospheric views Yorkshire had to offer.

'Oh, look!' Kitt shouted from the front passenger seat in such an abrupt manner that Banks jumped. 'It's the *Frederick William Kitson!*'

Banks glanced for a split second down to where Kitt had gestured to. The only article that might be said to be of particular interest was a large, coal-black steam engine sitting quietly in a siding at the station. The front of the train boasted attractive streamline curves, and several vintage coaches painted in maroon and cream were attached to the back of it.

'Are you talking about the steam train? Is that the name of it? I wouldn't have had you down as a trainspotter.' In spite of the dark events that had drawn her to Andaby, Banks felt a chuckle brewing at the thought.

'Not me,' said Kitt, 'Mal hasn't stopped talking about this train since they announced its launch two years ago. He's even had his train set down from the attic in recent months – I'll be honest, I didn't notice him smuggle that in with him when he started living with me at the cottage. He and Iago have almost come to blows on several occasions because of the feline tendency to chase things that seemingly run away from them. I've been informed more than once that model trains are not cat toys. Iago seems utterly disinterested in any rules Mal might lay down for him, and it's not like I've ever had much sway over that cat's levels of obedience.'

'When this is all over, I'm going to need a lot more information on Halloran and his model train habit,' Banks said. 'In order to effectively ridicule and tease him about it in a workplace setting, you understand.'

Kitt laughed but paused the conversation while Banks navigated the steep slope into town, punctuated with several hairpin curves.

'Don't tell Mal I said this,' Kitt said as they passed onto a flatter stretch of road and approached the town boundary. 'But I must admit that steam train is a bonny sight. And it will no doubt draw in a fair few tourists.'

'I'll get a proper look when we pull up to the museum,' said Banks. 'But I bet she's no *Flying Scotsman*.'

'And no bias whatsoever there, from the born and bred Glaswegian,' Kitt teased.

Banks managed a smirk in response and wished she could have been even more responsive to Kitt's admirable attempts to keep the atmosphere light. It had been a ninety-minute drive to Andaby from York and in that time the pair had thankfully settled into a relatively easy rhythm with each other. A promising sign considering things were only likely to get more tense during their time in West Yorkshire.

'At this rate, we're definitely going to be early enough to

take a quick scout around the industrial museum before the meeting with your colleague,' Kitt said, glancing at her watch. 'And who knows, maybe there'll be a little time to potter about too. I don't think I'm going to have time for a visit through to Heptonstall to visit Sylvia Plath's gravestone while we're here, but perhaps there's a bookshop in Andaby?'

'There is,' Banks said, her smirk broadening into a smile. 'But I'm on strict orders from Halloran not to let you inside.'

'Bless him,' Kitt said, 'almost six years we've been together and he still thinks he has some vague hope of controlling my book buying habit. Some might be offended that their partner doesn't know them better, but I can only admire his enduring optimism.'

Banks chuckled. Down at the nick in York, what Halloran said, went. Unless he was overruled by a superior officer. It always amused Banks to think of him navigating a situation where people weren't compelled to follow orders. From what Banks knew of Kitt, following orders wasn't high on her agenda.

'Do you think DS Robinson will be forthcoming with any more useful details on the case?' Kitt said, her mind seemingly re-focusing on the business at hand now that the industrial museum, at which the crime took place, was in view.

'I hope so. There are a few things going for us in that respect, even though she's compartmentalizing information.

She knows Ewan is my brother. She knows I can get close to him and keep an eye on him in a way nobody else can. Hopefully, she'll see me as an asset and give me something to work with. I suggested she look me up on the system after our first conversation. My service record is pretty much impeccable. Yes, there was obviously that attempt to frame me but it was disproved, so with a bit of luck she'll understand she's got nothing to worry about when it comes to where my loyalty lies. But, in terms of whether or not she'll give us anything more to work with than she already has . . . I don't know, is the honest answer. She agreed to meet with me when I arrived here, off the record. Which is a good sign. But I can't overstep. If word gets back to York Station . . . well, Ricci thinks I'm busy picking out chair covers for the wedding.'

Kitt raised a suspicious eyebrow. 'Chair covers? You're not really bothering with those, are you?'

'At forty quid a shot? Not a chance. People are only sitting on the bloody things. They're not eating their dinner off them.'

'We think alike, you and I,' Kitt said with a wry smile.

'There won't be any chair covers at your wedding then?' Banks said. It was a risky comment. She and Kitt were hardly close. But Halloran never mentioned marriage when he talked about Kitt and she was secretly a little bit curious about whether the two would ever tie the knot. It seemed unfair to try and get answers out of Evie. What was said between Evie and Kitt about their relationships was between them. Banks had no desire to come between the two, which meant that this trip might be her only opportunity to find out a little bit more.

Kitt's nose crinkled. 'No weddings for me, thank you very much.'

'And Halloran?'

'Mal . . . well, he did ask me once. And I asked him what he was playing at. He's already done that dance before, with someone else, and I've no desire to be part of such an archaic institution that does so very little for those involved, except maybe make things a little easier should one of you tragically and suddenly die . . . ' Kitt trailed off then. Noticing the bemused expression on Banks's face. 'Oh . . . but I'm sure *your* wedding, and marriage, will be a glorious exception.'

It was Banks's turn to chuckle this time. 'Very convincing.'

'I'm sorry Charley, really, I am. There's only so many books on gender studies you can read and still find the prospect of marriage a welcome one. Don't mind me. I really couldn't be happier for you and Evie, you know that don't you?'

'I know,' she said, making sure their eyes met at least briefly so her sincerity would be clear.

At the mention of her betrothed, Banks couldn't help but smile. Most of the people who knew Banks wouldn't have described her as a smiley person, but that's just the effect Evie had on her. She cast her mind back to the evening before when she had sat down with Evie and explained the true nature of Ewan's crime. Evie had been left with facial scars after her own run-in with a murderer some years ago, and thus murder was a rather sensitive subject in their household. True to form, however, Evie had been her usual loving, warm and understanding self. Banks had never had any doubt that Evie was the woman she wanted to marry, but after the compassion she'd shown over her family's chequered past last night, Banks was more certain of her life choices than ever.

Pulling the car up outside the museum, Banks turned off the engine and looked across at Kitt. 'I sincerely doubt we'll have a cat in hell's chance of seeing the room where Siobhan was murdered, but I at least want to get a look at the room where they found her. So, how do you want to play it in there?'

'Oh,' said Kitt. 'I'm allowed to call the shots, am I? I didn't want to presume anything.'

'Technically, this is your investigation,' said Banks. 'I'll obviously speak up if I think there's a better way but given my personal attachment to the case, the less I instigate things the better. Without my warrant card on me, I'm not going to be able to identify myself as an officer. I'm on a career break so, essentially, I'm a civilian and that's the way I'm going to introduce myself.'

'That makes sense,' said Kitt. 'But letting me call the shots on the investigation, well, that really is quite different from working with Mal . . . who, by the way, said he'll meet us at the guest house in Halifax at seven. He was talking about having an evening meal at the Piece Hall. He's giving Evie a lift over and, I'm afraid, Grace too.'

'You don't have to apologize for her,' Banks said, feeling slightly guilty that her distaste for Grace's wilder antics must have been more than apparent for Kitt to say something like that. 'She's part of your team. And she is good at what she does. Some of the leads she's generated on the cases I've been involved with have played a crucial part in convicting the perpetrator.'

'Yes, but a bit of peace and quiet on the journey here this morning hasn't gone amiss, has it? At least not for me. Anyway, factoring in the drive over to Halifax, that gives us about five hours to get some preliminary information from Siobhan's colleagues here at the museum, and for you to meet with DS Robinson and get any insider details that might help us draw up a list of suspects to monitor and interview.'

'In short, you're taking it easy on me on the first day, eh?'

Kitt part sighed, part smiled. 'I should have guessed that nothing would get past you. Obviously, I've got to go back to York for my shift on Friday evening, so we want to have as much tied up before then as we can, but I think taking it as easy as possible, at least on the first day of our initial inquiries is probably a good idea. I don't want to say something out of line when it's not my place but, in my experience, the personal cases can do real damage if you're not careful. So do me a favour this week, and just be kind to yourself. OK?'

'You're the boss.' Banks flashed what she was sure was a pretty convincing smile as she unclipped her seatbelt and climbed out of the car. She made her way to the main entrance of the building, and as she did so she remembered the picture she'd seen of Siobhan Lange in an online news report. In the photograph she was holding a red cocktail in a nightclub. Her long, blonde hair had been styled poker straight and she had these big blue eyes, framed by fake eyelashes, that had felt to Banks as though they were staring not just at her, but through her. Siobhan Lange had been only thirty-eight years old when she died. Which was no age at all.

Banks stared up at Andaby Industrial Museum and tried to breathe through the sting of the knowledge that a woman had died in there. Plus, there was more than a passing chance that the woman died at the hands of her brother. With this in mind, Banks began to wonder if her promise to Kitt, to take things easy and be kind to herself this week, was a promise she could keep.

CHAPTER FOUR

The scent of sawdust and oil was the first thing Banks noticed about the inside of the old mill. With her case load and working hours, cultural pursuits were never exactly a top priority. In fact, the last time she'd been anywhere that might be considered a cultural space was when she had proposed to Evie nine months ago. She had hired out The Ritz Cinema in Evie's home town of Thirsk for a special screening of *Breakfast at Tiffany's*. Evie made no secret of her love of all things vintage – including vintage words which she tried to squeeze into conversation whenever she could – and Banks couldn't think of a better place to pop the question than at a picture palace first opened in 1912.

Banks smiled to herself, remembering how Evie's jaw had dropped when she presented her with a small blue Tiffany box of her own as the credits rolled. She felt so far away from all that happiness right now. Stuck in an old, draughty building. Hunting down possible murder suspects when she should have been selecting the wines for their wedding reception. With every passing moment, the contempt Banks felt for her brother deepened. If he had made different choices, she might have had some chance of enjoying the normal things other people did without even thinking about it.

Taking a deep breath in an attempt to steel herself for the day that lay ahead, Banks followed Kitt as she approached a woman in costume standing close to the entrance. Her high collared shirt almost gave the impression that she had no neck, and the long navy skirt, fitted with a white apron, similarly eclipsed her feet. To Banks's eyes the woman almost looked like a ghost that might appear in some paint-by-numbers horror film about an abandoned mill. A thought she tried to push out of her mind as she digested the somewhat creepy atmosphere of the building. The wooden beams somehow created a sense of the ceiling pressing down on her. Every floorboard creaked underfoot and there was a decided dampness hanging in the air. Banks would rather be on desk duty from now to the end of time than work in a place like this.

'Mornin' folks, my name's Deborah,' said the woman. 'Come to explore our exhibitions?'

'Well, actually . . . ' Kitt began but it seemed Deborah had asked the question rhetorically.

'Just lovely to receive visitors, it really is a joy. I've got a map for you right 'ere – everything you need to know about the building's in there. There'll be a live demonstration of the spinning wheel at two o'clock so don't miss out on that. There's no fee for entry to the museum but we do welcome donations in the boxes next to the displays. If you have any questions, you're welcome to ask one of our staff members.'

'Thank you,' Kitt said, without making it sound much like a thank you at all. She paused for a moment, and when Deborah didn't at once leap to fill the silence with more visitor's information it was clear she hadn't missed Kitt's tone. 'As it stands, I do have one or two questions I'd like to ask. About the death of your colleague, Siobhan Lange.'

'Oh! I'm . . . I'm not really supposed to talk about that,' Deborah said, her once cheery smile evaporating. She crossed her arms and eyed Kitt. 'Are you from the papers or something?'

'Oh, no, nothing like that,' said Kitt, reaching into her satchel, producing a business card and handing it to Deborah. 'I'm conducting an independent investigation into the death of your colleague. I run a private agency based in York and have worked on several prominent cases in the region.'

'Edwards and 'artley Investigations.' Deborah read aloud from the card.

'Yes, er, wait. What? No. Er . . . may I?' Kitt reached for the card so she could read it for herself. Promptly after her cheeks reddened.

'That's a bit of a misprint,' Kitt said, returning her card to

Deborah. Was she gritting her teeth? 'It should read Hartley and Edwards Investigations.'

Banks pursed her lips to keep from smiling. From what Evie had said, Grace was forever playing pranks on Kitt. It seemed her latest was to switch around their surnames on the business cards. Evie had also made it clear to Banks on more than one occasion that Kitt had no problem in disciplining her assistant when she went too far. Banks had no idea what the penalty was for meddling with Kitt's status in the company but judging by the librarian's ever darkening expression, she really wouldn't want to be in Grace's shoes next time the pair were face to face.

'I've already gone through all the details to do with Siobhan's death with the police,' Deborah said with a laboured sigh. 'Do I really have to go over it again?'

This statement gave Banks pause. If Deborah had already gone over everything with the police, as she claimed, that sounded as though they were systematically approaching staff members and questioning them about their relationship with Siobhan. Perhaps this wasn't surprising, taking into account the nature of Siobhan's death and the place at which it happened. Robinson's team were probably working on the principle that the killer knew their way round the museum and thus likely worked there. The museum was only open until five and Siobhan was murdered between seven and nine. Who else but fellow employees would have access to the building after hours?

'You don't have to go through it again at all if you really can't stand to,' Kitt said, her voice suddenly lulling, gentle. 'If discussing the issue is too painful, I'd understand completely. You're under no obligation to talk to me. It's just, anything you can tell me might well help me bring Siobhan's killer to justice. So really, it's not for me, you see, it's for her and her family.'

Although Banks had worked quite loosely with Kitt on a few cases in the past, she'd never seen her in investigative action first-hand. Her manner was impressively disarming and underlining the subject's choice in doing the right thing had the desired effect.

'Well,' Deborah said, briefly looking over her shoulder as though she were expecting somebody to be listening in. 'I suppose, if you're working to catch Siobhan's killer and help her family find closure, it won't 'urt to go over things again.'

Banks let out a short sigh of relief. She would have been willing to push a little harder if necessary but she couldn't evoke her status as a police officer for a small errand like this. She was on thin ice as it was stepping over the lines of jurisdiction. Mercifully, early Monday afternoon didn't seem to be a busy time for the museum, nobody was queuing behind them to get in, so Deborah had no real excuse not to talk to them.

'I'll try and keep the number of questions to a minimum. I've no desire to disrupt your work day any longer than necessary,' said Kitt. 'The biggest question is whether you noticed Siobhan acting strangely, or if she perhaps seemed under any duress before her demise?'

Deborah shook her head in an abrupt manner that spoke more to anger than to grief. 'The police asked the same question. No, sadly there was no change in the way Siobhan acted around here before she died.'

'What exactly do you mean, sadly?' said Banks. She'd let Kitt take the lead. That had been the deal. But there was something off about Deborah's behaviour that Banks couldn't quite put her finger on. She'd been doing the job long enough to know that when her instincts kicked in, she should follow them.

'I – I didn't dwell on this with the police,' Deborah said. 'I didn't want them to think me or anyone else 'ere had anything to do with what 'appened. Because they wouldn't do anything like this, you know? With the exception of Siobhan, everyone 'ere is just lovely and wouldn't 'urt a soul. So, I didn't want to give them reason to suspect any of us, but the truth is that Siobhan managed this place and her methods of doing so were . . . brusque to put it politely.'

'You mean, she wasn't well-liked by the staff here?' Kitt pushed. Just like Banks, it seemed Kitt was getting increasingly suspicious about the way Deborah was describing her former boss.

'Nobody would have wished this on 'er, well not so far as I know anyway,' said Deborah. 'But she didn't treat us very nicely. And that didn't change one bit before the murder. She was her usual self. Quite nit-picky, you know? She'd take any excuse to tell you what you were doing wrong and somehow never noticed when you did things right.'

'Yes,' said Kitt. 'I'm not unfamiliar with that management style. Doesn't exactly inspire good feeling, does it?'

'No,' Deborah said, just as a small smile formed on her lips. She appeared relieved that Kitt empathized with overbearing bosses. Or perhaps she took Kitt's commiserations as a sign she believed her story about the staff here being innocent of any retaliatory wrongdoing. 'Thing is, someone on the staff must have let the police in on what we all really thought of 'er because we were all asked for our alibis and were told we might be brought in for further questioning depending on the outcome of certain enquiries . . . which I have to say, I don't much like the sound of.'

'I'm sure it's just routine,' Kitt said with a dismissive wave of her hand. 'When they said "certain enquiries" I'm assuming they simply meant forensic investigation. Unless the police recovered some CCTV footage from somewhere on site? Something that might, upon analysis, reveal the killer was somebody who worked here.'

'If there's any footage, it won't be from cameras on-site,' said Deborah. 'We do 'ave cameras up but some of them are older than some of the items on display and none of them are in working order. Funding has been squeezed, you know. And the council put pressure on us to keep admission free to attract visitors to the area. But people are 'ard up at the minute, so it's not like the donations are rolling in.'

Something in Banks's chest tightened at this information. Deborah was quite insistent that nobody who worked here could possibly have anything to do with Siobhan's death. And yet, in the same breath, she also had told them that Siobhan was not well-liked by her colleagues. The fact that there was no video footage of the murder because the cameras weren't working only seemed to make it more likely that someone who worked at the mill was responsible for the murder, and had potentially planned the attack in meticulous detail. Whoever had carried out the killing must have known that the cameras wouldn't capture anything and that they would be safe to commit their crime without CCTV footage leading the police straight to them.

'That's a real shame about the cameras,' Kitt said, the disappointment evident in her voice.

Deborah offered a sympathetic nod. 'I know, but we're not exactly displaying Picassos 'ere, you know. We've not had any security problems or even any minor thefts to speak of. So, we just left the cameras up as a visual deterrent, as it were, and kept it quiet that they weren't actually taking any footage.'

'Can't be helped I suppose,' Kitt said, taking out a notebook from her satchel and making a note Banks was too far away to read. 'Is the room where the body was found at least open to the public again?'

'Only just. And only because the police think the actual murder took place in the back office. That's still off limits for now.'

'I see,' Kitt said, snapping her notebook closed again and offering Deborah a measured smile.

Deborah had just unwittingly revealed a piece of information that Robinson hadn't volunteered – that the murder took place in the back office. After hours and in a staff-only area, no wonder Robinson and her team had decided Siobhan's colleagues were the best starting place in their hunt for the culprit.

Banks wondered how many other people Deborah had relayed this information to, and thus how long Robinson could expect to keep information about the case compartmentalized.

'I think I've taken up quite enough of your time for one day,' Kitt said to Deborah. 'So, we'll just have a look around the room where the body was found by ourselves. We'll be sure to make a generous donation to the museum, of course.'

'I appreciate it. Jobs in culture aren't exactly ten a penny around 'ere. But the room where Siobhan was found has been forensically examined, like. So, if you're hoping to find something other than some fine examples of industrial 'eritage, I think you'll be out of luck.'

'Don't worry about that,' said Kitt. 'We haven't got our hopes up too high about cracking the case on the first day.'

Shrugging, Deborah pointed them in the right direction and Kitt and Banks headed directly to the room where Siobhan had suffered the indignity of being crushed by a yarn tub after she had already breathed her last.

'What did you think of that?' Kitt asked Banks when Deborah was well out of earshot.

Banks cleared her throat. 'I've got one big question for you.'

'I'm listening.'

'Other than staff, who do you think would have known all the CCTV cameras in here were ornamental only?'

'Off the top of my head, I'm guessing nobody,' said Kitt.

Banks nodded her agreement. 'DS Robinson won't be wasting her time checking the alibis of everyone from the cleaner to the curator for nothing. She must suspect the killer is on the payroll here. And given those little nuggets of information Deborah just so kindly shared with us, I'd say she's got every reason to.'

CHAPTER FIVE

'I'm not used to being without a badge,' Banks admitted as she and Kitt looked around the space labelled The Loom Room. 'If I'd been officially investigating, I could have got us inside the room where Siobhan was killed no problem. Under these circumstances it wasn't even worth asking to be admitted into that part of the museum, especially as Robinson's team have got it cordoned off. We can't do anything that interferes with their investigation. I very much need to keep her on side . . . you know, I'm starting to understand how tricky it is to get to the truth in a case without access to police resources.'

Kitt smiled at Banks, who had so regularly stood on the other side of the cordon line to Kitt during past investigations. 'With a bit of luck DS Robinson will be able to give you a hint about whether they found anything of use in the back office. Or offer some insight into whether their research into Siobhan's colleagues has turned anything up.

It's true, we can only do so much when we don't have police access to the crime scene but there are other creative ways of getting the information we need, and some people, of course, are just helpful of their own accord without the need for any prompting at all. It's one of the benefits of investigating in Yorkshire, you know, we are rather known for talking the hind legs off donkeys.'

'I'd never really thought about it that way, but of course you're right,' said Banks. 'And I thought it was my skill at interrogation that caused so many criminals to spill their guts to me over the years. Now I find out I just chose to work in the right county.'

Kitt laughed at Banks's remark but noticeably didn't rush to correct her logic.

'I'm surprised Deborah was willing to tell you quite as much as she did,' said Banks.

'If there's one thing I've learned doing this kind of work it's that people can and will always surprise you. I went through a phase not so long ago of feeling quite jaded. The cases were starting to get to me, you know?' said Kitt.

'I am more than familiar with that problem,' Banks said. Considering the personal nature of this case it was a feeling Banks was doing everything in her power to ignore right now.

'But the truth is,' Kitt said, 'most people want to help when something bad has happened. You know what it's like when something really significant and terrible unfolds.

Something global that none of us can ignore. Certainly, you see some of humanity's worst colours but you also see some of their best. When I'm running investigations like these, after a bit of nudging, the vast majority of folk I interview will start talking. It's just a matter of finding the right way into the conversation. From what Mal tells me, you use many of the same techniques in the interrogation room.'

'Yeah, we probably do. But even then we've got the weight of the law behind us. Coaxing people to volunteer information without the formality of my job title playing its part is going to take some getting used to.'

'Well hopefully, we'll catch a break sooner rather than later. And then you won't have to think about anything crime-related for a couple of months.'

'I love your optimism,' Banks said scanning the contents of the large, rectangular room, which chiefly comprised of a row of looms that had not seen any action in decades, a series of information boards and a stack of large steel canisters arranged in the corner.

'Those must be the yarn tubs used to crush Siobhan,' Kitt said, following Banks's gaze.

Banks paused for a moment. 'It's an awful lot of trouble you know. To drag a dead body from one room to another. You'd have to be pretty strong to do that, even before you start messing around with yarn tubs. And then there's the issue that while you're moving the body from one place to

44

the other, anyone might discover you at any second. Why wouldn't you just leave the body strangled and get out of there?'

'You're right,' said Kitt. 'The nature of this crime raises so many questions. Even if you were strong enough to pull a body from one room to another on your own single-handedly, it's still beyond me how they managed to topple one of those yarn tubs on their own. I mean, look at them. You'd probably need a forklift to move them when they were full.'

'And imagine working here in a time before forklifts existed,' said Banks.

'Oof, no thank you,' said Kitt. 'No wonder people were in a terrible state by the time they got to fifty back then. I'm not sure if there's anything in them now but, even empty, they must be heavy enough.'

Banks narrowed her eyes. 'Either the person was very strong or they had an accomplice and we're looking for two killers, or possibly more.'

'You mean we could be looking at *Murder on the Orient Express*, but in a mill instead of on a train?'

Banks's expression must have conveyed that this statement didn't mean a lot to her as Kitt continued to explain.

'In that story, everyone on the train collaborates to commit the murder. Everyone's the culprit. You don't think the employees at the mill might have clubbed together to see Siobhan off, do you?'

Banks, trying to be polite, did what she could to temper her amusement at the idea. 'I think that's perhaps a little bit far-fetched. And if it is the case, Robinson's going to have an unenviable job on her hands.'

'Well, I suppose it doesn't have to be a group of people. Perhaps there's another explanation. Maybe you could use something to knock the yarn tub over with for example . . . what about that broom in the corner?'

Banks's eyes settled on the broom. 'Aye, I suppose if you managed to find a space between two of the tubs you could use the handle to lever one of them forward and knock it down, if you were smart enough.'

'If that broom, or anything else in here, played a part in what happened to Siobhan however, the police will likely know won't they? Surely everything in this room will have been tested for fingerprints by the forensics team?' said Kitt.

'I would think so,' said Banks, 'but I will mention it to Robinson anyway. Just to be sure.'

'Or, just in case, I could save her a job,' Kitt said, pulling out a small, hard plastic case from her satchel and proceeding to put on some plastic gloves.

'What, you've got a fingerprint testing kit in there, have you?' Evie had mentioned that Kitt always came overprepared when working a case but it hadn't dawned on Banks that such preparation would stretch to low-grade forensic testing.

'Of course I have. That's just an investigative basic. What kind of Mickey Mouse operation do you think I'm running?'

Banks opened her mouth to reply.

'On second thoughts, don't answer that,' Kitt said before Banks could get a word out. Instead, she watched Kitt work. She could tell from the manner in which she set about the task that Halloran had likely given her a lesson or two on how to prevent contamination and ensure an even spread of the powder. Not that either Halloran or Banks were recovering fingerprints for themselves on a regular basis. But they had both watched the forensics team work at so many crime scenes that the movements and process were deeply etched into their minds.

'Hmmm,' Kitt said after a moment.

'What? Have you only got partials? Because even that can be enough.'

'No. It's stranger than that. There are no fingerprints on this broom handle at all. Not even one partial.'

Banks pressed her lips together, thinking. 'That's . . . an unlikely discovery. A broom in this kind of place, it must be used every day. Deborah said the room only opened again today so the post-closing time sweep hasn't taken place yet.'

'It's likely, then, that it hasn't been touched since Siobhan was murdered,' Kitt said, following Banks's line of logic.

'If the killer did use that broom to lever the tubs on top of the victim, they would have wiped it down afterwards.'

'That's my guess too,' said Kitt.

'OK,' Banks said with a shake of her head. 'So, we know the how. Or certainly we've got a working theory. One that points more at someone working solo than with an accomplice. But why, why when the woman is already dead would you do that?'

At this juncture a man in a long grey coat entered the room with a toddler who had obviously only just learned how to walk. Banks and Kitt paused their conversation while the man heavily enunciated the names of the different machines to the kid before moving onto the next room. There weren't many people milling about, but the man's appearance was a reminder to both of them that they needed to be careful about just how loudly they were speaking, and exactly how explicit they were being. There may be friends, family or colleagues who were close to Siobhan in the vicinity and the last thing they needed to hear was a forensic deconstruction of her death.

'And why take the time to drag a body from one room into another like that?' Banks asked once she was sure sensitive ears wouldn't overhear her. 'Even after hours, anyone could have noticed activity from outside. Or someone who works here could have passed by and noticed something untoward, like the door still being unlocked and come in to check things out. So much could have gone wrong for the killer. Why take the risk of getting caught?'

'Difficult to say,' Kitt mused. 'If the killer is somebody

Siobhan managed here at the mill, perhaps it was their way of humiliating her after the belittlement she put them through?'

'Possibly,' said Banks. 'But it's a pretty violent act. I mean, you've already strangled the person to death. And you go to the trouble of crushing them to boot? That goes beyond the description of calculation. You'd have to be consumed by rage to do something like this.'

'After months, possibly years, of workplace intimidation, it's not completely unthinkable,' said Kitt. 'Although if anything happens to Michelle back at the library, I'd appreciate you vouching for my virtuous character in a court of law. Yes, she is irritating and narrow-minded and makes a fuss over the smallest thing . . . '

'Anything else for that list, while you're on?' Banks teased.

Kitt took a deep breath before replying, seemingly trying to regain composure. 'The fact remains, Michelle is not worth going to prison for. But if Siobhan was just as bad or worse, I can see how someone might start to think that it was worth it. Especially if work was a big part of their life and they didn't have much going on outside it.'

'I take your point,' Banks conceded. 'I've never seen a case along those lines that's quite like this but I have definitely brushed up against that motive in the past. Usually, it's a GBH case. It hasn't gone so far as murder and especially not one this brutal. But I suppose the principle is the same. Some people, understandably, can't take being worn down every day. They'll do just about anything not to feel like the victim any more and finally they snap.'

'I suspect that's why DS Robinson's team are taking the time to investigate Siobhan's work colleagues,' said Kitt. 'And if Siobhan was murdered by someone at work, well, at least you can rest easy knowing your brother wasn't involved. Unless he's just started a new job here and you failed to mention it?'

'No,' said Banks, 'he doesn't work here. It's quite difficult to find work right out of prison so he's on benefits. But right now, the idea that one of Siobhan's workmates is the murderer is really just a theory. There is another possibility.'

'The misdirection tactic you mentioned back at the library?'

Banks nodded. 'The toppling of the yarn tub might have been a calculated move to place suspicion on a work colleague rather than an act of revenge. Admittedly, they'd still have to know enough about this place to understand that there was a feud between the staff. But Andaby is a small town. People talk in the streets. In coffee shops and pubs, without thinking about the fact that they're likely being overheard by somebody. Word gets around. And, perhaps especially after consorting with criminals for twenty years, Ewan is smart enough to try to mislead the investigation like that.'

'Just remember, we haven't found anything concrete that points to him yet,' Kitt said.

'*Yet* being the operative word.'

'Let's keep an open mind for now, OK? Come on, I don't think we're going to learn anything else by staying here and it's almost two o'clock. I'm assuming you don't need me on comms while you meet DS Robinson and I can go for a cuppa?'

'You mean you're not going to dash to the demonstration of the spinning wheel? I thought that'd be right up your street.' Banks was teasing but to her surprise Kitt answered her earnestly.

'I would rather have enjoyed that, but I haven't had a cup of tea in a few hours and my tea habit always comes first . . . followed closely by my bookshop habit so perhaps it's best to find me in the bookshop when you're done?'

'Of course, that's fine,' said Banks. 'I'll drop you a text to confirm you're in the bookshop and pick you up from there, or wherever you are, after I'm done with Robinson.'

'Will do,' said Kitt. 'In the meantime, I'll call Grace and ask her to start looking into the employees at the mill and their closest online connections. While the police are focusing on the people who worked with Siobhan, it might be good for us to slightly widen our scope. Maybe it wasn't somebody who worked at the mill who committed the crime but someone related to an employee, or who was otherwise close to someone on the payroll. Like you say, Andaby is a small town. People likely have similar routines from day to day and for this killing to take place we're really looking for two possible kinds of suspects. A disgruntled work colleague who knew Siobhan's movements and had motive to kill her. Or someone outside with a motive we've yet to uncover. Someone who's been watching her, following her and waiting for just the right moment to strike.'

CHAPTER SIX

'All right Jo?' Banks said to DS Robinson as she took a seat next to the officer on a wooden bench by The Rochdale Canal. It was one of those glorious May days where wispy white clouds drifted lazily across the blue sky and seemed to admire their own reflections in the waters below.

Banks had always thought there was something quite enchanting about canals. Living in nearby York, she had done a bit of walking along the Rochdale Canal in her time and the view along that glistening liquid pathway never ceased to utterly entrance her. Even more mesmerizing was watching people on their narrow boats navigating the locks. A strange science to somebody who had never worked with them. Not every narrow-boat driver was an expert with them of course, and occasionally a dog dressed in its own little life jacket would create some kind of ruckus by jumping into the canal while the people on the boat were busy trying to pass through the lock, which often created much anguished shouting and barking. A narrow boat sailed by just as Banks sat down but it did so smoothly and quietly without any racket from human or beast.

Although this was the first time the pair had met face to face, Banks had been able to look up Robinson's photo on the database back at York so she knew to look out for a woman with shoulder-length blonde hair and a pointed nose. Truth be told, the uniform was also a bit of a giveaway. 'Thanks for meeting me,' Banks said, keen to underline just how grateful she was that Robinson was engaging with her at all; she certainly wasn't forced to. 'And for agreeing to meet here rather than at the station. Probably best I'm not seen at any official police building right now.'

'It works better this way for both of us,' said Robinson. 'I'm not sure how I'd explain your input to the temporary DI they've installed here.'

'Who is it?'

'Graves. From Leeds. He's up into everything. I had to tell him I was getting a bikini wax so he didn't follow me here.'

'You didn't.'

Robinson looked at Banks out of the corner of her eye and then a little smirk formed on her lips. 'No, I didn't quite have to go that far. But he's enjoying throwing his weight around a bit too much. You know how it is with DI's who are reassigned to a different patch. They like to make sure you know who's boss from the get go.'

'Aye, I've seen it once or twice,' said Banks. 'And I'm

genuinely not trying to cause any trouble for you. I've worked murder cases myself, many times over. I know distraction is the last thing you need. I'm really just here to make sure that if any evidence comes to light suggesting Ewan might be involved that he comes in quietly, and to underline that I have no associations or dealings with any illegal activities – including those potentially perpetrated by a family member.'

Robinson pursed her lips, nodding along to Banks's explanation. 'You know, Charley, if your brother is guilty, and I'm not saying he is, but if he is, I sincerely doubt you'll be implicated. You've only been in very loose contact with him. And the allegations of corruption made against you in recent years were disproven. Discounting that, you've got an impeccable record so I'd be surprised if you had anything to worry about.'

'I'd like to believe that but I can't risk it.' Banks raked her hands through the front of her brown hair. 'I was going to go for a DI position in Bradford. I got a bit comfortable working with my partner, Halloran, you know. I was long overdue a career move. So, I was going to push myself and take a step up. Bring home a bit more for me and my fiancé, Evie. But, right now I feel like I'll be lucky to stay in post as DS if any suspicion at all falls on me. The thing is, I know I've done nothing wrong. But I wouldn't put it past Ewan to find some way of framing me.'

Robinson frowned. 'He was cooperative when we spoke

to him. I didn't get the sense that he was up to anything untoward, otherwise we'd have been straight into his phone records. Do you really think he'd try something like that?'

How to answer that question? It was a worst-case scenario, Banks had to admit that. But after all she'd been through with Ewan she couldn't discount it as a possibility. Ever since he had been first convicted, he'd always made it seem like he wanted to win her forgiveness. But maybe a twenty-year prison stint had left him bitter when it came down to it. And Banks couldn't be sure how he would express that resentment.

She shrugged in response to Robinson's question, as though the idea of Ewan betraying her yet again didn't fill her with the most profound sense of dread she'd ever experienced. 'He's been in prison for twenty years. His little sister became a copper. Essentially started working for the side who put him away. I'm trying not to talk about it too much because it almost feels like saying it out loud will make it happen, but that's my worst fear. That this recon-ciliation – him moving to Yorkshire, allegedly to be closer to me and resurrect our fractured relationship – it's part of a bigger plan I didn't see coming.'

Banks had only just recovered from the last time some-body tried to set her up. Wondering if the life she had worked towards for so long was going to be stripped away had been nothing short of hell. She didn't relish going through all that again, especially at the hands of a blood relative.

'Does Ewan know you're in town, looking into him?' Robinson said.

'No. If he is up to something I don't want to give him the chance to dispose of any evidence, cover anything up or otherwise alter his behaviour. If we turn up something that decidedly points to him though, I will relay it to you, and I'll happily take your lead on how to confront him over it.'

Banks's desire to keep the investigation she was running a secret from her brother was part of the reason she and Kitt had chosen lodgings in nearby Halifax, rather than staying in Andaby itself. There was a strong likelihood that, at some point, Banks would be forced to reveal the fact that she had suspected Ewan all along, and had engaged a private investigator to get to the truth. But it was in her interests to put off that moment for as long as possible. Staying in Andaby would only have increased the likelihood of a confrontation with her brother. And of him spotting her before she was ready to talk to him. If she had run into him while stepping out of the guest house, for example, it certainly wouldn't have been very easy to explain why she was staying in the town where he was now living and hadn't been in touch with him. Halifax was neutral ground and it was also a place that offered a little distance from whatever might unfold during their daily enquiries into Siobhan's passing.

'Well, right now I don't have any evidence that your

brother's involved,' said Robinson. 'His girlfriend, Nancy, confirmed that she was with him that night having a cosy night in.'

'And she seemed to be on the level? I mean, you believed her?'

Robinson nodded. 'According to other people I've worked with, Nancy has lived in the town all of her life and is very low key. I've worked here a few years myself and have always found her to be a little bit on the quiet side . . . though not psychopath quiet, if you know what I mean. She works in the grocers. Sure, she's a bit shy but she's always been friendly and courteous. If anything, I would count yourself lucky that Ewan has taken up with some-body so good-natured. She could be just what he needs after a stint inside.'

Banks folded her arms, thinking. 'Did you get the impression she knew the truth . . . about Ewan's past I mean? I've been wondering what story he's fed her about that. And if she knows who she's sleeping next to.'

'She definitely knows,' Robinson said. 'She made a point of saying that we all make mistakes and just because Ewan made a terrible mistake all those years ago doesn't mean he should be unfairly treated now. Keen as I am to get whoever killed Siobhan Lange into custody, I can't deny that she's got a point.'

'It is surprisingly forgiving of her considering they've only been dating a couple of months though,' said Banks.

'Maybe he was honest with her from the get go,' Robinson said with a shrug. 'And she just admired that. Like I said, Charley, your brother wasn't defensive when we interviewed him. He cooperated completely. We didn't get any of that usual backchat you get with parolees. He told us everything we needed to know. And he's got an alibi. So, I do think you're worrying needlessly when it comes to him. Unless you've seen him wearing anything dark blue lately.'

'What do you mean? Have you got some footage of the killer?'

DS Robinson pulled her phone from her pocket and scrolled to a photograph before holding the screen up for Banks to examine. 'Not footage. But we did find some fibres on the body that didn't match anything she was wearing. They are the tiniest threads. They were found at the nape of her neck, which is probably why the killer missed them. But there's just enough to make out the colour. If we can find whatever garment matches these fibres, we'll find the killer. Given that the item was used to strangle, our first instincts were that it was likely to be some kind of scarf.'

'That would be my guess too,' said Banks. 'Though I suppose it could be a belt. All factors considered, I imagine you're expecting the garment to belong to somebody Siobhan worked with.'

'That's the theory we're working on at the moment,' said Robinson. 'Whoever did this knew a lot about the ins and outs of life at that museum. But of course, we can't just go around every employee in the place and ask them to open their wardrobes and sock drawers.'

'If only it was that easy,' said Banks.

'We're going through the phone records and financials for her work colleagues to see if anything pops out. Some kind of connection between them and the victim. But so far, we've got nothing. There are still a few people to work through though. If we make an arrest, I will let you know.'

'I appreciate it,' said Banks. 'I appreciate all you've shared, more than you know. And if you're focused on the work colleagues, we'll pursue other leads. Make sure we stay out of your way . . . I know it's a bit of an ask but could you send me that photo of the fibres?'

Robinson shot a look at Banks that made it clear that she thought they were playing with fire, but she obliged and Banks's phone pinged with the message.

'Don't worry. I'm not going to cause any trouble for you. If anything, I'm hoping I'll be of help. The private investigator I've hired, well I've known her for some years now and she can be trusted to be discreet. We're going to continue our unofficial investigation into peripheral lines of enquiry. We would have looked into staff but you're already on that.'

'That's been the most logical starting point,' said Robinson. 'But there are twelve different employees on the payroll so it's going to take us a bit of time to get through checking their alibis and look into their records.'

'We'll do what we can to dig up any alternative leads or

theories,' said Banks. 'While I think to mention it though, the investigator I'm working with conducted a rudimentary fingerprint test on the broom handle in the loom room and it looked as though it had been wiped down – she didn't even get one partial.'

Robinson frowned. 'The forensics team tested every logical surface. I don't remember that detail jumping out at me though.'

'Probably because you're busy looking at the prints that *were* there.'

'Aye, that's why we had to think carefully about which surfaces to test though,' said Robinson with a sigh. 'It's a museum. There are people in there all the time leaving their fingerprints everywhere. So, we concentrated on the yarn tubs, the area directly around where the body was found and the body itself.'

'Makes sense,' said Banks. 'It just struck us as odd that something you have to hold to use had not one print on it.'

'It is odd.'

'We wondered if the killer used it to lever the yarn tub and then wiped it down.'

'I'll make sure to log this when I get back to the station. It might serve to give us a clue about the strength or size of the killer.'

'It's definitely something I'll keep in mind as we're looking into suspects outside the museum's payroll. And, you never know, someone we talk to might have something to say about one of the employees. If anything shakes out, I'll obviously feed it back to you.'

Robinson nodded. 'Thanks. If anyone asks, I don't know what you're up to though, yeah?'

'I won't let on that you knew anything about it if we get caught out.'

As Banks said these words, however, she transmitted a silent prayer to whoever might be listening. Appealing to some invisible, greater power to guard her and Kitt against being caught out during their time in Calderdale. Secretly investigating a crime that was both out of her jurisdiction and had a personal conflict of interest was not going to endear her to her superiors to say the least. There were strict rules prohibiting that kind of behaviour. But Banks could not just ignore the fact that her brother might be implicated in a murder investigation. Anger rose in her at the reminder of the unenviable position she was in. Perhaps the most infuriating aspect of this case was that Banks did not want to be working it. She didn't want to be doing something behind the back of her chief superintendent. Or spending time she should be using to plan a jolly wedding reception on catching her brother out in a lie. Granted, she had no real reason to believe Ewan had lied to her, or would lie to her. But likewise, she had no way of knowing how prison had changed him. How it had hardened him. Every minute she worked this case she was putting her whole future at risk and all because she couldn't trust him. She had to tread carefully and cautiously at all times while they were in Calderdale. If Ricci found out about what she was really up to, it would be her badge.

'I'm assuming you will still let me take full credit for anything you find, though?' Robinson said, a wry smile surfacing.

'You can help yourself to the credit. Even if I set some kind of record for cracking a murder case, we both know that Ricci would not be offering me a promotion. I'd be on desk duty for the rest of my natural life. If I was lucky.'

'Great life being a DS isn't it?' Robinson said, emitting a short snort of laughter.

'It might not be perfect,' said Banks. 'But if it's all the same to you, I'd like to hold onto my job.'

CHAPTER SEVEN

It was half past six when a knock came to the door of Banks's room in the Pennine View Bed and Breakfast. It was one of those guest houses where every floorboard seemed to creak, every surface was covered in florals and every lampshade had tassels. It was also safe to say that this particular boarding house wasn't necessarily going to win any awards for its hospitality.

On arrival the landlady had made it quite clear that she did not keep the water heater on all day, and thus any hot showers would have to be taken in the morning or between the hours of nine and ten at night. It seemed to Banks that whenever she went away somewhere she always managed to book into hotels that ran tighter ships than she and Evie did at home. Wasn't a holiday supposed to be about cutting loose a bit? Granted that's not why Banks, Kitt and Grace had come to Calderdale, but presumably some other people came with agendas more relaxing than solving a local murder. Quite what they must think when they were quoted times of the day during which they were permitted to enjoy the luxury of hot water was anyone's guess. One day Banks would book into a hotel where breakfast was served at a reasonable hour and you could have a hot bath anytime you chose. Oh, to have such giddy dreams!

At the sound of the knock to her door, however, Banks forgot about the strict rules and the never-ending supply of bedroom chintz. She smiled as she crossed the room and unlatched the lock. There was only one person she was expecting.

No sooner had she opened the door than Evie bustled her way in. Carrying two large vintage suitcases. Banks watched her drop the bulging luggage with a sigh and blow a blonde curl out of her face.

'Don't take this the wrong way,' Banks said. 'But I thought you were only staying the night.' She helped Evie hoist the bags onto the bed, which had been advertised as a double but was very obviously a bit narrower than that.

'I *am* only staying for one night,' Evie replied.

'This is how much you bring for one night?'

'Well, jinkies,' Evie said, sliding her trademark vintage slang into the conversation. 'I wasn't expecting an interrogation over it. You know I always bring a range of outfit choices whenever we go away.'

'Yes ... when we're going away for a long weekend or a

week. I didn't realize the same principle would apply to an overnight stay. Exactly how much luggage are you planning to take away with you for three months when we go on our honeymoon?'

Evie giggled and put her arms around Banks's neck. 'There is no way on this earth I'm telling you that before I've safely got a wedding ring on my finger.'

With that, Evie leaned in and gave Banks a soft, slow kiss. Not one to waste an invitation, Banks put her hands on Evie's waist and lowered her down onto the bed. Enjoying the way in which her broad frame completely covered Evie's petite form.

'Are you OK?' Evie asked when they at last broke the kiss. 'I haven't been able to stop thinking about what you're going through all day.'

'The seventeen messages you sent between midday and five were a bit of a clue to that,' Charley said, brushing aside Evie's hair and kissing the scars that still scored deep at her temples. A reminder to both of them that not catching a killer in time could be costly.

'Oh, you really are the mistress of dodging questions, you know,' said Evie. 'I can't help if you don't let me in.'

'I'm sorry love,' Charley said, stroking Evie's cheek. 'The truth is I'm pretty frightened right now. Of what we'll find. Or what we might not find till it's too late.'

'You've struggled with this for so long, I don't know how you've coped with it all,' Evie said.

Banks pursed her lips. There was so much going on inside at any given moment it was difficult to both contain it and talk about it. But she didn't want Evie to feel like she was holding back from her, so she had to try. 'When Ewan was first convicted, the pain of it was so profound, it didn't feel real. I felt completely separated from the world in a way that's difficult to explain. Everyone else was just going about their business as usual. But I was carrying this huge weight around. My brother had ended somebody else's life. And nothing any of us did could change that fact. When I heard about this murder, it was like all those feelings hit me at once. All over again.'

'It's totally understandable that it would feel like déjà vu. And of all the feelings to relive that kind of pain is not one anyone would choose,' said Evie.

Banks shook her head. 'For years, I just kept expecting things to snap into focus again. I genuinely felt like I was living some kind of nightmare. It was easier to believe it wasn't real. That none of this was real. Things did eventually snap into focus for me again. But not until the day I met you. When we crossed paths for the first time, I realized I wanted to get a hold on myself again. Wanted to have something to offer you besides avoidance and shame. I'm still working on it.'

Evie took a deep breath and looked deep into Banks's eyes. 'I love you, Charley. For who you are. You're not facing it alone this time. No matter what, I will always stand by you. We can work through each problem together. I really am here for you.'

At those words, the tightness that had clenched in Charley's chest released. 'You have no idea how much it means to hear that. I don't know what I'd do without you.'

Evie shook her head. 'You'll never have to find out, you daft thing. You went and proposed like a proper chump. You're stuck with me now.'

Charley leaned in for another kiss but before her lips could meet with Evie's, Kitt's voice came booming down through the ceiling.

'The business card debacle was bad enough, Grace. So don't play games with me. What have you done with my teapot? You know better than to come between me and a caffeinated beverage.'

'I haven't touched it!' came Grace's somewhat unconvincing reply.

'Don't give me that. What's that under your jumper?'

'Nothing . . . I mean I'm pregnant.'

'Pregnant with a teapot. Give over will you.'

Some scuffling sounds ensued and the subsequent bubbling of a kettle coming to the boil betrayed the fact that the teapot had been recovered.

'Are them two sharing a room?' Charley asked, not quite able to believe her bad luck to be stuck in the room below in a guest house that seemingly had crêpe paper floor boards. 'What about Halloran? Where's he sleeping?'

'He's caught a case so he can't stay over after all. He's going to drive back to York once we've had dinner and I'll get the train back tomorrow morning. But, to be honest, if it's a choice between hearing Halloran and Kitt getting busy or Kitt and Grace bickering I know which I'd prefer.'

'Fair point,' said Banks, trying to block out the images that had surfaced in her head at the mention of her boss's sex life.

'And on the plus side, you won't have to ask either of them for an update on the case,' said Evie. 'You'll be able to hear everything they say through the ceiling. From what Grace said on the way here though, she's had some kind of breakthrough with the photo of those fibres Kitt sent her.'

'Really? What's that then?' said Banks.

Evie shook her head. 'I don't know. You know what Grace is like, she loves to be in the spotlight so she probably won't do the big reveal until we're all sitting around the dinner table tonight.'

Banks's mind at once started to race in anticipation of the various discoveries Grace could have made. She had been tasked by Kitt to spend the day researching anyone closely connected with Siobhan's work colleagues while also looking into the victim's history online to see if anything interesting surfaced about their lives and interactions. Grace had not been directed to look into Ewan. There wasn't likely to be much on the internet anyway considering he'd been in prison for twenty years and didn't have a computer in his home. Consequently, whatever Grace had found probably didn't relate to him. Still, Banks would breathe a little easier once she knew what Grace had found. Regardless of the circumstances, as a general rule, knowing was better than not knowing.

'It is a shame that the walls are so thin here though,' Evie said, re-establishing Banks's attention with an impish smile. 'I had hoped we'd have some fun tonight. Get in a little practice for the honeymoon.'

'Oh, we will,' Charley said. 'You'll just have to be very, very quiet.'

Evie chuckled and pressed her forehead against Charley's. They managed to enjoy the moment for all of three seconds before another argument broke out above. This time about a life-sized cardboard cut-out of Ryan Reynolds Grace had ordered on the company stationery budget. Which, though it no doubt brightened the work space of Hartley and Edwards Investigations, Banks had to concede didn't sound like an essential business expense.

'Come on,' Charley said, grudgingly accepting that the Punch and Judy show raining down on them from above was going to ruin any moment right now. 'Let's get ourselves ready and down to the Piece Hall for dinner. If Halloran has to drive back tonight, I want to go through everything we've got so far before he leaves. Considering the personal nature of the case, I can't exactly count on myself to be objective.'

Pecking Charley on the nose, Evie helped herself up off

the bed and tottered into the bathroom to freshen up. Banks was left to sit on the bed to contemplate what they had learned so far about the killing of Siobhan Lange. For all the circumstantial evidence pointing towards Siobhan's colleagues, Banks had a feeling that the blue fibres were going to be what led to unmasking the killer. It was usually some concrete detail of that nature that cracked a case. A small piece of physical evidence overlooked by whoever was perpetrating the crime. If Grace had already had a break-through on that score, then maybe they could wrap up this case sooner than Banks had hoped.

She hadn't been exaggerating in what she'd told Evie. For so long, she'd felt the gravity of her brother's crimes bearing down on her. If she was really honest with herself, that was one of the reasons she had joined the police force in the first place. To somehow atone for what her brother had done. To save lives. To help people. After all the work she'd put in over the last decade, didn't she deserve a chance to find release from these chains?

CHAPTER EIGHT

The Piece Hall was a somewhat peculiar sight to the modern eye, though there was no denying its unique, and antique, beauty. The structure was rectangular in shape and three storeys high. On the outer rim of the building stood rows of shops, once inhabited by textile vendors who would sell their 'pieces' of cloth to locals and visitors alike. Now, the small retail units were filled with quirky independent businesses that sold everything from vintage jewellery to cupcakes. At the centre of all this was a piazza that wouldn't have been out of place in Italy, though the weather in Calderdale wasn't quite in competition with continental temperatures.

Dusk would not fall for another couple of hours but the May sunshine was decidedly on the wane as Banks, Evie, Kitt, Grace and Halloran sat at a table at a restaurant overlooking a gurgling water feature.

'So, what's this Evie tells me about a breakthrough on those fibres?' Banks said the second they'd ordered their food. When Banks had shared the photograph of the fibres with Kitt, Kitt had in turn shared it with Grace. The idea being that while researching any persons connected with Siobhan's colleagues, she would be on a particular look out for anyone wearing that darker shade of blue. Given Banks had never really given Kitt's assistant much of her time, it seemed a bit rude to just launch straight into business the moment after they'd ordered their food but she couldn't keep her impatience in check any longer. Kitt had been up front about the fact that they were going to take the first day relatively easy. But their conversation with Deborah and Banks's conversation with Robinson had yet to throw up any suspects outside those on the museum payroll. Tomorrow, they would definitely need to step things up if they wanted to significantly move the case forward before Kitt returned to York on Friday.

As transparent as Banks's desperation might be to get the shop talk rolling, it likely wasn't entirely unwelcome. Halloran had spent most of his time at the table bemoaning the fact that since he wouldn't be staying the night in Halifax with the rest of them he'd been robbed of an opportunity to nip over to Andaby and get a look at the *Frederick William Kitson* locomotive for himself. There was only so much sympathizing the rest of them had been able to do considering the stakes of the wider situation they were dealing with. A change of subject was definitely in order.

'I had hoped to have a drink in my hand before getting

to that . . . ' Grace started but trailed off when she saw the expression on Kitt's face. After their bickering back at the hotel it seems she'd made it clear she wasn't in the mood for any more of her assistant's usual schtick.

'But, yes, I have turned up something,' Grace said quickly, tucking a curl of brown hair behind her ear as she spoke, 'though it's not quite in the direction we were hoping for.'

'How do you mean?' said Banks. Her muscles tensed. Was she gently trying to break the news that something in her research *had* pointed to her brother's involvement after all?

'I mean, I haven't found anything untoward on the social media accounts of her work colleagues. I've made a list of the twelve that appear on the website for the industrial museum and I've also made a list of their most common connections on social media, but there have been no online altercations with the victim. No dodgy or aggressive comments. Despite not being on the best of terms with the deceased, they've all posted about how shocked they are about her death. Now, that could be a ploy of course. If someone she worked with is behind it, they're hardly going to announce it on Facebook. But, if there is anything going on with those people, I think the police might well find it before us – through bank or financial records.'

'Robinson is already on that,' said Banks.

'As you'd expect given the nature of the crime and where it took place,' said Halloran.

'So, if your breakthrough didn't relate to work colleagues,

then what did it relate to?' Banks said, trying to keep her cool whilst at the same time trying to prepare herself for the worst. 'Whatever you've found, please do share it.'

Grace offered a gentle smile and wrapped the turquoise pashmina she was wearing a little tighter around her shoulders. 'I've been doing some digging on the victim, you see. Trying to find out everything I can about her. My hope was to discover a motive for Siobhan's killing. But instead, I saw something suspicious in an old school photograph I dug up on Facebook.'

'What was it?' Banks said, pretty desperate to cut to the chase now.

'The picture was from the day she left secondary school. Obviously, Facebook wasn't a thing at the time they left school, but someone had dug into their photo albums at some point and scanned the photo. Siobhan and her year group were all lined up in rows – class photo style, you know. There were about a hundred of them in total. And they were all wearing dark blue sashes as part of their graduation uniform. As soon as I saw them, there was something about the colour that struck me as familiar. That's when, on a whim, I compared the Facebook photograph with the photo of the fibres you sent through . . . they look like an exact match to me.'

Banks looked at Halloran and then her eyes drifted back to Grace. 'But, I mean, Siobhan must have left school twenty years ago.'

'Nineteen to be precise,' said Grace.

'It's not something to be completely discounted given the similarity of the colours, Grace,' said Halloran. 'It's just, in our experience, it's quite unlikely that something the victim wore nineteen years ago would be the murder weapon. It's more likely that it's a garment worn by the killer the day they struck. Or even something belonging to the victim, like a handbag strap for example.'

'I hear what you're saying,' said Grace. 'But I didn't find any other colour matches to those fibres, and I was trawling through photographs all day. Right now, those graduation sashes are the only thing we have to go on.'

Banks paused, thinking. On the one hand, that graduation ceremony was a long time ago and likely to have very little bearing on the here and now. On the other hand, there were roughly a hundred people associated with a school the victim had attended who possessed a garment that matched the fibres Robinson and her team had found. Of course, if the school used the same colour of sash every year a student graduated then the number of potential suspects would shoot up considerably.

'The police will be looking into the most up-to-date aspects of the case,' said Kitt, 'and working backwards. From what I've understood about the way you and Mal work, that would be their priority.'

'It's true that we tend to dive into the most recent records to pull up a suspect list, yes,' said Banks.

'So, if that's the case, it's going to be a long time before the police prioritize something like this,' said Kitt. 'In the cases we've worked there have been a few instances where the motive isn't derived from recent interactions. It's been something that's gone way back. And there's something about small-town life that can make some people quite insular or inward looking. Grudges can be held for a long time under such circumstances.'

'Take it from a Thirsk girl,' said Evie. 'It's not everyone by any means, but you do see it.'

'So, what are you proposing?' said Banks, after offering Evie a grudging smile.

'That we pay a visit to Andaby Comprehensive tomorrow and find someone who can tell us something about the people in the photograph,' said Kitt. 'I know it was a long time ago but some teachers and administrative staff stay in post in the same school for thirty or forty years. Especially in small places. Or one of the parents might have gone to school with Siobhan, someone who's never moved away from the town. We could also talk to them, see if they remember anything about the relationships of that year group. Perhaps we'll get a couple of new suspects out of it.'

Banks tried not to let her scepticism show but she suspected she wasn't doing a very good job of hiding her feelings. She knew that Kitt and Grace had their own unique way of working, to put it politely; an approach that perhaps wasn't exactly the most logical of procedures to someone who had had police training. But when she had hired them, she had been expecting them to propose something a little more plausible than delving back into the victim's twenty-year-old school history. That said, Kitt was right about the fact that the police were already following the most likely lead – Siobhan's work colleagues. Their visit to the mill, the online research Grace had conducted and their conversation with Robinson hadn't given them any other avenues for exploration. There was also the fact that she had promised to stay out of Robinson's way. Following a lead like this one would almost certainly ensure that. For now, at least, Banks had to acknowledge that this was their only break.

'Feels like a long-shot,' she said at last. 'But I suppose if we find someone we can talk to, we'll either get a few suggested suspects out of them, or rule out the idea that the fibres came from the sash completely. Which is progress in its own way.'

'Without police access to financials and phone data, I do agree that it's your strongest lead at the minute,' said Halloran. 'And you're better off pursuing avenues that neither Robinson or Graves have thought of. I don't know Graves personally but from what I've heard on the grapevine he'll be straight on the phone to Ricci if he thinks you've tampered with his investigation. Not to get sentimental but I would miss you if you weren't around.'

'I didn't know you had such schmaltz in you, sir.'

'Well, someone's got to fix the printer when it goes on

the blink,' Halloran said. Banks could tell from his over-confident grin that Halloran thought himself the wittiest person at the table just then. It seemed a shame not to seize the opportunity to prove him wrong.

'*You* certainly can't do it, can you? Not unsupervised at least,' said Banks. 'Though it is entertaining to watch you try for a good half-hour before I swoop in.'

'Yes, all right, that joke has backfired on me, let's move on.'

'Don't worry, sir, I'm sure it's just a matter of time before the whole office is powered by model trains in some ingenious energy-saving move from head office. Then you'll really be on top of things.'

Slowly, Halloran turned and glared at Kitt.

'You told Banks about my train set?' Halloran said, while everyone else at the table did what they could to keep a straight face. Evie, unable to keep from giggling, looked away and pretended to be deeply interested in some potted trees arranged in the middle of the piazza.

'I didn't know it was some big secret,' said Kitt. 'How many times have I told you to embrace your inner geek?'

'Now that is something I can imagine Kitt saying,' said Grace. 'I think she came out of the womb wearing glasses.'

'I don't wear glasses, Grace.'

'I think you'll find my logic stands. And, I don't wish to discuss the matter any further,' Grace said, and then changed the subject before Kitt could argue with her. 'I'm glad the trip to Andaby Comprehensive has been settled for tomorrow, however, as I believe that in the space of just a few hours I've cracked this case wide open.'

'Yes,' Kitt said, her tone more than a little bit dubious. 'We'll see about that.'

From there, the conversation moved on to arrangements for Evie and Banks's wedding. It was clear the next step for the case had been decided, whether Banks agreed with it or not. Maybe it was to the good that they were all there to offer her some steer, given the circumstances. She wasn't exactly thinking clearly just now. And, like Halloran said, she also had to avoid a run-in with DI Graves at all costs. In the pit of her stomach, however, Banks had a grudging feeling that their field trip to Andaby Comprehensive was likely going to be a waste of time. If their investigation wasn't urgent, that might not have mattered too much. But in this instance, with every second they squandered, Siobhan's true killer came closer to slipping through the cracks completely.

CHAPTER NINE

Banks did her utmost not to breathe in too much of the industrial-strength bleach that had clearly been used to clean the corridors of Andaby Comprehensive early that morning. Having already identified themselves at the locked school gate and explained their plight, the pair had been promptly buzzed in by Maya Garrison who, she had explained over the telecom, was the headteacher's assistant.

'Maya?' Kitt said to a woman standing behind a desk in a hijab.

'That's me,' Maya said, the warmth of her smile reflecting in her dark brown eyes. She was quite a short woman and Banks imagined some of the older kids at the school might underestimate her as a result. There was a definite firmness to her tone, however, that spoke of a desire to get things done efficiently. In summary, she had the air of a woman who could make people fall into line should she want or need them too. A valuable quality in a secondary school secretary.

'I appreciate you agreeing to talk to us,' said Kitt. 'We won't take much of your time. We just wanted to show you a photograph of Siobhan's year group and ask if anyone in the school might be able to talk to us about who was close to her back then and what their relationships were like at the time of leaving the school.'

'Oh, you don't need to show me a photograph of Siobhan's year group. I was in the year above,' Maya said. 'I mean, if you want to show me a photograph to refresh my memory, that's fine – it has been twenty years since I left school now – though I try to keep that quiet.'

'Don't we all,' said Kitt. 'Not that we should feel obliged to bow to the societal pressure to look young. But old, less enlightened habits do die hard.'

'Er . . . yes, I – I suppose so,' said Maya.

Banks couldn't help but smile at the rather bemused look on Maya's face. As far as Maya was concerned, Kitt was a private investigator. She had no idea about the fact that she managed the Women's Studies section of the local university library two days a week and was prone to dishing out unsolicited mini-lectures associated with the subject should the opportunity arise.

'Anyway,' Kitt said, not quite wrapped up in her feminist monologue enough to have missed Maya's slight surprise. 'You're brave, going to work in a school you used to attend as a student. I'm not sure I could do that myself. Too many memories lurking in the corridors!'

'Oh, well, it's not quite like that for me,' said Maya. 'This is a relatively new building as you can probably tell. The school moved campuses about a decade ago. The old building was crumbling to nothing after decades of Yorkshire rain and never quite enough money to maintain the stonework. You know how it is with these things, it just became cheaper to build a new one on the opposite side of the canal than it would have been to fix the old one. I came to work here a couple of years after the transition. I think I prefer it that way, you know. Separates teenage-hood and adulthood just a little bit more.'

'I understand completely,' said Kitt. I wouldn't go back to my teenage years if you paid me . . . but enough of my personal history. I'll just pull up the photo I mentioned on my phone in case it jogs anything about Siobhan's year group.'

Once the photo had been retrieved Kitt handed the phone to Maya.

'Oh, yes,' she said as she looked along the line-up. 'Look at that hair, we hadn't quite let go of the nineties even after the turn of the millennium, had we? How horrendous. Well, in our defence we didn't know any better.'

Kitt chuckled. 'It is a bit that way when a decade changes. I don't think I let go of the eighties until about 1993. I was admiring the colour of the graduation sashes in that photo though. Do they do those every year? Is it the school colour?'

'No, I know some schools do have colours, like associated

with their uniforms and that. We don't at this school. The head just decides on a different shade each year for the graduation sashes. We got lucky and had crimson ones. Siobhan's year had that deep blue. But while I've been here we've had years when the budget's running tight, so the colour has been determined by the cheapest available fabric. I've seen some years that graduate with muddy brown sashes, or some sickly colour between yellow and green. I've got two boys who attend here and neither are eager to find out what their colours are going to be.'

Banks nodded along to what Maya was saying. If there was anything to this whole sash theory then at least they could focus their efforts on Siobhan's year group. It didn't sound as though any other cohort had graduated in quite the same colours. That was their suspect list whittled down to about a hundred people. But they'd have to do better than that.

'I'm not sure if you'll have any direct insights given that you were in the year above,' said Banks. 'But do you know if there was anyone in that photograph who didn't get on with Siobhan, or perhaps maybe even had a serious altercation with her?'

'Hmmm,' Maya said, scanning her eyes across the photograph once again. 'Siobhan appeared to be one of the more popular girls. But, of course, that doesn't mean she was actually liked by that many people. Most of them envied her, I would say. I know I certainly did and I was a year older than she was. From what I knew about her she had a little bit of a clique going on with her friend Emily Cook.'

'Which one is she in this photograph?' Kitt said, holding it up again so Maya might pick her out.

'Ummm, there she is,' Maya said. Banks leaned in to take a look for herself. Maya was pointing to a slim girl with freckles and blonde hair.

'There were a couple of others involved but Emily was without doubt Siobhan's wing woman,' said Maya. 'The pair were very close all the way through school. Everywhere one went you'd find the other, they were inseparable. But pretty much anyone else, as far as Siobhan was concerned, was a fair target for some of her crueller acts. You know what kids are like, they're not really fully developed people, at least the two I've got at home aren't! They're still learning that kindness is the most valuable asset in this world.'

'And some people haven't even learned that by the time they're adults,' said Kitt.

'Too true,' said Maya. 'Sorry if this is jumping the gun a bit, but why are you asking about people Siobhan went to school with? You . . . you don't think one of her classmates had something to do with her death, do you?'

'Oh, no, nothing so concrete at this stage,' said Kitt, while Banks admired her ability to lie through her teeth for the sake of the investigation. 'We're just gathering background information about the victim's life and then once we've done that, we'll analyse the whole picture for leads.'

'Nineteen years of history is certainly a lot of background information,' Maya said, seemingly not all that convinced by Kitt's explanation. 'But if you're really looking for the full picture, there are definitely a couple of people in this photograph it might be worth your while looking into. Craig Norris, for starters.'

'Boyfriend?' Banks said.

Maya nodded. 'They were the hot couple for about three years. Which is, of course, a lifetime when you're eighteen. But she did something really terrible to Craig. I'd already left school by that point, but since I never moved away from Andaby, I still heard about it. The whole town did.'

'What did she do?' said Kitt.

'Due to Siobhan's popularity, she was asked to give the graduation speech. It was supposed to be motivational, maybe even inspiring. I know it sounds really American, but that was about the time schools over here started to adopt some of the more Americanized customs like proms and graduation ceremonies, all that stuff, you know? Our year was the first at this school to have any of that stuff. And the year after I left, Siobhan gave the graduation speech and decided that while she had access to a microphone she was going to break up with Craig.'

'What? In front of the whole year group?' said Banks.

'And teachers and parents. Who knows what possessed her to do it? I think she was just trying to prove how much she could get away with by that point. And, of course, it was the end of the school year so there was nothing the staff could really do to punish her for it even if they had wanted to.'

'It must have been quite a scene,' Kitt said, shaking her head.

'You're not wrong. The incident was the talk of the school and the town for weeks after,' said Maya. 'I didn't hear the exact wording but, from what I was told after the fact, she made it clear that she thought Craig wasn't good enough for her.'

Banks exchanged a look with Kitt. Depending on how Craig's life had panned out, that could be motive for murder. If he felt like his best years were behind him and Siobhan's public break-up scene had been the start of his life going downhill, Banks couldn't discount the idea that he might decide to teach Siobhan a lesson in cruelty. Certainly, in her time as a DS she had seen people kill for a lot less. The sad truth about murder cases was that boyfriends were suspects a lot of the time. Granted, it was usually people who had broken up with each other last week or last month who were most likely to be victims and perps in these kinds of situations. But school was a formative time for everyone, and Craig might blame Siobhan for any lack of success in his love life if he still hadn't struck it lucky with the right girl. An event like that could dent a person's confidence for life. Perhaps he had decided it was time for a little payback?

'I must say, that is quite a dramatic end to your school

years by anyone's standards,' Kitt said. 'We'll definitely track Craig down. See how he's doing.'

'I always thought there was something a bit off about him to be honest,' said Maya. 'I know that's hardly concrete evidence but he was quite a big guy and a bit of a bully himself. I wouldn't have liked to be left alone in a room with him if you know what I mean.'

'Was he ever violent at school?' asked Banks.

'He was an eighteen-year-old rugby player and yeah, not all of the tackles were on the pitch from what I saw. Lots of the younger kids lived in fear of him, but to be honest I never saw him direct his violence at Siobhan herself. I suppose that doesn't mean it didn't happen . . . she did wear a lot of make-up. I never thought to wonder why, just thought she was being an insecure teenager like all the rest of us, you know?'

At this, Banks began to reconsider her previous reservations about just how useful this visit was going to be. It had been obvious from what Deborah told them back at the mill that there was no love lost between Siobhan and the people she worked with. But now Maya was telling them that there were other people in Siobhan's history that hadn't been well-disposed towards her. In fact, she had actively made enemies on her graduation day – a day on which everyone had been wearing dark blue sashes that matched fibres found on the victim. So perhaps there was a chance that the motive did stretch as far back as Siobhan's school days after all. One thing was for sure, after hearing all this Banks would definitely be seeking out Craig Norris.

'There is someone else I'd recommend you talking to, though,' said Maya, snapping Banks out of her thoughts.

'Who's that?' asked Kitt.

'Well, Craig wasn't the only one who was a bully. As I said, Siobhan could be cruel. And, between them, Craig and Siobhan were quite a pair. Siobhan bullied quite a few of the girls but out of everyone who attended the school, there was one person she bullied more than anyone else.'

'Can you remember their name?' Banks said.

'Oh, yeah, she was one of those people pretty much everyone pitied. I never would have forgotten her but, as it happens, she still lives in town now. Her name's Nancy Murphy.'

'Nancy Murphy? A– are you sure?' Banks stuttered, feeling all the colour drain from her face.

'Oh, yes, as I say, she still lives in town. Works in the grocers. Poor old Nancy,' Maya said, a sorrowful look crossing her face. 'When I was at school, changing places with her was one of my worst nightmares. Siobhan was always dreaming up new ways to torment the poor lass. I don't pretend to know her very well, but from what I see and hear from a distance I don't think she ever really got over it.'

Banks glanced over at Kitt who had already adopted a pained expression.

So, she recognized the name just as well as Banks did.

Could it be coincidence that Ewan's new girlfriend had been mentioned in relation to this murder by someone who knew next to nothing about the case? A churning feeling in her gut told Banks that coincidence had nothing to do with it.

CHAPTER TEN

'Charley!' Kitt called after Banks.

Banks didn't slow. Couldn't slow. What on earth must Maya have thought of her rushing out of there like that? As she burst out of the main entrance doors of the school, however, she decided she didn't much care what anyone thought. She didn't have the resources just then. She could barely breathe, let alone care about appearances. The fresh, blossom-filled May air was a welcome presence in her lungs and she sucked it in deep. Only after taking in a good few breaths did she slacken her pace. For a second, she thought she was going to be sick but she leaned against the nearest wall and managed to steady herself. Closing her eyes, she tried to collect her thoughts.

She had been dubious of Ewan's alibi from the get go. But to hear his girlfriend's name mentioned as a potential suspect, she hadn't been prepared for that. She hadn't expected today's trip to lead anywhere at all. It was supposed to be

a box ticking exercise at best. Part of the process of elim-
ination.

'I'm so sorry,' Kitt said, catching her up. 'If I'd thought
there was even half a chance that Nancy was going to be
implicated, I would have suggested you wait in the car until
I had a clearer picture of how she fits into it all. But I just
didn't clock that she was even the same age as Siobhan. I
only knew her name, not what she looked like, so we had no
chance of picking her out of this photograph ahead of time.'

'I've never met her either,' said Banks. 'I did find a Facebook profile for her but the photo wasn't of her – it was
a vase filled with daffodils and there were no other photographs available due to her privacy settings. So, I didn't
know what she looked like.'

'This is the danger of working a case with such a personal
angle,' said Kitt. 'I'm going to have to work a little bit harder
at protecting you, aren't I?'

Banks shook her head and tried to stand upright of her
own accord. She looked around the small playing field for a
moment, taking in the view. The school had done a pretty
good job of making the new campus a charming place to
be when the sun was shining. A small court with basketball
hoops stood off to the right. To her left there was a grassed
area with blossom and sycamore trees planted every so
often to provide shade from the sun. Banks had no idea
what the old campus looked like but if it was anything like
this then it was hard to believe that any form of cruelty and

mean-spiritedness played out in such beautiful surroundings. Though, of course, Banks knew objectively that many a child will have experienced humiliation on these patches of tarmac and grass. Right now, the whole scene looked peaceful and just at this moment that's exactly what she needed. A place serene enough to collect her thoughts.

'It's not your fault,' Banks said. 'If I work cases on a daily basis and couldn't see that coming there's really no reason you should've. But this is not a good sign when it comes to the involvement of my brother. What if Nancy told Ewan about how Siobhan tortured her in school and he put the idea in her head to do something? What if they planned this together? He has been consorting with criminals for the last two decades, I have no idea what he's capable of any more.'

'We've no evidence of either of those things just yet,' said Kitt. 'Remember, Nancy wasn't the only name Maya mentioned. And, to be quite frank, from what I've understood so far about her, Siobhan seems to have made far more enemies than friends during her contracted time on this planet. The probability that she bullied, or was otherwise cruel to someone more recently and that they took it upon themselves to murder her, is much more probable.'

'I – I suppose that's true,' Banks said, grudgingly. Her head was spinning after hearing those words fall out of Maya's mouth. When she was younger, before they began their epic battle as teenagers to see who could come up with the most innovative insult, she had always looked up to her older brother. Not just that. He'd sort of been her hero. Always there to protect her and support her. Even when they bickered during their teenage years, it always felt like more of a game than anything else.

But when he lost control that night and a man ended up dead, the illusion of her brother the hero was shattered. Banks had never quite overcome the sense of betrayal she had felt, and perhaps that's why her first instinct was to assume he had betrayed her once again.

'We'll follow up with both Craig Norris and Nancy Murphy because we need to eliminate them from the list of suspects, but remember, we're talking about almost a twenty-year history here. The police are already on the most likely track to success; after all, by the sound of things Siobhan wasn't liked at work any more than she was at school. And if I had to bet one way or the other, I'd say the killer was likely to be someone with a current grudge against the deceased. We just have to check out these historical threads to tie up the loose ends.'

'All right,' Banks said, even though she knew Kitt probably didn't believe what she was saying. At least not one hundred per cent. From what she knew about Kitt, she wasn't a fan of wasting her own time, so she must think that this was a lead worth following despite her protestations, no doubt designed to protect Banks from being overwhelmed. 'Before we go to either Craig or Nancy, I need to let DS Robinson know about this, and then have a conversation with Ewan,' said Banks. 'I wasn't expecting to talk to him this early. But I promised myself I would act upon the earliest sign that he might have played a part in this woman's death. The right thing to do, even if there's nothing to this whole theory, is to inform Robinson about what we've uncovered and get her to agree to me having a firm conversation with my brother. They've already had a run at him and it hasn't yielded the results they needed. It's my turn to try and get the truth out of him.'

'But haven't you already tried that, Charley? You said that he just told you the same story he told Robinson. I think it might be time to face the fact that right now your brother views you more as a police officer than as a sister. And as long as that's the case, there may be little hope of getting him to open up, even if he is hiding something.'

Banks pressed her lips together, thinking. 'You're right. He did tell me the same story he told the police last time. Probably, as you say, because right now he's just thinking of me as another badge. But maybe I can work another angle, find another way in and get him to tell me something he wouldn't ordinarily let slip.'

Kitt paused and looked hard at Banks. 'You're going to challenge him over his alibi, aren't you?'

Banks nodded. 'I'm going to try and get Robinson's permission to, yes. This is her case so if she vetoes it, I'll just have to step away. I know it might seem a rash move at this early stage but I've just got that gut feeling you get when something isn't right. You know what it's like trying to solve a murder – it's like the world's most impossible jigsaw puzzle. Because if one piece isn't right it skews all the others. If my brother hasn't been honest about where he was that night or has lied about something else, that could seriously affect Robinson's chances of finding the real killer. So regardless of exactly how involved he is, I need to make sure that alibi is watertight.'

'I'm not going to suggest you're being rash,' said Kitt. 'That would be equal parts insulting and hypocritical given some of the things we've resorted to in past investigations. You are a very experienced officer – you don't need me second-guessing what you're doing. I suppose I just wouldn't be doing my job right unless I underlined the fact that calling his bluff might tip him off and enable him to destroy evidence if he is up to something.'

Banks took a deep breath and let it out slowly. 'I know, but I also know how to handle him. He likes to think he's the clever one in the room. If he denies any wrongdoing, I'll just pretend he's got me completely fooled. Set him at ease. I know it's a risk and Robinson might not let me within a mile of him after she hears what I've got to say. But I just can't go any further with this case without at least trying to find out once and for all if he's telling the truth about where he was that night.'

'I take it this is something you want to do alone,' said Kitt, seemingly resigned to the fact that Banks was going to go ahead with this meeting, regardless of her cautions.

'It's probably best if I don't go with an entourage, yeah. I need him to trust me. Even though I don't trust him. He needs to think that he's on safe ground, otherwise I don't stand a chance of coaxing him into talking. Understandably, after being in prison for so long, he's sort of always on full alert. If he spots anyone watching us it's game over.'

'OK. While you're doing that, we'll be doing our best to make ourselves useful,' said Kitt. 'We'll look into Craig Norris, see if he's still living in the area. If he's moved to the Highlands, he might not be the most probable suspect. But if he's living anywhere within a couple of hours drive, we might even be able to track him down today. Find out one way or another if he's got an alibi and such.'

'Thanks, Kitt,' said Banks. 'What you must think of me, I don't know.'

'I think you are a person in a very difficult situation who is doing a very admirable job of managing it. But be careful, Charley. Remember you can step back from this case any-time you choose. And it's worth considering the idea that at some point that might be the best option. No matter how much you want to get to the truth, you need to think of your future, with Evie. You're too close to having everything you want to risk it all now. Evie hasn't said it outright because she's too loyal. But I can tell she is worried about you, and frankly, so am I. So, this is just your friendly reminder that

Grace and I are perfectly capable of working this case on our own and reporting back to you should it ever get too much.'

'Thank you,' Banks said, blinking back tears. She could have taken offence at the lecture, of course. But everything Kitt said was pretty much on the money, so what was there to argue about? Except the fact that she had no hope of following Kitt's sage advice. 'I can't step back, not now,' Banks said. 'I know I wasn't the one who committed murder all those years ago but somehow I've always felt responsible. And there's nothing I can do to shake that feeling. My only hope of getting closure on this is to find out if Ewan killed that woman. Yes, it will be painful if I find out he did. But at least he'll be back behind bars and unable to hurt anyone else, including me. Until I've got to the categorical truth there's no way I'm giving this up.'

CHAPTER ELEVEN

'I thought you quit smoking,' Banks said. She watched Ewan hastily stub out his cigarette on the dry-stone wall of the small bridge on which he stood. Since the investigation began, Banks had been careful to only meet with Ewan in public places. In this instance, she'd suggested the green at the centre of town which had cricket lines etched onto it at one end and a stream running through it at the other. The little bridge running over the beck had seemed the perfect landmark at which to arrange a meeting. The last thing Banks needed was footage or photographs taken by another officer depicting her and Ewan having what might have looked like a covert conversation down some dark alley.

Given that her brother's true part in this killing, and any nefarious plans he might have as to the future of her career, were yet unclear, she had to do everything possible to underline to her fellow officers that she had nothing to hide. Moreover, she had to ensure that any conversations she had with her brother were to ascertain facts about the case in support of the team investigating the crime, rather than to cover up any wrongdoing for which Ewan might be culpable.

To this end, Banks had taken the precaution of calling DS Robinson, updating her on their suspicions about the source of the blue fibres and convincing her to allow her to have a preliminary conversation with her brother about the relationship between Nancy and Siobhan. Particularly, Banks had explained, she would seek to put pressure on Ewan to reveal the truth if he had fudged anything surrounding his alibi. At present, as far as Robinson was concerned, there wasn't anything concrete to suspect Nancy. They would need a warrant to search her home for a school sash, but they needed to persuade a judge to get a warrant and neither Robinson nor Banks were convinced that a judge would grant such a warrant on the basis that the victim had bullied Nancy at school almost two decades ago. Even when you threw in Nancy's poor choice of boyfriend, in an ex-murderer, the pair said they were together on the night of Siobhan's murder so, unless they could find evidence to the contrary, a search warrant wasn't likely to materialize. If Ewan did reveal anything even remotely damning, however, Banks was to escort Ewan to Andaby Police Station so he could be questioned under caution.

That was the plan. Exactly whether it would yield any results in practice, Banks had no idea.

Ewan scratched the side of his head as she approached him. 'Give me a break about the ciggys, eh, Charley? It's been a difficult week as it is without a public health lecture from my own sister.'

'Has it been a difficult week?' Banks said, while wondering if he had felt on edge because he had lied about his true whereabouts on the night of Siobhan's murder.

A flash of confusion stirred in his dark brown eyes as he looked at her. 'You know it has been. Only I could get released from prison and move to a place where I'm back on the suspect list within a matter of months.'

Banks took a breath, contemplating the various strategies she could use to get the information she needed, and landed on pretending it was his interests she was most concerned about.

'What are you doing on this side of Yorkshire, anyway? Missed me since last week, have you?' Ewan asked. There was definitely a note of suspicion in his voice. Something Banks was going to have to diffuse if she was to find out the truth about his alibi.

'You know I'm not the sentimental type,' she said, and he at once grinned back at her. Considering how long he'd been in prison, where personal hygiene was perhaps not the chief concern, Ewan had a good set of teeth on him. They were a bit yellow, but unlike so many people Banks had dealt with who had seen long stints behind bars, they were all at least still intact.

Banks took a breath and delivered the story she'd practised on the way here. 'The truth is my partner at work is obsessed with trains and wanted to come and see the new steam engine they've commissioned. Apparently, it starts running this week.'

Though not the gospel truth, this wasn't an outright lie either. Halloran had made a point of saying before he left them at The Piece Hall last night that he would definitely be across to Andaby at the first opportunity to get a glimpse of the *Frederick William Kitson* for himself. In truth, Banks had rarely seen her superior so animated as when the subject of the steam train had come up at the dinner table.

'Aye, I pass it most days. I try to get out every day for a walk, you know, since such liberties have been restricted for a long time. I've seen them getting it ready for its special launch. Looks impressive.'

'Yeah, well, I had planned to just catch you for a quick cuppa while I was in the area but something's come up and, truth be told, I'm a bit worried about you.'

Ewan frowned. Understandably so. Banks hadn't been cruel to him since his release from prison, but she had been cold. Distant. Unsure whether a reconciliation between them was really the best idea. This was the first show of concern she had made towards him since he had moved to Andaby, and it wasn't even all that genuine.

'What's going on?'

'I'm not certain of absolutely all the ins and outs yet,' Banks said, 'but I think your girlfriend has become a suspect in the murder case.'

'What? Why would she be a suspect?'

'Like I say,' said Banks, 'I'm not clued up about it all because it isn't my case and I can't go into details about what I do know. I shouldn't have told you that much. But I had to come and make sure you hadn't been . . . duped into anything, I suppose.'

'Pretty difficult to be duped into murder, Charley. Even for the likes of me.'

'I wasn't suggesting that. I mean, were you really together the night the murder happened? Because now that she's on the suspect list, the police are going to be checking into her movements that day. If they find anything that doesn't match the statement you've given, then you'll be implicated too.'

Ewan paused for a moment. It seemed Banks's words had given him much to think about. 'When you say they'll be checking into her movements, what exactly do you mean?'

Ewan's eyelashes fluttered a little as he spoke. She recognized that tick from their younger years. He was definitely lying about something.

'I mean they'll be checking CCTV cameras in the town. Questioning her work colleagues, her friends. Checking bank records and phone records. The whole shebang. If they find anything that contradicts what she told the police, well, I wouldn't like to be in her shoes.'

So far as she knew, DS Robinson had no immediate plans to do any of this but something about the prospect of the police looking into Nancy's movements more closely had Ewan rattled, so Banks had to lay it on as thick as she could in the hope he would break and talk.

At present, however, Ewan wasn't doing any talking at all. He was just standing there, brooding.

'If this goes to court and they find Nancy wasn't where she said she was, the judge won't think twice about the idea that you were an accomplice,' Banks added. 'With your record you'll be straight back in the slammer. So, if you're covering for her, in any way, it's best to get it cleared up now so that no matter what the police find out about Nancy, they know you had nothing to do with it. I can't watch you go to prison a second time, Ewan, I just can't.'

Ewan swallowed hard. 'I don't know what the police think they know, but there is no way Nancy had anything to do with this murder. I decided to go out with her because she was shy, and kind and gentle. She's not capable of doing that to another person, I don't care what evidence you turn up. That said, if she really is on the suspect list, then the police are going to be knocking on her door. When they do, she will need a better alibi than me.'

Banks could barely breathe as she said her next sentence.

'Oh, Ewan, you – you weren't with her that night, were you?'

Ewan opened his mouth to speak but then caught Banks's eye and, at once, closed his mouth again. It was almost as though he couldn't bring himself to say the words. Slowly, he shook his head in response to her question.

The May sunshine couldn't reach Banks as she digested the unsavoury truth. Her brother had lied to the police. Her brother had lied to her. Even if he wasn't guilty of the murder, that looked terrible, on both of them.

'How could you do that? After everything, what the hell do you think you're doing, lying to the police about where you were on the night of a murder? Why don't you just go down there and get the handcuffs slapped on you right now?' Banks knew her outburst was unlikely to serve her well, but just then, she couldn't hold back.

'It's not Nancy's fault, and she shouldn't be on any suspect list.'

'Be careful what you're saying, Ewan. Because if the deceit isn't Nancy's fault, then there's really only one other person to blame.'

'It wasn't meant as any grand deceit. It just seemed like the easiest thing to do at the time,' Ewan said.

Banks sighed and closed her eyes for just a moment. She opened them before speaking again. She had to. Otherwise, she might miss a sign that her brother was feeding her yet more lies. 'Please tell me you didn't put pressure on that girl to say she was with you?'

'I didn't pressure anyone, she offered to help me because I was innocent.'

'If you're innocent then why did you lie? And this time I want the truth. It's not just your neck on the line here.'

'I'm aware of that,' he said. 'You really think I want to cause you any more pain after everything? I lied 'cause I don't have an alibi. At least not one that will get the police off my back. I didn't commit any murder but I can't prove that I didn't. I was at home that night. Nancy was at her knitting club. Though if she's a suspect I'm sure you'll hear that from her yourself and you will go to the people who she knits with and they will tell you where she really was. That's the kind of person you're accusing. Someone who knits in their spare time.'

Banks shrugged. She was in a petulant mood, an attitude Ewan seemed to bring out in her. 'They're sharp them needles. You could do any amount of damage with them.'

'Oh, come on, Charley, be serious. Don't go on the warpath with her just because you're angry at me. The only reason I lied is that I knew neither you nor the police would believe me if I said I was home alone. That's not an alibi. But it is exactly where I was on the night that that woman was murdered. And I couldn't tell them that, could I? I was scared about going back to prison. I survived the last twenty years by the skin of my teeth. If they'd decided, for any reason, not to let me out I wouldn't have wanted to see another sunrise. The meals, the violence, even the haircuts.'

'Right now, you wouldn't know you'd ever had a haircut,' Banks said, glaring at Ewan's chin-length black hair.

'For good reason. I'm trying to forget two decades' worth of buzzcuts. In fact, I want to forget I was ever there entirely. No, I couldn't go back. Not when I was innocent. That's why I lied.'

Ewan sighed and looked back at Banks.

'And look, it wasn't a total lie. It was only a lie for the precise time frame they gave us. I did see Nancy that night, later after she'd finished at her knitting club. But that was no good to me because the police were asking where I was between seven and nine.'

Banks rubbed a hand over her face and tried to think. On one level, she knew that what Ewan was saying was spot on. The police would have been suspicious of him if he told them he was home alone at the time of Siobhan's murder. They would have essentially chalked that up as him not having an alibi. And although, if he was innocent, there would be no physical evidence, he had flirted with Siobhan in the bar when he first came to live in Andaby. So, it's not as though the victim was completely unknown to him. Those two things alone were not enough to win a conviction. But in a small town, who knows how many other threads of circumstantial evidence the investigative team could have teased out if they really worked hard to build a case against him? Ewan and Siobhan's movements might have easily overlapped without either of them knowing about it. In that sense, Banks understood why Ewan might have felt lying was the right option. The bottom line was, however, that the truth always came out, and in this case his lies had been very quickly revealed. Which meant he hadn't just risked his own freedom but Nancy's reputation and standing in a job she'd worked at for over a decade.

'I'm glad prison was a bad time for you,' she said at last. 'I'm glad it's left you with no desire to return. But you went about this the wrong way. You should have told the truth and now I've got to go to the police officers investigating this and tell them that my own brother has given a false alibi.'

'You don't have to.'

'What? Keep it a secret so you can drag me down with you? If you had any idea how long it took me to get over what you did ... the shame of you going to prison. Mam never got over it. Dad died ashamed.'

Ewan cursed under his breath. 'That ... is the coldest thing you've ever said to me.'

'Yeah, well, it might actually be the most honest thing I've ever said to you too. You'd better hope that your girlfriend has a watertight alibi, because if neither of you can provide convincing proof of where you were that night, people might start to suspect you were both in on it together. Come on, we really don't have time for any more of this polite chit-chat. I'm taking you down to Andaby Police Station, now.'

CHAPTER TWELVE

The greengrocers in Andaby was situated on Brightstone Road, a side street off the main square. It was only a poky little shop but there was space enough for Banks and Kitt to squeeze in there and casually stroll along the narrow aisles. Banks pulled a packet of crisps off the shelf and opened a fridge in the corner to grab a bottle of water, all the while examining the woman sitting at the counter. The woman they had come here to question.

Kitt had protested about launching straight into a questioning of Nancy. It was only early afternoon and it had already been quite the day. When Banks had delivered Ewan at Andaby Police Station, Robinson made it clear to Ewan that although they had no forensic evidence to hold him on, and there was seemingly nothing concrete that linked him and the victim, she would be notifying his probation officer about his behaviour, who would in turn contact the parole board and there would most definitely be consequences to his actions. A member of Robinson's team also rang Nancy on her mobile to ascertain her true alibi for the night of Siobhan's murder – as Ewan had said, she had named her knitting group and that was being verified now.

From what Robinson already knew about Nancy, and given how long it had been since Nancy and Siobhan had had any regular interactions, she was expecting Nancy's alibi to be confirmed. But Banks wasn't going to leave anything to chance when it came to her brother. Moreover, should Robinson inform her that Nancy's alibi hadn't checked out, she would be in a much better position to apprehend her if she was in close proximity to the suspect.

While Banks and Kitt questioned Nancy, Grace had agreed to try and locate Craig Norris. One way or another, Banks wanted to know if there was anything to this sash theory by the end of the day. Robinson had suggested to Banks that if a graduation sash had been used to strangle Siobhan, then it most likely was the sash that belonged to her, rather than somebody else. But that begged the question, why would Siobhan have that on her person when it had been so long since she graduated from school? Moreover, Nancy had graduated the same year as Siobhan and would have been given her own blue sash all those years ago. If the killing had been payback for bullying suffered at school, Nancy could have used her own sash to commit the murder and then disposed of it. They had no evidence of this, of course. But until Robinson confirmed Nancy's alibi, Banks was inclined to keep a very open mind on the subject.

Banks had never met Nancy so there was no guarantee necessarily that the shop assistant on shift with the frizzy brown hair that reached her shoulders and a thick pair of glasses perched on her nose was in fact her brother's girl-friend. But the woman was occupying the space between customers with a knitting project. A solid clue that this was the next person they needed to talk to on their shortlist of potential suspects.

If she was honest about it, Nancy's appearance somewhat surprised Banks. On first impressions, she didn't look like the kind of woman who would have turned Ewan's head before his time inside. The married woman he had been seeing back in Glasgow was all long legs and long blonde locks. Nancy was her polar opposite. She wasn't wearing any make-up and there wasn't a hint of cleavage. Her body was completely swamped by a thick forest-green cardigan, even though it was far too warm outside for layers.

Many aspects of Banks's job relied on her working know-ledge of psychological profiling. The way in which Nancy's head dipped as she hunched over her knitting needles, and the extra layer of clothing serving as a cocoon from the world, suggested to Banks that Nancy was unlikely to be high on confidence. Then again, if Maya Garrison's descrip-tion of Nancy's school years were anything to go by, then perhaps that wasn't such a surprise. Kids were notoriously cruel, and, by the sound of things, Nancy had endured years of torment at the hands of Siobhan. Perhaps she still carried the weight of that cruelty all these years later, and it had made her somewhat withdrawn. The question was whether she had reached the point where she had decided it was time to turn the tables and show Siobhan the true meaning of cruelty.

The only thing Banks couldn't square away in her head when it came to that theory was, why now? If Nancy really had been waiting to pay Siobhan back for all the bullying, why on earth had she waited so long? A five-year gap, that might be believable to make sure suspicion didn't fall on you. But nineteen years? It wasn't even a significant anniversary of them leaving school. This was a question they needed to ask when it came to considering Craig Norris as a suspect as well. Both he and Nancy had been in some way humiliated by Siobhan, but in both cases the malice they endured was almost two decades ago. One would expect that if somebody was going to hurt someone who had caused them grief, they would do it sooner rather than later. There was no legitimate reason to wait all that time before carrying out a plan of this kind.

Still, she and Kitt were here now so they may as well question Nancy, and at least find out what she knew. Maybe their conversation would reveal something, or betray something that explained the delay between the murder and the original acts of degradation that potentially prompted such a brutal response.

'Just let me know if there's anything you can't find, loves, all right,' Nancy said, offering a smile and a nod, first to Kitt and then to Banks.

'I'm just picking up a couple of snacks,' Banks said, seizing on Nancy's invitation to start a conversation. 'But to be honest, shopping isn't the reason we're stopping by.'

'Oh, need directions or something?' said Nancy. 'The signposting could be better around here, I know. There's sort of a local knowledge assumed, which is weird for a place that's so keen to attract tourists when you think about it.'

'Thank you, but we don't need directions,' Kitt said with a warm smile. 'We've actually come to town for a much more serious purpose, and we wondered if you could help us.'

Nancy at last stopped working the needles. She looked first at Kitt and then at Banks as they slowly approached the counter.

'Is there some kind of trouble? I mean, am I in some kind of trouble?'

'I don't know yet,' Banks said. 'You see, we are conducting a private investigation into the death of Siobhan Lange, and we're following up on the fact that you originally gave the police a false alibi.'

'Oh,' Nancy said, pressing a palm against her chest. 'It's about that, I see. I know this might seem like an odd response, especially as I'm probably in a lot of trouble for not being one hundred per cent truthful, but I am so relieved Ewan's finally told the truth.'

'So, it was his idea to lie to the police?' said Banks. This was not what Ewan had claimed, and so often when it came to catching criminals out, you had to pick at those small details for the whole house of cards to collapse.

'Oh, no, it were my idea,' Nancy said. 'I didn't know what else to do, you see? He's just got out of prison and he's trying to make a fresh go of things . . . with me. But then, this murder happened. And the police singled him out first, even though I know he wouldn't have made the same mistake again, and . . . well, I thought they were going to take him away.'

'So, you lied to the police.'

Tears filled Nancy's eyes. 'Please, try to understand. I've only been seeing him a couple of months. Might not seem a lot to most folk. But, I mean, well, look at me. I'm not exactly the lass all the boys go running to when they're looking for someone to take out on a Saturday night. But Ewan, he didn't care about the superficial stuff some men care about, you know? He was upfront about his time in prison. Said he was trying to build a new life, and now that Siobhan was dead, he would be implicated and . . . I just panicked. He's the best thing that's happened to me in a very, very long time. I didn't want him to leave.'

'That's a very understandable feeling,' said Kitt, her voice soft, soothing. 'And we should be clear here that we are not the police. We're just independently trying to support the police in bringing Siobhan's killer to justice.'

Nancy gave a half smile, 'I see. Well, I didn't want to lie or keep secrets. It just seemed like the only way to deal with a terrible situation, you know.'

'It may not have been the soundest choice, but as far as I know there aren't any plans to press charges for obstruction of justice this time,' said Banks. 'Though when the dust settles that might change, and it will be at their discretion. The fact that you lied about your whereabouts might even make you a suspect in the case of Siobhan's death. I assume you've been asked to give a full, and truthful, alibi?'

Nancy nodded. 'I understand there might be consequences for what I did. If there are, I'll just have to face them. But as for the alibi, it's not a problem. I do have one, unlike Ewan, I just kept it to myself while I was protecting him. I'm part of a local knitting club, you see. And it was on during the times the police asked me about. All the regulars in the group will vouch for the fact that I was there. I told the police all this and I think they're confirming it now. I can understand how lying about where I was when Siobhan died might make me a suspect but I don't regret protecting Ewan . . . although . . . have I always been a suspect and just not realized it? Did they suspect me anyway just because I'm Ewan's girlfriend?'

'That association may well have placed you on the police's radar,' Kitt said. 'But I also understand from the interviews we've conducted so far that you've lived in Andaby for a long time and went to school with the victim. I think with a case like this the police are likely to look at all the people in the town who have a long history with Siobhan. So long as you got on OK with her, there shouldn't be any problems. It's only if the police find . . . '

Kitt trailed off because Nancy's hand had leapt to her mouth.

'But Siobhan hated me!' she said. 'I don't know why. Well, I do know why. Because I'm different. I never fit in, you see, and she didn't like people who didn't fit in. Nobody at that school did. So, if the police are looking for people that Siobhan didn't get on with and they're really going that far back, I could be in big trouble. Big, big trouble . . . although I have got an alibi . . . that will make it OK, won't it? I mean, if I was somewhere else at the time Siobhan died then they can't say I did it, can they?'

It was obvious from the way Nancy's pitch was getting higher and higher as she spoke that real panic about the possible consequences of being in a relationship with Banks's brother was starting to set in. Although she had no plans to do the same for him herself, Banks felt she owed something to the woman who had tried to keep her brother out of prison, even if it had been a deeply dubious choice.

'The police can't charge you without hard evidence,' Banks said, in the same calm, soothing voice she always used when she was trying to appease someone. 'And I'm sure you weren't the only one Siobhan didn't get on with at school.'

Nancy shook her head. 'No, that much is true. I don't know what it was with her, really, I don't. Her behaviour was . . . inexplicable at times. She even drove away her best friend.'

'Who was that?' asked Banks.

'Um . . . Emily Cook, yes that was her name,' said Nancy. 'Oh, they went everywhere together, the two of them. They were friends all the way through school. Then at the end of the graduation ceremony they got into this big public fight. Not just strong words, they were rolling around on the playground, pulling each other's hair out. Siobhan looked like she was really relishing it, mind.'

'Relishing it how?' asked Kitt.

'She was laughing. But Emily really wasn't. Her face was redder than any face I've ever seen. I mean, it was practically purple. Because they were friends for so long, I had thought that maybe I'd misunderstood what played out that day. That maybe it was a joke, you know? Or a strange attention-seeking stunt of some kind. But Emily's tears looked pretty real to me.'

'A fight?' said Banks. Maya Garrison hadn't mentioned anything about a fight between Siobhan and Emily. Then again, she was in the year group above and would already have left the school by then. The humiliation that Siobhan put Craig Norris through was definitely the kind of thing people would chat about in the town square given half a chance. But a story about two young girls having a bit of a tussle on the playground, that would hardly count as gossip even in a place as small as Andaby. Perhaps Maya was not aware of the disagreement. At this rate, however, it felt like it might soon be more pertinent to ask who in Siobhan's year group *didn't* have a motive to kill her.

'Did you ever learn what the fight was about?' said Kitt.

Nancy shook her head. 'I wasn't exactly part of their inner circle. But, then again, I don't think they ever did let slip what had passed between them. Certainly, there weren't any rumours that I heard. Everyone wanted to know what had caused the fight after the fact but we couldn't get any gossip whatsoever out of either of them. Which is rare for Andaby. There are very few things in this town that the gossips aren't aware of within mere hours of something happening. Take it from someone who overhears a lot of conversations in here as people do their shopping. Not that I'm eavesdropping, you under-stand. Some people forget where they are and don't think to lower their voice. But there was nothing said about their fight at the time, and I've not heard anything since either way. They might still be friends, or they might still be locked in a bitter feud refusing to talk to each other. I'm afraid I'm not the one to ask when it comes to the popular people.'

'If they never made up, maybe we need to let the police know,' said Kitt.

'I . . . seriously doubt Emily has anything to do with Siobhan's death,' said Nancy. 'She left Andaby a long time ago.'

'Do you know where she moved to?' said Banks.

'I . . . I don't, I'm afraid. Possibly the other side of the Pennines, or maybe it was a bit further south than that, the Midlands somewhere. But we're talking about something that happened almost twenty years ago. They may have buried the hatchet since then, and I wouldn't know if they had. But even if they hadn't made amends, I really would be surprised if Emily had anything to do with what happened to Siobhan. All that – school, I mean – it's just such ancient history. I imagine they'd both moved on from that unfortunate incident at graduation a long time ago.'

Banks exchanged a look with Kitt. Emily and Siobhan had not just had a verbal altercation on that last day of school, things had got physical. Sure, Maya had said that Craig Norris had been aggressive off the rugby pitch but, so far as they knew, his aggression wasn't channelled at Siobhan. Nancy's description of what had passed between Emily and the victim was the first time anyone had mentioned a physical attack on the woman now lying in the local morgue.

Nancy was right, of course. It was a long time ago. But, as

Banks had found out when her brother was released from prison and forgiveness didn't flood out of her the moment she saw him again, ill-feeling had a long shelf-life. And, for the aggrieved in such situations, twenty years was really no time at all.

CHAPTER THIRTEEN

'Will I get to come along and actually interview Craig Norris for myself?' Grace asked from the back seat of Banks's car. 'I've been on research duty all day. You know I get antsy if I don't get out and about.'

'Actually, you get antsy regardless of how much you get out and about,' Kitt called back from the passenger seat. But then, as if sensing that she was rather putting on her assistant by cutting her out of the interviews, her tone softened. 'I know research isn't necessarily the most exciting thing in the world, Grace, but you know it is really important to what we do. And I am grateful for all the time you spend doing it.'

'Yeah, I know that. I just like to hear it once in a while.'

The trio had been sitting outside Body Power Gym on the outskirts of Leeds, where Craig Norris worked as a personal trainer, for about half an hour now. In the distance, Banks could see the high-rise buildings and lurching cranes of the city, looming tall against the backdrop of a grey sky. She had never really been able to put her finger on why, presumably it had something to do with the close proximity of the Pennines, but whenever Banks visited Leeds, it never failed to rain. Sure enough, even as these thoughts drifted through her mind, just as the clouds drifted through the atmosphere, moisture from a light drizzle splashed against the windscreen and she hit the button for the wipers to make sure they maintained a clear view of the gym's entrance.

After leaving the grocers, Banks had picked up a message from Robinson to say that Nancy's alibi had been confirmed by the woman who led Andaby Knitting Circle. Now that Nancy's alibi had been confirmed, they could focus on other suspects.

Which is why it had been fortuitous that Kitt had also had a message from Grace waiting on her phone to say that she'd managed to track down Craig Norris with relative ease. His posts to social media had indicated he had been into work at the gym for the early shift, so would likely finish for the day in the next hour or so. If he didn't materialize, they'd have to go to the reception desk and ask for him directly. Given that this was just a hunch, however, they were trying to avoid that if possible. Rumours spread quickly in a workplace, and for all they knew Craig Norris was innocent.

'And as for your question about whether or not you can come and interview Craig,' Kitt said, seemingly only just remembering that Grace had asked a question, 'you already know the answer to that. You're here chiefly for research purposes and to keep in the back pocket in case we need a fresh face for a sting operation.'

'You always get to have all the fun,' said Grace.

'You have a very strange definition of fun,' said Kitt. 'Now, come on. You know we need your expertise when it comes to social media tracking. So, how are you doing on looking up Emily Cook?'

'I've only just got my signal back. Andaby is a bit of a black hole in that respect. Thank goodness that B&B has reliable Wi-Fi, otherwise any kind of internet research would have been a bust. I'm looking through her Twitter and Facebook feeds now. If she's moved away from the area then maybe we can arrange some kind of video call with her rather than traipse all the way to wherever she might be living. Do you not think the pair might have buried the hatchet by now, if they were so close at school?'

'We don't know either way,' said Kitt. 'That's what we want to find out.'

'This twenty-year, or nineteen-year gap to be precise, between all these happenings and Siobhan's murder is really starting to nag at me, I have to admit,' said Banks. 'I know you've worked cases where there's a lot of history to them but that's actually quite rare. What on earth could prompt somebody to wait precisely nineteen years before dishing out their long-awaited payback? It just seems to me that there would have been opportunities before now if that's what this is about. I can't really think of any rational explanation for it.'

'I know what you mean,' said Kitt. 'That thought has crossed my mind too. But I suppose one of the ways I've justified it is that the perpetrator of a crime like this doesn't necessarily adhere to rational explanations. A person can be triggered at any given time, sometimes that might lead to a violent act, other times nothing will happen at all. I think when we're doing work like this, we're prone to try and find logic, when in fact logic went out the window the moment taking another person's life seemed like the most prudent option.'

Banks paused, digesting what Kitt had to say. On a surface level, she was right of course. Someone who goes to the lengths of committing murder isn't necessarily operating within any kind of rational framework. But, in Banks's experience, most killers did in fact have some kind of warped logic and justification for the acts they were carrying out. That was the only way they could convince themselves that they had no choice but to take another person's life. Perhaps this was just one of those cases where random elements played more of a part. But, as it stood, Banks wasn't ready to fully commit to the idea that someone who attended school with Siobhan nineteen years ago could be a prime suspect. Not until she could figure out what might cause somebody to wait that specific length of time before acting.

'I'll admit that the timing is a little odd,' said Grace. 'But you saw the picture of Siobhan's year group wearing those sashes. They were the same colour of those fibres, exactly.'

'They were,' Banks grudgingly agreed. 'And I can't think of a reason why Siobhan would have her own sash with her at work, so if one of those sashes was used maybe it is more likely that it belonged to the killer.'

'We may not have all the answers when it comes to this element of the case, but given the colour match I'm convinced we're on the right track somehow. I . . . Oh!'

'What?' said Kitt.

'Oh, dear.' Grace said. 'Oh dear, oh dear, oh dear.'

'Grace,' Kitt said, closing her eyes in an attempt to keep her patience.

'Sorry, I just wasn't quite expecting this. It's Emily Cook, she's gone missing.'

'What? How long for?' said Banks, glancing at Grace through the rear-view mirror.

'According to a post that her mother tagged on her Facebook page, she's been missing for about two weeks now.'

Grace held up the phone while Banks and Kitt turned to get a look at Emily's profile. She still had blonde hair and freckles but it looked as though she bleached her hair these days. Sure enough, the top post was a plea from her mother.

'The post says the police have searched but so far haven't found any traces of her,' said Grace. She left work for the evening a couple of weeks ago and that was the last anyone saw of her.'

'Strange, I haven't seen anything on the news,' said Kitt, turning back to face the front of the vehicle. 'Where is she based?'

'Her about info says she's in Lincoln at the minute, or was until she disappeared,' said Grace.

'When it's an adult that goes missing like that it doesn't always make national news,' said Banks. 'The local news outlets will cover it but it's rare that news of something like that stretches further unless it's a child or a teenager.'

'Do you think her disappearance has anything to do with the case?' said Grace. 'You said Nancy had described Siobhan and Emily as best friends. Can it really be a coincidence that Emily disappears two weeks ago and Siobhan dies in quick succession?'

'Off the top of my head, I can think of two possible theories,' said Banks.

'Let me guess,' said Kitt. 'The first one is that the same person who murdered Siobhan has murdered Emily in a more covert fashion and her remains have not been found.'

Banks nodded. 'I'm sorry to say, that's definitely the first thing that comes to mind. People are sometimes found alive after two weeks, but it becomes less likely with each passing day. Still, there's also a chance that Emily disappeared of her own accord in order to put into motion something she'd been planning for a long time.'

'The murder of Siobhan?' said Grace.

'It's a possibility we can't rule out,' Banks said. 'At least not until we know what their relationship status was at the time of Siobhan's death.'

'But we don't even know what they fought about,' said Grace. 'Kids will fight over absolutely anything sometimes.'

'I know,' said Banks. 'And I'm not saying that the idea that Emily murdered Siobhan is the world's most probable theory, I'm just saying it's something to hold in our minds as we take the investigation forward. I'll give Robinson a text now and let her know that Siobhan Lange's best friend, Emily Cook, disappeared two weeks ago. Hopefully she'll be able to get in touch with Lincoln police station and collaborate with them to share any useful pieces of information. Emily might have further significance in this case either as a perpetrator or as a victim. We can't leave anything to chance.'

'And it really couldn't be a coincidence? You're certain about that?' said Grace.

Banks considered Grace's question for a moment before responding. 'I suppose that there's a small chance that Emily's disappearance and Siobhan's murder have nothing to do with each other. But in my experience, when it comes to murder cases, it's best not to treat anything as a coincidence.'

CHAPTER FOURTEEN

Another hour passed before Craig cut across the car park where his Fiat was waiting quietly to carry him home. The second Banks and Kitt clocked him, they started off in his direction and managed to get to him just as he was starting the ignition in his car.

'Craig Norris?' said Banks, tapping on the glass at the driver's side.

The man wound down the window, turned towards them, and seemed to fill the whole frame with his width. 'Yeah . . . ?'

'Sorry to bother you,' said Kitt. 'We were just wondering if we could ask you a few questions. You see, we are investigating the death of Siobhan Lange.'

Craig turned off his ignition and eyed Kitt and Banks. 'Are you the police or something?'

Although, if he'd left school the same time as Siobhan, Craig couldn't have been more than thirty-eight, he actually looked a little bit older than that. Banks got the impression that he had potentially spent one too many hours on the tanning bed at the gym. His skin had a leathery quality and a buzz cut barely disguised the fact that his hair was receding at the front.

'No,' said Kitt. 'I've been paid to investigate the matter privately in the hope of supporting the police in closing the case as quickly as possible.'

Not quite the truth. Banks had tried to pay Kitt for her services but since Banks was about to marry her best friend, and in fact she was Evie's maid of honour, she wouldn't hear of it. She had said that if Banks needed some way to justify her waiving the fee, she should consider it an early wedding present.

Craig nodded. 'I see, well . . . I couldn't believe it when I saw her picture on the news. Got the shock of my life, I did. It was like seeing a ghost. When you're at school, you just think everyone is going to go off and live relatively happy lives. You don't think about the real world, you know? You sort of take it for granted that everyone will make it to old age. You never think about something like this happening.'

While he was talking, Banks took the opportunity to examine Norris's physique. Being a personal trainer at the gym, he was more muscled than most. And, although the broom handle would undoubtedly have helped anyone topple those canisters at the museum, having biceps like his would also certainly be an advantage when completing such a task. Not to mention how useful they would be in dragging a dead body from one room to another. A move that still mystified Banks, and likely Robinson's team too. Hanging around like that at a murder scene is a sure way of getting caught. And most killers have watched enough television to know that.

'I know just what you mean,' said Kitt. 'And I don't want to take up too much of your time with such morbid matters, so I'll make it quick,' she added, while Banks admired her ability to make it seem as though she was there to pander to Norris's every need and whim. There was something deeply unassuming about Kitt and her manner that had no doubt caught a lot of people off guard during the time she'd been investigating. She was just one of those people who seemed safe to talk to. Disarming you might say. Her charms were certainly working on Norris. His whole body had tensed as they'd approached him, but now he leaned an elbow out of the car window, showing off his tanned biceps.

'While the police focus on the suspects who have had the most recent contact with the victim,' said Kitt, 'we are focusing on ruling out lower priority suspects. The kind of people who have been in the victim's life at some point and perhaps didn't part on the best of terms, but no longer have any connection to her.'

'Wait a minute,' said Norris, his eyes suddenly narrowing. 'Me and Siobhan didn't part on the best of terms. But Jesus, that was twenty years ago. Are you saying I'm a suspect?'

'Oh, no, well I don't think so,' Kitt said, doing what she could to calm Norris back down again. 'The people we've spoken to verify that you haven't even talked to Siobhan in a very long time.'

'That's right, not since graduation.'

'The only reason we're here is to ask for your alibi on the night of the murder so that you can be ruled out,' Kitt explained.

'I'm still a bit hazy on why I am being ruled in?'

Banks watched in quiet amazement as, despite Norris's reluctance to cooperate, Kitt's smile became even gentler than it had before. 'One of the people we spoke to from your school said that Siobhan did something very cruel to you at the graduation ceremony. And if all other avenues in the case get exhausted the police would look at those kinds of incidents as motive, or potential motive, for killing Siobhan. So, to save them doing that, which would probably be a huge waste of time, we're just collecting alibis now and will pass on that information to the police to save a more official visit, if you get my meaning.'

'So, you think because Siobhan dumped me over a microphone all those years ago, I could be considered a suspect for her murder twenty years later? Like I would still be bitter about that or something?'

'It seems an unlikely story to us,' said Kitt, 'but we have to rule out all possibilities in a case like this. That way we can focus on the people whose stories really don't add up.'

Banks was all out of patience now. Craig kept posing questions, when he knew all they wanted was his alibi. Was he stalling for time? Trying to think of something on the spot? 'Siobhan was murdered last Wednesday,' Banks cut in. 'The police are saying the murder likely took place between seven p.m. and nine p.m. Do you have an alibi?'

'I was at work,' Norris replied, an unmissable edge to his voice. Seemingly, he didn't appreciate Banks's more direct approach. 'I always work the late shifts on a Wednesday. It's not the best schedule because then I'm expected to be in again for the early shift on a Thursday. I don't get a lot of sleep. But I suppose I can get my boss to give you a ring and confirm it if you really need her to. Though I think this whole thing is bloody ridiculous.'

'Here's my card,' said Kitt, presenting him with one and ignoring his protestations now that she had the information she wanted. 'We'd be grateful if you could ask your manager to call us and confirm. Especially as it has just come to our attention that another one of your classmates, Emily Cook, has gone missing.'

'Emily? Missing? Oh, God, I hadn't heard,' said Norris. 'She's . . . she's not dead as well, is she?'

'We don't know,' said Banks, wondering if she should read anything into the fact that this was Norris's first assumption. Did he know something? Or was he just guessing? Perhaps Robinson's team also needed to start checking alibis for the night Emily Cook went missing. When Norris's boss rang to confirm his alibi for last Wednesday, Banks made a mental note to also double check with his boss, while they had her on the phone, if he was working the night Emily Cooke went missing.

If Emily's mother had posted details to her Facebook page as Grace suggested, it would be fairly easy to pin down the exact date and the rough time Emily went missing. Banks wished she could be more optimistic about Emily turning up alive and well somewhere but that was just so rare in a case like this. Under the circumstances, it made much more sense to treat that incident as though it were another murder and ask people for their whereabouts.

'We hope that nothing bad has befallen Emily, obviously,' Kitt said. 'It's not like a body has been found, so there is still hope. As for not hearing about it, I don't think the news has made it this far north. She was living in Lincoln when she disappeared a couple of weeks back now. Chiefly, my card is there to verify your alibi, but first Emily goes missing and then Siobhan is murdered – we can't rule out the possibility that someone may be targeting your circle of friends from school for reasons we don't yet understand. So, if you notice anybody out of the ordinary following you or behaving in an unusual manner, please call me straight away. I will be with you as soon as I can and will also notify the police as we do have direct contact with the investigation team.'

Craig frowned. 'Do you really think somebody could be targeting the people I went to school with? Why would anyone do a thing like that? After all these years?'

'That's what we're trying to ascertain,' said Kitt. 'We can't rule it out under the circumstances, I'm afraid. But the first thing is to get you struck off any suspect list by confirming your alibi.'

'I'll get back inside now, ask my boss to give you a ring sometime this evening. I would invite you in but she's in training sessions all this afternoon so she wouldn't welcome being interrupted by a member of the public.'

'We don't want to be a disruption to your life,' said Kitt.

'It's so strange to think I could be a suspect because of something like that,' Norris said, shaking his head. 'Something that happened years and years ago, and that frankly I thought was a favour.'

'Not many people would think that,' said Banks. 'I certainly wouldn't thank someone for breaking up with me that way.'

Norris shrugged. 'I think I was well shot of her to be honest. Not that I wish her dead, before you move me up the suspect list. I had a suspicion at the time that she had some kind of relationship going with our physics teacher,

Mr DuPont. There were rumours that Siobhan didn't deny when I pushed her about them. Siobhan and Emily also had a massive fight at the graduation ceremony, and I think it was over Mr DuPont's affections. Bit weird if you ask me. I mean I know it happens, teachers and students getting together. But still . . . why either of them would have been interested in the guy, I've no idea. Mind you, I think he actually did end up marrying an ex-student. Someone in the year above us.'

The strange tingling in her gut Banks had when an important piece of information fell into her lap suddenly started nagging at her as Norris said those words. 'You don't remember who, do you?'

'Uh,' Norris's eyes darted to the ceiling of his car as he tried to dredge the name from his memory. A name he probably hadn't spoken out loud in more than a decade. 'Maya-something, I think.'

'Maya Garrison?' Kitt said, the disbelief sounding out in her tone as she did.

'Yes!' Norris pointed at Kitt as though she'd just correctly answered the tie-breaker on a game show. 'That's it. Yeah, I didn't know her much myself, like, but she seemed all right from a distance. It doesn't half make you wonder though, doesn't it? Marrying a teacher. It's all a bit creepy if you ask me.'

Banks and Kitt exchanged a look. All the information

they'd been working on so far was based on leads given to them by Maya. She had neglected to tell them about the rumours surrounding the victim and her now husband. Something told Banks that was no accident.

CHAPTER FIFTEEN

The school day had already finished and the gates were open so that the children could amble home by the time Kitt, Banks and Grace arrived back at Andaby Comprehensive. The journey between Leeds and Andaby had been spent discussing the possible implications of Maya withholding information from them. Though they had discussed the ins and outs of several different theories, there were two that seemed particularly probable under the circumstances. The first was that Maya suspected DuPont of murdering Siobhan but rather than face the truth she had decided to shield her husband, and her children, from the consequences when Kitt and Banks had come knocking for answers. Exactly why DuPont might have murdered Siobhan, they weren't sure. But an affair gone awry was certainly one possibility they had deliberated given the rumours Norris had mentioned.

The other main theory they had discussed was that

Maya may have learned of some kind of affair between DuPont and Siobhan. Either one that had endured since they first met each other twenty years ago or, more likely, that the pair had rekindled their earlier attraction in recent months. In either scenario, Maya may have decided to protect her family by getting rid of the outside influence that, to her mind, was causing the trouble. Banks had seen quite a few cases where affairs had resulted in violent interactions. Especially between the wife and the mistress. It was likely easier for a married woman to focus on hating the woman her husband had turned to, rather than placing blame on the husband himself. Between them, Kitt, Banks and Grace had imagined a similar turn of events between Maya, Siobhan and DuPont. The only problem with all this was evidence.

If DuPont had committed the murder, how had he acquired a sash from Siobhan's graduating year? It didn't seem like the kind of thing a teacher would be given. Had he used Siobhan's own sash to strangle her? If so, where was that sash now?

Considering the kinds of rumours that were circulating about Siobhan and DuPont while Siobhan was still at school, they couldn't discount the idea that the pair might have crossed the professional student–teacher boundaries even then. Had Siobhan given her sash to DuPont as a memento of their time together when she left school? If something had happened all those years ago, it wasn't so much of a stretch to imagine that they might have reunited in adult-hood to live out something they weren't able to fully realize when Siobhan was a student.

Moreover, it didn't seem such a wild idea that at some point Siobhan would do something to anger or provoke either DuPont or his wife, or both. The more they learned about Siobhan the clearer it became that she wasn't a particularly likeable person and that many of her actions seemed to be driven by spite or a desire to feel superior. Not that Banks, Kitt or Grace thought that was reason to kill Siobhan, but it might explain why somebody else had.

Once they had reached the school, Grace had agreed, with only minor reluctance, to stay in the car and look up anything she could about DuPont, whose first name, Craig Norris had relayed once he'd done some more raking of his memory, was Adam. Grace understood that if they all went into the school together to confront Maya, she may feel ganged up on and go on the defensive, or even make a run for it. Banks had had enough of the run around for one day. She wanted to make this process as painless as possible.

Maya was just packing up her handbag as the pair pushed through the double doors that led into the reception area. She looked up at the sound of their footsteps along the lino-leum corridor and, at once, seemed to gauge the expression of her visitors. The fear in her eyes could not be missed but she tried to smile and put on a brave face in preparation for the conflict she must have known was coming, even as she had stood in that exact spot, misdirecting them, only this morning.

'Back again so soon?' The singsong tone in Maya's voice only betrayed just how nervous she was. 'Is there something else I can help you with?'

'Yes,' said Banks, before Kitt had a chance to swoop in with the softly softly approach. It was bad enough that she suspected her brother might have had a part in this without interviewees sending them on wild goose chases. She was all out of patience and needed to get to the truth, fast. 'You can tell us why you neglected to mention that your husband was rumoured to have had a relationship with the victim while she was still at school.'

Maya's eyes lowered to the desk. 'I didn't mention it because there was nothing to those rumours. Siobhan just spread them. Out of viciousness. Trying to get Adam in trouble. He was in trouble with the school board because of it, you know? But she didn't care about stuff like that. Consequences weren't something she gave much thought to at all, in fact. Everything was just a good time to her. Adam told me that the matter was settled, though. That it was proven that there was nothing to the rumours back then and their relationship was completely professional.'

'If you really believed that, why weren't you upfront about it?' said Banks. 'We all know kids can be cruel. Or that sometimes they can tell tall stories, trying to stir up trouble just for something to do in some cases. If you had told us the truth, we could have looked into it and verified your story. Now, we've found you've misled us and we can't be sure that any of the information you've given us is worth our time.' Banks tried to keep the volume of her voice under control as she spoke but there was no holding back on the tone. Livid didn't even come close to describing how she was feeling just now. And she didn't mind one bit if Maya knew that.

If she was really honest with herself, she might have admitted that she was taking out some of the anger she felt towards her brother for lying about his alibi on Maya. But the truth was she was tired of deceit altogether. It was an element she dealt with on an almost daily basis. Very few of the people who crossed Banks's paths were one hundred per cent honest when they talked to the police for fear of what might happen to them if they said something that incriminated them by accident.

But a woman was dead. Whether or not she was a nice person was irrelevant. Nobody had the right to take another person's life. And nobody, no matter how spiteful, deserved to die the way Siobhan had died.

'I didn't lie about the other stuff Siobhan did when she was at school,' said Maya. 'She really did bully Nancy and she did break up with Craig over the microphone like that. I just omitted some information because me and Adam have two young kids and I don't want his name dragged through the mud when I know he's not guilty.'

'While you were so busy trying to protect your own family, you completely forgot about Siobhan's family. Her parents are now grieving the loss of a thirty-eight-year-old daughter. Her life cut short, like that.' Banks snapped her fingers. 'They didn't factor into your equation when you lied to us. But they should have. As a mother, surely you can imagine how terrible it would be to lose a child like that. Yet, you let a fellow woman and mother suffer longer than she needed to. To save your own.'

Maya at least had the decency to look shame-faced after Banks had finished her lecture. 'I wasn't trying to send you off in completely the wrong direction, quite the opposite. I was trying to think of people who might have felt strongly enough about Siobhan to do something like that to her. Adam does not fall into that category. It would have been a complete waste of time to even bring him in for questioning.'

'I see,' Banks said. 'So, are you sticking with the story that there was never any relationship between Adam and Siobhan? Not now and not in the past? You didn't find out that your husband and Siobhan had become close? Or that those rumours all those years ago weren't just rumours?'

'Adam loves me and he loves his kids,' Maya said with a sigh. 'He wouldn't throw that away for something as frivolous as an affair with an old student. He already got to relish the thrill of that taboo when he married me. That thrill included friends disowning him because they didn't agree with our relationship. And, in case you're wondering, me and Adam didn't start a relationship until many years after I'd left school. I wasn't even taught by him when I attended as a student. It was one of those small-town romances where you meet someone in the pub and then find out that they're not quite the age you thought they were, and as it happens you have a shared history. We just clicked and Adam's never had any reason to stray like that.'

'You need to think really carefully about what you do and say next,' Banks said. 'Are you telling me that your husband is innocent and that he'd never stray, because that's what you truly believe, or because it's what is easier for you to believe. There's an incredible amount riding on your answer to that question, Maya. So, I'd think carefully before you answer.'

'I don't need to delude myself, if that's what you're asking,' said Maya. 'Me and Adam have been together long enough that I know him and adultery, murder – he'd have nothing to do with any of that. Remember that you're basing all this on some rumour a kid made up twenty years ago. That's not the kind of evidence that will stand up in court.'

'I'm not basing it on a rumour from twenty years ago,' said Banks. 'I'm basing it on your determination to make sure we didn't find out about a rumour from twenty years ago. If there was nothing in it, there was no need to deceive us. But you did.'

'Adam went through hell when those rumours started,'

said Maya. 'I'm not about to put him through another round of that unnecessarily. What's the point in dredging up the past? He wouldn't hurt anyone. You've got this one wrong.'

'I'd like to believe you, really I would,' said Banks. 'But the fact that you misled us like that makes it very difficult to give any credit to what you're saying. You've really made things a lot worse. For both you and Adam.'

'It's true,' said Kitt. 'It's not just your husband that looks guilty because of what you withheld from us. You chose to hide the fact that Siobhan had spread these rumours about your husband. That she tried to make people believe the worst in him. Some investigators would read jeopardy to a loved one's reputation as a possible motive for murder. The fact that you tried to cover it up makes it all the more suspicious. You could be in a significant amount of trouble over this.'

'Now just hang on a minute,' Maya said. 'I might be protective of my family and husband but I'm not a murderer. I've never hurt anyone in my life. Anyone who knows me would vouch for that.'

Banks and Kitt shared a look. They couldn't take anything Maya had said at face value, but it was her husband who was rumoured to have had some kind of unsavoury relationship with the deceased, not her. Whether or not Siobhan spread those rumours without any basis, or whether they had been having a relationship, in the past or in the present, and something had gone awry, it was a plausible motive for murder any way you looked at it. People's reputations were precious, and someone who taught physics would be smart enough to know that.

'You seem very convinced of your husband's innocence,' Banks said.

'When you really love someone and know them well, it's not difficult to believe in their innocence,' Maya said.

'You were with him the night of the murder then, were you?' Banks pushed.

Maya looked up at Banks but didn't verbally respond. By the expression on her face, Banks would wager this was the part of the conversation she'd really been dreading.

'You *can* vouch for your husband's whereabouts on the night of the murder, can't you, Maya?' Banks said again.

Maya shook her head. 'He was out that night with his telescope. There wasn't anyone with him. And I know how that looks. But I know he didn't do it.'

'Maya, it's really important you answer this next question honestly. When we came to visit you earlier today, did you tell Adam about what we've been asking you? Did you contact him, tip him off?'

Maya pursed her lips and tears rose to her eyes.

CHAPTER SIXTEEN

'Robinson is looking for DuPont's phone location now and she's getting in touch with Lincoln about Emily Cook's disappearance,' Banks said, handing Grace and Kitt a takeaway tea apiece as they sat on the green in the centre of town awaiting news from the local constabulary. Now that she was sitting still for more than five minutes, it dawned on Banks what an incredibly long and gruelling day it had been. Her head pulsed trying to separate all the different strands of the mystery they had explored so far. Nancy Murphy, Craig Norris, Adam DuPont, Maya Garrison, not to mention Banks's brother. Yes, Banks had been hoping that the pace would pick up today, but that was more potential suspects than she'd rather deal with on any given Tuesday. Especially when she didn't have access to police resources in order to get a better sense of which one might be worth pursuing.

Banks took some deep breaths in a bid to steady herself. Luckily the green at the centre of Andaby was a tranquil place. It was mostly populated with people walking their dogs, couples enjoying picnics under trees and in the distance local teams were playing cricket. No doubt relishing the latest round of some intense rivalry that had raged on for decades between neighbouring towns in the valley. There were worse places to be when you weren't feeling your best but Banks would feel a lot happier when they located Adam DuPont. All breadcrumb trails were currently leading to him. Once Robinson had had the opportunity to question him about his relationship with Siobhan, not to mention analyse his phone for any suggestions that he might have been having an affair with her, they would all be able to regroup and ascertain what the next best step would be.

'I'm glad Robinson is in touch with Lincoln about Emily's disappearance,' said Kitt. 'Her disappearance is unnerving, make no mistake. While you were on the phone, I also received a phone call from Norris's boss at the gym.'

'What's the verdict?'

'Norris was at work on the night of Siobhan's murder, just like he said he was,' said Kitt. 'I also asked about the second of May, the night that Emily disappeared. But again, Norris was at work from four p.m. that day and Emily didn't go missing until after five p.m. when she left work.'

'Thanks for confirming all that,' said Banks. 'And for thinking to check about the alibi the night Emily disappeared. I suppose if he's got alibis for both of those dates, we can pretty much rule him out as either a murderer or an accomplice.'

'I think so,' said Kitt. 'An alibi from work is pretty water-tight. It looks as though this strange situation with Maya, Siobhan and DuPont is the one that needs our attention.'

'Robinson surprised me on the phone. She said that since we gave her that tip about the sashes, they've been looking for it in Siobhan's belongings. I honestly didn't think they'd given our theory enough credit to warrant that amount of police time.'

'Have they found Siobhan's graduation sash?' asked Kitt.

Banks shook her head. 'Not yet, but apparently Siobhan had a lot of stuff and it's taking time to sort through it all. Something like that could be buried in a box in her parent's attic. If they don't find it, then there's a chance it was used by the murderer to kill her. If they do find it, then we know the odds are that it was someone else who graduated the same year who killed Siobhan.'

'Assuming she didn't throw it out at some point,' said Grace. 'Not sure that Siobhan strikes me as the sentimental type from what we know about her.'

'We're operating on the hope that she liked to be reminded of her glory days,' said Banks. 'From the picture that's building it's clear that Siobhan was popular at school. She might have viewed it as a sort of golden era in her life and held on to articles like the sash. But you're right of course, she's not forced to have held on to something like that. If Siobhan's sash wasn't used as the murder weapon, then it seems clear now that the killer was in possession of their own or somebody else's. How DuPont might have got hold of one, or Maya for that matter, I don't know.'

'I couldn't see any online connections between DuPont and Siobhan,' said Grace. 'If they were having some kind of secret affair for all these years, they've done a pretty good job of making sure there's no digital trail between the two of them.'

'Thanks for checking into that,' said Banks. 'It's one avenue of exploration ruled out, although it doesn't necessarily lower the chances of them having some kind of secret relationship. Some people who do that kind of thing are smart enough not to leave any evidence on their phone, or in their social media accounts, where messages might be found by a significant other. They both live in a small town, they'll run into each other from time to time or pass each other in the street. It's quite possible they arranged meetings face to face so there's no evidence of it. We'll know more once Robinson has DuPont in custody and has seized his phone.'

'I assume they're taking Maya in for questioning too? I know that Maya wasn't officially on Robinson's suspect list but the fact that she's chosen to mislead an investigation about Siobhan's murder in this way is surely ringing some alarm bells?' said Kitt.

Banks nodded. 'They'll need to get everything she told

us on the record and Robinson also thinks, as I do, that she still might not be telling us the whole story. You were right when you laid it out for her that this turn of events makes her more of a suspect, just as it does him. She said herself that she is very protective over her family.'

'But how would Emily Cook's disappearance fit into that theory?' asked Grace.

'I'm not sure yet,' said Banks. 'I know you asked me before if it could be coincidence. It's very unlikely. But it does happen that two people who were once related suffer terrible events around the same time. The thing to remember when it comes to how Emily's disappearance fits into all this is that Norris said Emily and Siobhan were fighting over DuPont's affections at that graduation ceremony. I don't exactly know what he meant by that. Whether Emily was jealous of DuPont's relationship with Siobhan, or whether he'd been leading both of them on and rather than turning on him they turned on each other, but something was going on between them and it involved DuPont.'

'Yes, that line of thinking invites all kinds of complicated possibilities,' said Kitt. 'Emily could have disappeared because she found out that Siobhan had started seeing DuPont again and decided to take Siobhan out of the running once and for all. DuPont could have killed either or both of them if they threatened to expose any affairs he'd had with them, now or in the past. I must admit, though, that I'm still struggling with the idea that this disturbing little love triangle has endured for nineteen years. Something about it just doesn't add up to me.'

'I'm with you,' said Banks. 'That's why I think that there's a possibility that Maya was at least telling the truth about the rumours not being true while Siobhan was at school. The odds of a murder and a disappearance taking place because of what went down at the graduation ceremony all those years ago seems highly unlikely. But if there's been more recent interactions between them all that we've yet to find evidence of, perhaps that makes a little more sense. Essentially, we're missing a piece to the puzzle, and that missing piece is Adam DuPont.'

'I suppose,' said Kitt, 'that there's also a chance that if Maya is involved in the killings then she might have effectively made Emily disappear in the hopes that Emily would seem like a more viable suspect than herself.'

'I still can't believe that there were open rumours about a student and a teacher like that,' said Grace. 'I really don't feel like that would have even been tolerated at our school. You said that Maya suggested there was some kind of run-in with the school board about it but I don't get the impression that the consequences were in any way grand. Did people just turn a blind eye? Or was it dismissed as the fantasies of a silly school girl? It seems unlikely to me that something like that wouldn't have been taken more seriously. But maybe things were a bit different at the time that Siobhan and Emily went to school here. Even if it is just a rumour, it completely creeps me out that a teacher might be thought to have taken advantage of that position of responsibility and nobody really bothered to do anything about it.'

'Small towns never change their spots,' said Kitt. 'The rumour mill in a place like this must be off the chart. It doesn't mean that there's anything to the rumours, which is possibly why nothing significant happened in this case. DuPont did after all protest to his wife that the rumours were proven to be false. But in terms of this investigation, the rumours that were circulating back then wouldn't have to be true to keep Maya in the frame. Maybe there was nothing going on all those years ago, like she said. Maybe Siobhan did make all that up. But perhaps that isn't the case any more and something had started up between the two of them. If Maya found out about such a relationship, that would be motive for murder, especially given she's got two boys to protect.'

'On the plus side, this line of enquiry does not involve your brother,' said Grace. 'That's something to be grateful for at least.'

'No, it doesn't, but it is only early days,' Banks said, not quite willing to permit herself any sense of relief just yet. She hoped, more than anything, that the investigation continued to steer away from her brother, but she was nowhere near idealistic enough to believe that she could dismiss the idea of his involvement so soon. A second later her phone rang and she answered.

'Robinson?'

'We've tracked him down,' Robinson said. 'He's at Andaby Industrial Museum.'

'The industrial museum? Well, that's not exactly a brilliant hiding place given it's where the murder took place. Maybe he's not on the run after all if he's got time for cultural pursuits.'

'Wait a minute,' said Kitt, who, alongside Grace, had overheard this back and forth.

'Hang on, Robinson.'

'What time is it?' said Kitt

'It's uh, twenty to six,' Grace said, checking her phone.

'Charley, the Kitson train. It leaves at six o'clock passing through Leeds on to Settle through to Carlisle. I think he might be going to board the train.'

Banks scrunched her eyes shut in disbelief. Of course, he was going to board the train. That's why Maya hadn't wanted to answer their questions about whether she'd tipped off DuPont.

'Robinson, did you hear that?'

'Aye. Looks like he might be making a run for it after all. All my units are out on jobs but I'll redirect them straight away, see if we can catch him.'

'I'm headed that way now and will try to apprehend him,' said Banks. 'We've probably still got just enough time to make it to the station before the train leaves.

'I'll get in touch with the British Transport Police. See if they can hold the train. I don't know if they'll be able to do that in time but it's worth a try.'

'Definitely,' Banks said. 'We know what DuPont looks like from his social media pages, so we'll be able to identify him. We're leaving right now.'

CHAPTER SEVENTEEN

The sound of a train whistle echoing down the valley of Calderdale would usually have been heartening to anyone who heard it. In this instance, however, the hoot came just as Banks, Kitt and Grace clambered out of the car. A warning sign that the train was due to leave in five minutes.

With considerable haste, they jogged up the steps to the platform. If Banks had had time to digest it, the sight of a hulking great steam train that was hissing and huffing, and seemingly impatient to make its way along the tracks on its first official outing, would have been a spectacular view. As it was, Banks did not have time to admire the engineering magnificence before her. Due to the fact that this was the train's first journey, the platform was packed with people ready to board and already in the process of boarding. On any other day it would have been lovely to see such enthusiasm for tourism in Yorkshire. People were singing little tunes to themselves, and whistling and giggling. The atmosphere was understandably buoyant. For Banks, however, the crowds only presented an added challenge. Somewhere in this throng Adam DuPont was hiding. And if they didn't locate him soon, he may just slip through their fingers.

'Before we hop on, we have to make sure that he's actually on that train,' said Banks. 'With a bit of luck, we'll either catch him before he boards or we'll be able to get him off the train before it leaves. But we're going to have to keep our eyes peeled. It's nothing short of madness here today.'

All three of them started scanning the crowds. Banks had to hand it to him. With such short notice, DuPont had picked an excellent escape plan. Singling him out from all the other train enthusiasts, parents taking their families out and couples looking for an alternative romantic afternoon was no easy task. All in all, locating DuPont seemed to take a lifetime but, in truth, it couldn't have been more than a minute or so before Banks set eyes on the subject. He was carrying a small suitcase, which had likely been packed with whatever essentials he could throw in there before making his way to the train ahead of departure time. Since he had packed his bag for an extended trip it was clear he really was making a run for it and not just out for a jolly ride on a steam train by coincidence. He was about to board one of the carriages painted in maroon and cream.

'There he is,' Banks said, pointing to a man with blond hair and a large bald patch at the centre of his head.

'Damn it,' said Kitt. 'We're not going to get to him before he boards. There're too many people. We're going to have to think about a Plan B. It's just too busy here for us to grab him.'

'You're right,' Banks said. But they weren't finished just yet. Banks was already poised to put Plan B in motion. At once, she began searching the crowds for a different figure, the train guard.

She could just make out a lady wearing a uniform of midnight blue at the far end of the platform. Her red hair was tied back under a conductor's hat in a neat bun. It would be easier to explain the situation to her now than it would if the train set into motion and they were found to have no tickets, no police identification to warrant such a breach and some wild story about a possible murderer roaming through standard class.

Banks charged towards the conductor and the others followed. It was slow going, working and weaving their way through the crowd, but they did eventually manage to get close enough to the woman who would make or break their chances of apprehending Adam DuPont.

She had just finished answering a question from one of the passengers about the train's arrival time in Carlisle when Banks reached her.

'Hi there, I'm Detective Sergeant Charlotte Banks,' she said, catching her breath after all the hurrying. 'I'm off duty so I'm afraid I don't have a badge with me but

I've just had a call from the local constabulary led by DS Robinson, you might know her if you're local?' It wouldn't have been Banks's preference to identify herself as a police officer, especially without her badge, but this was a rather desperate situation. She had refrained from announcing her job title up until now, but she had the strong sense that if she didn't take some initiative Adam DuPont would be halfway to Settle very soon and they would be left behind.

The conductor shook her head. 'I'm not familiar with the lady.'

'I see,' said Banks, already sensing by the conductor's somewhat curt response, that she had an uphill battle on her hands. 'The thing is, we've got a bit of a situation. I don't want to cause a panic, so please don't react loudly when I tell you what I'm about to tell you. There's been a murder here recently and the prime suspect in the case has just boarded your train. I'm assuming all tickets for this train have sold out given how well advertised it's been?'

'They sold out months ago,' the conductor replied with a firm nod.

Banks would have expected a bit more of a reaction to the revelation that a murder suspect had just boarded the train but, still, did her best not to be unsettled by the woman's seeming indifference to their dilemma.

'In which case,' Banks said, 'there's at least one person on this train who doesn't have a ticket. He boarded this train on a whim in a bid to escape custody. He didn't know we were onto him until this afternoon, so he wouldn't have had time to purchase a ticket in advance. We want to apprehend him and get him off the train before it leaves.'

The conductor sighed, and looked at her watch. 'I wish I could help, and I don't mean to be rude, but I've no proof whatsoever that you are who you say you are. It's more than my job's worth to delay this train.'

Banks pursed her lips but tried to remain calm. The conductor was right after all. She didn't have any identification to prove her job title. And she couldn't blame anyone for wanting to hold on to a steady job.

'I really wouldn't ask if it wasn't an emergency,' said Banks. 'If this guy slips through our fingers now, I really don't know who else he might hurt.'

At the mention of other people being hurt the lines on the conductor's face softened, just a touch. 'I'm sorry, really. But your best bet is to meet the train at the next station in Todmorden and use the waiting time there to apprehend him. We're due to leave in less than two minutes. My managers have made it more than clear that I'll be held accountable if this service gets a reputation for being late on its maiden journey. Besides anything else, there'll no doubt be a scene if you apprehend him now. We can't afford that kind of publicity on our first ever passage. I'm not trying to be a nuisance, though I can tell by the look on your face you think I am. And I certainly don't want to think of a would-be murderer rattling around the carriages. But I can't delay this train.'

'Then can we at least get on to take him off quietly at the next stop?'

'I would let you. But you haven't got tickets or a badge that proves who you are.'

'I'm sorry, what's your name?' asked Kitt.

'Shelly . . . why?'

'Shelly, let me paint you a little picture. It's the maiden journey of the Kitson steam engine. It pulls up in Carlisle and, as people are disembarking, one of the train crew finds a dead body. One of the passengers didn't make it safely across the Pennines. Word soon spreads about The Death Train of the Dales . . . What kind of publicity will that be?'

'You're exaggerating,' Shelly said, waving a dismissive hand in Kitt's direction.

'All right, Shelly, let me paint you another picture,' said Grace. 'You're going about your conductorly duties as you always do. Checking people's tickets and giving them a stamp to validate their journey. Only one man you come to doesn't have a ticket. He happens to be a murderer who doesn't want to get caught. What do you think he's going to do when you ask him for a ticket he can't present?'

Shelly paused for a moment, looked between Kitt, Grace and Banks and then cleared her throat. 'On reflection, your best bet is to board and get him off quietly at the next stop in Todmorden. I'll pretend I saw your tickets. But there won't be a seat for any of you by the looks of things. Not expecting many no-shows given the crowd and I don't want you sitting in reserved seats for those yet to board. It'll only create a kerfuffle. The second we are on the tracks, I will be calling this into the British Transport Police to verify the threat. This is the last thing I need on a day like today, the last thing.'

'Make sure you do call it in to the BTP,' said Banks, doing all she could to ignore Shelly's irritatingly jobsworth comments. Obviously, the woman had a job to do. Banks could appreciate that more than most. But this wasn't some low-level drug dealer they were after. This was a man who had committed a violent crime. 'DS Robinson, who I mentioned earlier, should already have phoned them, so they should have some record of the issue. We'll apprehend him as quietly as possible.'

Banks turned back towards the grand old engine that by now was almost definitely harbouring a murderer. She walked back along the platform towards where the suspect had boarded.

'I watched where DuPont got on,' said Grace. 'It was the middle coach, F.'

'From what Mal's told me, and believe me, I'll never hear the end of the fact that I got to hunt down a murderer on a steam train – which I'm pretty sure is his ultimate dream – this train has those old-fashioned compartments.'

'I suppose that will give us a chance to systematically search each coach with relative ease,' said Banks.

'If the train is sold out, he won't be able to find a seat. Maybe we should head straight for the buffet car?' said Kitt.

Banks shook her head. 'We'll get to that, best to go with the last known sighting of the subject and start where he boarded, then if he's not there we'll devise a new plan. Just because the compartments are sold out, doesn't mean every last seat will be taken in them. He might be hoping to find a seat if there's been a no-show. Either way, we'd better get on board before Shelly changes her mind.'

Kitt and Grace hopped up into Coach D. As Banks followed them, she hoped for all that she was worth that Adam DuPont wouldn't give them any trouble. If this situation made the headlines, Ricci would be guaranteed to read about it. The last thing Banks needed was to be taken off this case, just when it looked like they were about to break it.

CHAPTER EIGHTEEN

Banks pulled open the door to the ninth compartment in Coach D, just as the train lurched into motion. She, Kitt and Grace were met with the sight of a startled young family with grandparents in tow. Although she had had little time to stop and admire her surroundings while searching the first eight compartments in this coach, Banks had to give the designers credit for the fact that the interiors were stylish and luxurious by almost anybody's standards. Each one was decked out in dark wood and furnished with thick red cushions to make train travel that little bit more comfortable. The only disappointing thing about this particular compartment was that Adam DuPont was nowhere to be seen.

'He's not here either,' said Kitt, the weariness in her voice already more than apparent and they hadn't yet really begun their search. 'Are you sure this is the right coach?'

'I'm absolutely certain,' Grace insisted, 'I saw him get on this coach and turn right. I made a mental note of it because

I knew we'd need the information, even if we did have to catch up with him at the next station.'

'Sorry to bother you folks,' Banks said to the family. 'But was there a man sitting in here with you?'

'A chap did poke his head in a few minutes ago,' the mother said. 'But he realized the compartment was full and moved on.'

Banks, Kitt and Grace exchanged looks. This was the first person who had mentioned anyone poking their heads into the compartment. Surely, that had been DuPont trying to blend in and find somewhere to sit while he contemplated his next move?

'Did you see which direction he went in?' said Kitt.

'I'm afraid not, I wasn't really paying attention. Why? Is there some kind of trouble?' the mother asked.

'No, no, no,' Banks lied. 'We're just looking for a friend of ours, that's all. I appreciate your help.'

She apologized again for bothering them before closing the compartment door. Perhaps it wasn't the kindest thing to leave that family there like sitting ducks, uninformed and unsuspecting, but Banks had already deliberated the alternatives. If she told people what was really going on, they might panic. Or worse, try to play the hero and apprehend DuPont if they came across him. Better to rely on the odds. If he'd already stuck his head through the door of that compartment and decided it wasn't for him, he probably wouldn't be back.

Banks felt her phone vibrate and took a quick look at the message. 'Robinson's sending officers to meet the train at Todmorden. We'll have to conduct a search and see if we can flush him out.'

'If he's sussed that the train is fully booked, or got spooked when he poked his head into that cabin, worried that someone might be able to identify him later, he might have gone to hide somewhere a little bit less conspicuous,' said Kitt.

'We'll need to check the toilets at the end of each carriage,' said Banks.

'Joy,' said Grace. 'So glad I came along for this outing.'

'Other than that, he may have put on a little disguise, you know, sunglasses, sun hat and sat himself in the buffet car, or there's the luggage car at the back of the train,' Banks said, ignoring Grace's comment, even though she rather agreed with the sentiment.

'All right, I'm happy to bow to your experience on this one Charley, you'll no doubt have conducted many more searches like this than I have,' said Kitt. 'How exactly should we go about it?'

'The main thing to be conscious of is that he may well suspect that people will already be looking for him. Maya may have had the opportunity to text, or otherwise contact him about the fact that we were on his trail before Robinson's team took her in for questioning. At any rate, it's important we find him. The last thing we need is a potential hostage situation on our hands.'

Banks tried to contain the feeling of nausea that washed over her at those words. That really would be the worst of all possible scenarios. Even if she, and the rest of the passengers, managed to make it out alive, there would be no plausible deniability left for her when it came to debriefing Ricci about her actions over the last few days. Even though Banks had done all she could to ensure she didn't interfere with Robinson's investigation directly, Ricci would no doubt argue that Banks had put the integrity of the investigation at risk by going rogue.

'Do you really think it would come to that?' said Grace, propping her hand up against the wall to steady herself as the train turned a sharp corner. The engine wasn't breaking any records for speed. That was for sure. But it was still quite rickety and all three of them were being knocked from side to side as the train ambled on.

Banks considered Grace's question, trying to gauge whether her fears were getting the better of her. But no, she didn't think so. Everything she had learned in her training told her this was exactly the kind of situation that could turn nasty very quickly. She was particularly concerned that they were tracking somebody who was believed to have committed such a violent crime. That was the unpredictable part of it all. She was very much relying on DuPont wanting to minimize any attention that might be drawn to him during his arrest. He was, after all, a figure of respect in the place where he lived. With this in mind, it seemed unlikely that he would want to create a public spectacle. But, of course, there really was no knowing what a person would ever do, especially when they felt like there was no way out. 'I think DuPont is likely to be feeling pretty desperate right now. I don't know exactly what Maya told him, or what crimes the two have committed, either separately or together, but he didn't hang around to clear everything up. His first instinct was to run. And that does not bode well. Certainly, it doesn't strike me as the reasonable actions of an innocent man.'

'There are eight coaches not including the luggage car at the back of the train and since we are roughly in the centre of the train do you think it might make sense for us to split up?' said Kitt. 'Cover more ground more quickly.'

Banks shook her head. 'I can't leave you two civilians on your own, not when there's a potential murder suspect on the loose.'

'If that's all that's stopping you, you should know Grace and I can handle ourselves,' said Kitt. 'If all else fails I'll just get Grace to annoy the suspect into submission.'

'Or I could get Kitt to bore them into submission with a lecture on the history of the Dewey Decimal System.'

'Oh, now that's unfair,' said Kitt. 'You're being unduly dismissive about the Dewey Decimal System, there's so much about it that most people don't know.'

'All right!' Banks said, trying to regain order. 'I concede the point. I don't envy any suspect that has to deal with you two.'

'I'm more worried about leaving you on your own,' said Kitt.

'Oh, trust me, there's no need for worrying about that either,' said Banks. 'It's been a tough week and I haven't been able to get to the gym to let off some steam. I've got more than enough energy to defend myself if he tries anything. He's a physics teacher, so he does quite a sedate job. Maybe that will work in our favour.'

'If you think teaching secondary physics is a sedate job you clearly haven't been hanging around on Coney Street right after the schools kick out,' said Kitt.

'You know what I mean,' Banks said, smiling in spite of herself. 'Unless he's secretly trained in the martial arts, we probably won't have too much to worry about on a physical level so long as we're all as careful as we can be. We don't know if he's carrying a weapon, that's the difficult thing, and I expect both of you to be sensible enough to keep your distance if you spot him. I really need to lead on this one, otherwise someone could get seriously hurt. So, don't move until we're all back together.'

'On that note, I know that we've got phones, but it's much better if we use these,' Kitt said, handing them earpieces and switching on a radio unit in her satchel. 'Keep us updated about where you are. We will do the same. If you find him, give a location and, if possible, wait until we're all back together before confronting him.'

'With a bit of luck, we'll find him sooner rather than later,' said Banks, who, after the fingerprint test at the industrial museum, was not surprised to see that Kitt kept radios and earpieces on her person. 'Try and look along the buffet car before you enter it. If you see him, just let me know and I'll be along as soon as possible to devise a plan,' Banks said, pressing the comms piece into her ear. 'Remember, if he had nothing to do with what happened to Siobhan, he wouldn't be running away like this. Based on his behaviour, I'd have to say we've probably found our killer. So, while you're conducting the search, always keep that at the front of your mind. Don't take any chances. Don't get backed into a corner. Stay alert. Stay alive.'

CHAPTER NINETEEN

Banks passed into Coach H and slowly placed a hand on the handle of the toilet door at the end of the carriage. The lock sign read VACANT but that didn't mean that DuPont wasn't hiding in there – hoping he'd go unnoticed until he could slope off the train at one of the stops and then disappear. Banks had come too far to let that happen. She would pull every part of this train to bits, screw by screw, if she had to, to find the man she could now only assume was the person who had killed Siobhan Lange.

Taking a deep breath, Banks pushed down the handle and whipped the door open in quick succession.

Nobody there.

Slowly, she exhaled, let the door fall shut and began to move towards the next set of compartments. This kind of search was better than any gym workout she'd ever known. Her heart rate must be through the roof.

'Anything?' Banks murmured into the comms receiver.

She still wasn't sure quite how sensible it had been to let Kitt and Grace form their own search unit. But she had them on comms so if anything untoward did happen, at least she'd know right away.

'Nothing yet,' Kitt replied. 'We're just leaving Coach B. If we get to the end of Coach A and don't find anything we'll double back. We're not making ourselves very popular pretending to have the wrong compartment all the way along, mind. If looks could kill, well let's just say you'd have a couple more bodies on your hands.'

'Well, we've got bigger fish to fry than worrying about ruining people's grand day out on the railway, I'm afraid,' said Banks, opening yet another compartment door. The couple inside, who had obviously been engaged in some serious heavy petting, jumped and looked surprised for a second.

'Sorry,' was all Banks gave them by way of explanation, only taking the time to check that there weren't any obvious hiding places for DuPont, before sliding the door shut once more and moving on to the next compartment.

'If we don't find DuPont in any of these coaches, maybe you wouldn't mind if me and Kitt stopped off for a bacon sandwich in the buffet car, hey Banks? They looked really good, they did. I could practically taste the butter melting over the bacon,' said Grace.

'Just make sure you bring back one for me,' Banks said. 'I'm bloody starving.'

'What happens if we don't find DuPont before Todmorden?' Kitt asked. From this statement, Banks knew that Kitt was taking this situation very seriously indeed. Food was usually at the top of her agenda, but she didn't even acknowledge Grace's remarks about the bacon sandwiches.

'To be honest, I don't know,' said Banks. 'Robinson's team will likely be there when the train pulls in if her text messages are anything to go by. Luckily DI Graves has decided to sit this one out at the office and coordinate remotely, which means I won't have to explain myself to him at least. But if the train arrives at the next stop and we still haven't found DuPont, I'll have to ask Robinson what she wants us to do. It's her investigation at the end of the day. We just happened to have stumbled onto a prime suspect by taking a slightly different angle. The odds are that uniformed officers would be able to put enough pressure on our friend Shelly to delay the train until the suspect is in custody.'

'Oh, for goodness' sake,' Kitt said over the comms.

'What? What is it?' said Banks.

'Grace, did you give Ruby Barnett my new mobile phone number?'

'I thought you wanted me to give Ruby your new phone number.'

'Ruby is the reason I got a new phone number in the first place!'

Banks tried not to get too distracted by what was going on at the other end of the comms line, but it was difficult.

173

Ruby Barnett was a character rather well known to the York constabulary, and, from the various anecdotes about her that Halloran had shared, it seemed she had latched onto Kitt. The woman, who had already lived to a grand old age and showed no signs of slowing down, considered herself a psychic and had phoned the station many a time with a 'hot tip' or two for a case she'd read they were working on in the newspapers.

'According to the text message I've just received, Ruby seems to have mysteriously found out about our trip to West Yorkshire, Banks,' said Kitt.

'Dare I even ask what a text message from Ruby Barnett looks like?' Banks said, opening the next compartment and then apologizing again when it became clear that DuPont was nowhere to be seen.

'She's suggesting that since the murder took place in a textiles mill that she should do a thread spell, whatever that is, to banish the evil spirits from the building,' said Kitt.

'She's unique in her approach to fighting crime, I'll give her that,' Banks said.

'That's not the only unique thing about Ruby,' said Kitt. 'We're pretty much at the end of the train now and there's no sign of DuPont at this end.'

'I'm almost at the back of the train myself,' Banks said. 'There's only the luggage car left to search after this one.'

'Whatever you do, wait for us before you search that one,' said Kitt. 'Since he's not in the buffet car and we haven't found him in any of the toilets, if you ask me that's now the most likely place for him to be hiding. He's unlikely to be discovered by the guard there.'

'Yeah, you might be right,' said Banks. 'The train is fully reserved but it is making stops along the way so there'll be empty seats waiting for the occupier to board. He could be sitting in one of those, hoping not to be noticed. But my money is on him finding somewhere to hide. DuPont is a teacher. Not your average perp. He's probably relying on his intellect to get him through this. Being a bit strategic. How exactly he's planning to evade the police at Carlisle, I don't know. If we don't catch him before then, the police will definitely be waiting there.'

'Well, if I am right about the luggage car, he's not going anywhere for at least another ten minutes,' said Kitt. 'We can reach you by that time and search the luggage car together, before we reach Todmorden.'

'Yeah, all right, sounds like a . . . ' Banks's voice cut out. For while she had been speaking, she had opened another compartment. And as she slid the door open, a man shoved her hard against the other side of the corridor and ran. Banks only just caught her breath in time to notice the colour of the man's hair: an ashen blond with a large bald patch, like a crop circle, right at the centre.

'Ugh. I've found him. Or should I say, he's found me. I think he overheard me saying his name. If he didn't know we were onto him before, he does now. He's running towards the luggage coach. I can't wait. The train is only going about five miles an hour at the moment. Not sure why we've slowed but if he's desperate enough he might jump off the back of it. Just come and catch me up as soon as you can,' Banks said, paying no attention to Kitt and Grace's protestations as she ran full pelt towards the luggage car.

CHAPTER TWENTY

'Running is only going to make it worse, Adam,' Banks shouted as she pulled open the door to the luggage car. She waited a moment to see if Adam materialized from the near darkness but nothing stirred.

'Banks,' Kit said over comms, 'we're not far away. Just hold him steady, no need to go on the offensive until we arrive. Apprehending him will be easier between the three of us.'

Banks didn't reply, but Kitt didn't push her to. Perhaps she understood that Banks didn't want to tip DuPont off to the fact that there were more people waiting for him if he managed to get past her. Though some part of him must have known Banks wasn't acting alone if he overheard her talking about him over comms, he had no idea whether or not those people were on the train. Banks wanted to keep it that way. So long as they knew more than DuPont did about the state of affairs, they had the upper hand.

To say that the luggage car wasn't an ideal place to hunt a murderer on the run was an understatement. The windows were much smaller than those in the carriages designed for passengers, so it was difficult to see more than a couple of feet inside. She could just make out a few stacks of suitcases on trolleys that were harnessed to the walls by bungee ropes. They creaked and rattled as the train trundled along the jointed track, through the valley of Calderdale. A strong scent of tobacco hung in the air, perhaps this carriage had once been used to transport freight?

'I'm innocent, I haven't done anything wrong!' came a call from somewhere inside. There was no more time to assess the environment and its potential pitfalls. She had to focus on DuPont now. Banks cocked her head, squinting into the dimness. She was relatively sure the call had come from behind a large stack of storage boxes off to the left.

'I'd like to believe you, really I would,' said Banks, taking her first, tentative step into the luggage car. Granted, when he'd shoved her before, she hadn't been expecting it but even taking that into account, she had been quite surprised by the force of it. A reminder that when people are desperate, adrenalin can completely overtake them. And before you know it, you're dealing with someone who could give Captain America a run for his money.

'If you're innocent, then why are you running? Surely an innocent person would want to straighten everything out. You've made things very difficult for yourself. And you haven't made the best choices so far, but it's still not too late to turn yourself in and explain everything that's been going on. If we've got the wrong idea, then I'd think that correcting the record is a better plan than this. I'm sure whatever the issue is you'll be given a fair hearing.'

'There'll be no fair hearing. Not after the police look at my phone. They're never going to believe I'm innocent.' There was no mistaking the panic in DuPont's voice. Whether he was panicking because he really did believe himself to be innocent and was scared about what might happen next, or simply because he had been caught, Banks couldn't say. Either way, she needed to try and get him on side.

Banks took another step closer to where she thought the calls were coming from. It was difficult to isolate the sound over the sway and clatter of the carriage but she was relatively sure she was in the right area at least.

'Adam, what's on your phone?' Banks called back. This time there was no response. 'Did you have some kind of relationship going with Siobhan, is that what this is all about? That alone isn't proof that you killed her, if that's what's worrying you? The police do have to have considerable evidence to convict. Especially in a case as complicated as this. You're an intelligent man, Adam, but you're not making an intelligent decision right now. Why don't you just tell me what's going on and then I can advise you on the best thing to do?'

Again, silence.

Trying to keep her breath steady, despite her uneasiness, Banks made another attempt to engage with DuPont. 'Look, I don't know what kind of relationship you had with Siobhan. But whatever the problem is, running away from it is not going to do you any good. I know you're not some hard-bitten criminal. You're a teacher. A science teacher no less. So, some part of you understands that there's no logical way out of this situation. The police are already closing in on the station at Todmorden. The train won't leave until you are off it. You won't get far if you jump off early either. It's really rugged terrain in this part of the valley. Even if you can navigate it for a while, you won't make quick enough progress to outrun the police helicopter that will undoubtedly be after you within the hour.'

Banks swallowed hard. She'd take anything over this silence. There was really only one last card she had in her pocket. It was time to play it.

'OK, I understand you don't want to talk to me. I'm not going to try and force it out of you. But before you do anything else, I want you to think about your children. They rely on having you around, and they love you no matter what you've done. So, before you do anything rash, consider them, and think about what kind of future they'll have if their father is taken away. You're increasing the likelihood of that happening by running from the police. Facing up to whatever is happening is the only way forward.'

Banks strained her ears but again DuPont did not respond. She took another step forward. Just as she did, however, one of the trolleys lurched towards her as though someone had given it a good push from the other side. She was swept hard against the opposite wall of the carriage but thankfully only her right arm was pinned. She easily managed to pull it free just as DuPont tried to make a run for the door.

'Oh, no you don't,' Banks said, grabbing the collar of his shirt. This, however, did little to slow him down. He twisted and writhed and swung his arms back at her. Unwilling to submit. In a split second, he had grabbed Banks by the arms and was shaking her with all of his might.

'I am thinking of my children! I am thinking of my children!' he shouted, over and over again. The light from the small windows flitting over his face made him look akin to some unhinged psycho in a horror film.

Although initially startled by DuPont's outburst, Banks had dealt with enough suspects resisting arrest in her time to know how to see such situations off quickly.

Hooking her leg around his ankle, she managed to push him backwards and watched him topple to the ground. He landed with an almighty thud. This dazed him for a moment or two, but then, without warning, he returned the favour and grabbed Banks's ankles. With unexpected force, he pulled them clean from underneath her.

She didn't have a second to brace. She didn't have a

moment to think. And it was her head that hit the hard planks of the carriage floor first. But she was barely even aware of that as everything around her went instantly black.

CHAPTER TWENTY-ONE

'Charley,' said a voice that seemed vaguely familiar. It was the first thing to permeate through the blankness. 'Come on, Charley, wake up now.'

Banks wanted to open her eyes. But just at that moment, she couldn't obey the instruction that had been given to her. It was too painful, and she didn't seem to have the strength to even lift her eyelids. There was breath in her lungs, that much she knew, and her head was definitely still attached to her body. That, she could deduce from the endless pulse touching every nerve in her skull, which showed no signs of stopping.

'Charley, wake up,' the voice came again.

Desperate to obey what seemed like a simple command, Banks battled to open her eyes. For a minute, the world around her spun but it did eventually stop with a sickening jolt.

DS Robinson was leaning over her, worry lines marking

her forehead. Banks's eyes darted to her left and she noticed Kitt and Grace standing close by, looking equally concerned. She was still in the luggage carriage, but no matter which way her eyes flitted, DuPont was nowhere to be seen.

Her head throbbed and she let out a little moan in an attempt to manage the pain. 'He ran away,' Banks managed to croak out.

'It's all right,' Robinson said. 'You may have done it the hard way, but you did succeed in slowing DuPont down. He's already in custody, Charley, so don't worry. Kitt, Grace and the guard managed to corner him and he locked himself in the toilets at the end of the carriage. Once the train stopped at Todmorden we managed to unlock the door and apprehend him. He is in quite the frenzy though. We're not too sure exactly what that means about his innocence or guilt at present, but once he's calmed down and had a sobering few hours in a cell, we'll ask him some questions about why he ran and his relationship with Siobhan Lange.'

'So, nobody got hurt?' Banks almost whispered.

There was no missing the admiration that shone in Robinson's eyes as she spoke. Perhaps Banks should be more concerned for her own well-being given the knock she'd taken. But she'd spent so long trying to protect the lives of others, above her own, her safety was rarely her first thought.

'No, Charley,' Robinson said, 'He didn't hurt anybody,

and if he is our murderer, I'll see to it that he never hurts anybody else again.'

Banks let out a breath she didn't realize she'd been holding onto. But then something nagged at the back of her mind. 'I don't know what . . .' she murmured. After her knock to the head, she had no idea if she was making sense, or was speaking clearly. She had to try and warn Robinson though. 'But there's something on his phone he doesn't want you to find. He was raving about it. Might be nothing. You've seen what he's like right now. Not exactly in the most coherent frame of mind, but I'd start there. Whatever is on that phone, I think it's the reason he ran.'

'We've already requested his phone records,' said Robinson. 'We did so the second we realized he was on the run. If he's already admitted to you that there's something on his phone, then we should be able to drag the truth out of him pretty quick once the records come through. Then we can put all this behind us.'

'He said he was innocent,' Banks said, her voice barely above a whisper now. 'But they all say that.'

'He's not innocent of grievous bodily harm, that much is for sure. And committed against a police officer no less,' said Kitt. 'Given his actions, I would say any protestations of innocence are more out of desperation than anything else. I heard you over the comms. You gave him ample opportunity to give himself up. Instead, he chose to attack you. It doesn't look good on him.'

Banks tried to sit up; Robinson helped her lean against a nearby case. Even that much movement made her feel nauseated but she did what she could to steady herself. 'If he's guilty, then why tip me off, about his phone?'

'That I don't know,' said Robinson. 'If he knows there's something incriminating on there, perhaps he's just trying to find a way of wriggling out of it by pretending it's not the whole story. Or perhaps, when the time is right, he wants to pretend that somebody is framing him. Either way, I think you've had enough excitement for one day. I've managed to fudge things with DI Graves. I told him that a fellow police officer was visiting her brother and stumbled across a tip about DuPont. It's not the most believable of stories, but considering how much you've done to bring DuPont in, I'll make it work in the report. Right now, you need to get to the hospital and have that head checked out.'

'I'm OK,' Banks said.

'Charley, you know that I have to send you to the doctor and make sure there's no lasting damage,' said Robinson. 'Don't make it a struggle. I've got quite enough on my plate as it is.'

'I know, sorry. It might surprise you to learn that I'm not the world's best patient,' said Banks.

'That is shocking,' Robinson said, her face registering absolutely no shock at all.

'Are there any journalists or camera crews out there?'

Banks asked. She wouldn't need to explain to Robinson why she was asking.

'There's a couple of journalists, and I'd imagine camera crews aren't far behind. So, you better keep your head down, unless you fancy going on the evening news and giving Chief Superintendent Ricci a little wave,' Robinson laughed at her own joke. Banks would have joined her if her head didn't feel like it was about to explode.

'That would certainly be an efficient way of extending my upcoming honeymoon – permanently.'

'Sounds like you've got more than one excuse for popping open a bottle tonight,' said Robinson. 'You should take the evening to relax and celebrate . . . assuming the doctors give you the all clear, of course. Given DuPont's aversion to law enforcement, it looks to me like you've caught yourself a killer.'

Banks offered Robinson a half-smile as Kitt and Grace helped her to her feet. On the surface, she agreed with Robinson's perception: Adam DuPont must have run for a reason, and already seemed to have admitted to at least one incriminating piece of evidence on his phone. He also had links to the school where the sashes were distributed and, according to other interviews they'd conducted, he had several possible motives for putting an end to Siobhan's life. As far as suspects went, he was definitely the best they had at the moment.

'Come on,' said Kitt. 'Mal is already sending me about

twenty texts a minute to find out if we were on the train hunting down the suspect, so clearly news of this incident has already reached York station. I expect he'll want a second-by-second breakdown of the whole adventure.'

'If word has already reached York, I really do need to get out of here pronto,' said Banks, hobbling a little bit faster than she had been before, until she made it out into the light at Todmorden platform.

As Kitt and Grace escorted Banks to a nearby ambulance, she could only hope Robinson was right and, despite his protests, DuPont was the real killer. Certainly, it would be a relief to know that Ewan had nothing to do with it. And if that had been decided once and for all, Banks could go back home, marry the woman she loved and put this terrible mess behind her. Maybe, given a little time, she could even consider rebuilding the trust between her and her brother.

Perhaps it was a little soon to pop the champagne as Robinson had suggested, just yet, however. They would know more once the phone records came through. Until then it was a matter of sitting tight and hoping whatever evidence soon to be uncovered on DuPont's phone spoke for itself.

CHAPTER TWENTY-TWO

'How's your noggin?' said Evie, gently stroking Banks's shoulder-length brown hair as they sat in the beer garden at the White Lion pub in Hebden Bridge.

'Same as it was when you asked three minutes ago,' Banks said, but made sure she coupled her comment with a smile and a kiss to Evie's cheek. She didn't really mind Evie coddling her. In fact, it was rather wonderful to know that another human being cared about her enough to do so. But Banks had always struggled with public displays of emotion – even with the woman she loved – so it was easier to offer her a wry comment and a smile.

The original plan had been that she and Evie wouldn't see each other again until Banks returned from her covert investigation in West Yorkshire. But Kitt had apprised Evie via text message of Banks's injury and, after that, Evie had insisted on coming out to see that her betrothed was still in one piece. Halloran had offered to drive her back to the area. He claimed it was to save Evie driving up and down dale in her vintage car, which might not take so kindly to some of the gradients, but it was pretty clear that he was only here in the hope that he would catch a glimpse of the *Frederick William Kitson* during his stay. Certainly, he'd asked many more questions about the steam engine than he had directly about the apprehension of DuPont.

Mercifully, the doctors had given Banks some meds for the unearthly headache that had only worsened on their way to Rochdale Infirmary. Apparently, she had quite the bump on the back of her head but the doctor assured her it would reduce after a couple of days. If it didn't, she was to report back post haste.

'I must admit, I'm glad we're all heading back to York tomorrow,' said Halloran, nursing the half a shandy he'd ordered when they arrived an hour ago. 'It's probably time you came back to your own turf. I think you've done enough damage to West Yorkshire, for now.'

'Oh, are you missing me already, sir?' Banks teased. 'I know you can barely go a day without me and I'm the centre of your otherwise bleak universe, but I have got other things going on right now.'

Halloran chuckled. 'Yes, all right. I don't have a life. Very funny.'

'Don't feel bad,' said Grace. Seemingly deliberately misunderstanding Halloran's tone. 'She doesn't like to talk about it, sore subject you know, but Kitt doesn't have a life either.'

'Yes, thank you Grace. I'm well aware of your thoughts on my out of office activities,' said Kitt, cutting in before her assistant could start her usual banter. 'But Mal does have a point. I'm sure DS Robinson can handle things from here. She's probably booking Adam DuPont right now. With this in mind, it's for the best we head back to York before we outstay our welcome.'

Banks nodded. 'What's this? An intervention?'

'Oh, no,' said Evie. 'Nothing that organized. It is us, after all. It's just we're getting married soon, you know, and the sooner we put this behind us the sooner we can start our future together.'

Banks smiled at her fiancée. 'Nothing would give me greater pleasure. I'm paid up at the guest house until tomorrow morning. Unless I hear from Robinson before then, I'll assume the matter is closed. After that, I'll consider whether or not I want to give Ewan an explicit apology for suspecting him, or just move on and then drive back to York.'

'You must be relieved,' Evie said. 'That Ewan didn't have anything to do with it after all. I know I'm relieved on your behalf.'

Banks wanted to agree with what Evie said. But she hadn't quite managed to convince herself that the case was really closed. And yet, all signs suggested that this was in fact true. That her brother had just been in the wrong place at the wrong time as, she supposed, ex-cons sometimes were.

'I think relief will come. Once it's official that DuPont was Siobhan's killer. Until then it's probably better to reserve judgement, but I'll admit I am right on the brink of being hopeful.'

'Steady on now!' said Evie, sporting that cheeky smile Banks loved so much.

'That's a vast improvement on how I felt four days ago!' said Banks. 'It means a lot to replace distrust with hope. So, I'm grateful to you for that.' Banks looked from Kitt to Grace. 'I'm grateful to all of you.'

Grace offered Banks a warm smile before taking a sip of her gin and tonic.

'We're glad to have helped,' said Kitt. 'I know from the hours Mal works that your routine is relentless, gruelling even. The idea of you working a case like that on your own, it doesn't bear thinking about. And, yes, I know that technically speaking you shouldn't be working cases outside your jurisdiction, but we all have times when we have to go with what feels right inside rather than stick to the rules. I think this was your time, Charley. And now that it's all over, you can put it behind you. Happily ever after awaits.'

'I didn't think you thought happily ever after and marriage went together?' said Banks. She was one hundred per cent stirring trouble now but it had been a trying few days. She needed to let off some steam.

Evie shot Kitt an accusatory look. 'What's that? Oh, no. Please don't tell me you've been giving my fiancée your standard lecture on the perils of matrimony? That's not cricket. I am trying to get this woman up the aisle, in case you missed it?'

'I think I just managed to catch myself before I put her off the idea completely,' said Kitt. It was the first occasion Banks had ever seen Kitt look apologetic, at least in the time she'd known her. It seemed it wasn't just Banks who was wrapped around Evie's little finger. 'But, I admit, my mouth did run away with me there. Must be Grace's influence.'

'Me? I'm a retiring soul,' said Grace, placing a hand against her chest as though Kitt's words had mortally offended her delicate sensibilities.

'And, if you don't mind,' said Halloran, 'I'd prefer you weren't going around telling everyone you meet what a terrible prospect marriage is. It doesn't really reflect well on your life partner, does it?'

'Don't hate the player, hate the game. I believe that's the expression,' said Kitt.

Grace's eyes widened. 'Katherine Hartley, where on earth did you hear that phrase? Have you been out on the town past nine o'clock in the eventide? I expect better!'

'You're not funny, Grace,' said Kitt.

'Oh, I don't know,' said Evie. 'Maybe she's a little funny.'

'Whatever possessed me to put you two in the same room as each other, I don't know,' said Kitt. 'I've had not a minute's peace since. But as we're talking about curfews, it's only nine now but I've got to pack everything back up at the guest house and, frankly, I've had more than enough excitement for one day.'

'It will be completely dark soon anyway,' said Banks. 'Best to nip back to Halifax now, go to bed and hopefully we'll be on our way home by lunchtime tomorrow.'

'Er, yes,' said Halloran. 'Although I have it on good authority that the *Frederick William Kitson* will be resting at Andaby station from nine tomorrow morning, so perhaps we could make one quick detour so the train enthusiast of the group could actually see a train?'

Banks chuckled. 'I suppose that could be arranged. I really should see Ewan tomorrow, even if it's just briefly, to check in on him after all he's been through this week. He'll be relieved to know an arrest has been made and we can both put Siobhan's murder, and all it stirred up, behind us.'

Banks did her best to sound convincing as she said these words. She tried so hard in fact that she did almost convince herself. No matter how hard she tried, however, she couldn't shake the feeling something wasn't quite right. Or forget Adam DuPont's words, which even now rang out in her ears. There was something about the tone of them that had stayed with her. Was it the tenor of an innocent man frightened he was about to go down for a murder he didn't commit? Or was it the notes a killer sings when he'll say anything to escape his fate?

CHAPTER TWENTY-THREE

When Charley awoke in the narrow bed at the bed and breakfast in Halifax, Evie was trying to restrain her wrists. She could hear whimpering, and then realized that it was she who was making the sound. She was aware, at once, that she was drenched in sweat and yet shivering from head to toe.

'Shh,' Evie said, stroking Banks's hair in the near darkness of the early hours. 'You had a nightmare, that's all.'

Banks took in a deep breath and tried to steady herself. It had been many years since she'd suffered a nightmare. She had always hated them with a passion. Not that anybody loved having nightmares, but when she described her own everyone else always commented how intense hers sounded; it seems she was gifted with a vivid subconscious that never missed an opportunity to really drum home how deeply insecure she was.

'Want to tell me about it?' Evie half-whispered.

'It was Ewan,' she said. The last thing she wanted was to

talk about it, but she knew it pained Evie when she kept things to herself.

'What about him?'

'He . . . was strangling me,' said Banks. 'And I couldn't make him stop. He was just too strong.'

'Hardly surprising you've had a dream like that, after a day like today,' said Evie. Banks felt Evie's head rest on her chest, and Banks wrapped her arms around her. 'Am I ever going to be able to let it go? What he did? What he put me through?' Banks whispered.

'That's not something I can answer for you,' said Evie. 'But, you know, they say that forgiveness isn't for the other person but for you. That the longer you hold onto these things the more they impact your life, not that of the person you hold the grudge against.'

'That makes sense,' Banks said. 'It's just that, we got the killer today. So, I feel like I shouldn't be having dreams about my brother strangling anybody. Given that we've all but proved that he wasn't involved in Siobhan's murder. Is it a sign that, no matter what, I'm never going to be able to forgive him for what he did?'

Evie turned on a small lamp on the bedside table but kept the dimmer switch low. She turned back to Charley, her eyes bleary and blinking in the unwelcome yellow light cast by what Banks would bet was the cheapest bulb the landlady had been able to find at the local hardware store.

'I think it's a sign that you got knocked hard on the

bonce. And that it's been a very emotional few days. And . . . that you're about to enter into pretty much the biggest commitment of your life.'

'No, no, no,' Charley said, holding Evie's face in her hands. 'This is not about you.'

'No, you're right, it's not,' said Evie. 'It's about your relationship with trust. Now that we're getting married, you're going to trust me with things that you haven't before. You're going to need to do that, or the relationship won't work out. And when you've trusted that deeply in the past, you've been burned. So, understandably, you're having dreams about being strangled to death by the last person you trusted deeply and who betrayed you.'

'I feel like you should be charging me for this,' Banks said, a small smile tugging at her lips.

'Oh, trust me, in twenty years you'll feel like you've paid dearly for these little nuggets of wisdom,' Evie said with a little chuckle. 'But the main thing to focus on right now is that your brother isn't trying to strangle you, or anyone else. You were worried he might have, but you went out and got to the truth. So, you can move forward now.'

'You're right,' Banks said, kissing Evie on the lips. 'Turn out the light, we've still got a good few hours sleep ahead of us.' Smiling, Evie tapped Banks on the nose with her finger and then, as directed, turned out the light.

Evie soon dropped off to sleep again, but Banks struggled to keep her eyes closed for long and instead focused on a shadow cast by the blinds across the ceiling. Even though she was wide awake now, she could still feel the weight of her brother's hands around her throat. Had Evie been right about the trust thing? Was she suffocating at the thought of letting somebody in again without any caveats? If so, she had to find a way to get over herself. She wouldn't let any of her hang-ups drive Evie away and, besides, the killer was in custody now. The many crises that she had so eagerly foreseen had all been averted. For once, rather than imagining every last thing that could go wrong, perhaps this time she should just take the win.

CHAPTER TWENTY-FOUR

'Where's Halloran?' Banks called, as she and Evie were loading the last of their belongings back into her car, which was parked next to the green in the main square in Andaby. As promised, they had hopped back to the small town so that Halloran could get a look at the *Frederick William Kitson*. Banks and the rest of them had hung back at the green. Those who had been on board the train during yesterday's ordeal weren't exactly desperate to see the train again, and, after the injury Banks had sustained the day before, Evie hadn't let her fiancée out of her sight.

Halloran's car was parked just behind Banks's, and Kitt and Grace were finishing up loading their coats and bags into the boot.

'He's still playing with the train, I think,' Kitt called back. 'Don't feel like you have to wait for us if you want to get on the road.'

'It's fine to wait,' Banks called over. 'Robinson said she would catch me here before we drove home.'

Kitt nodded and then turned back to arranging her bags in the car.

Banks checked her phone again. She'd sent Ewan a text message about meeting briefly this morning but had received no reply. Even though it was relatively early in the morning, this was quite odd for him. He was usually pretty quick to respond to Banks's messages, perhaps because during his twenty years inside she hadn't offered him much communication at all. She would like to put his radio silence down to the fact that he was just having a lie-in and hadn't looked at his phone yet, but she had a nagging feeling she just couldn't shake.

Just then a picture message popped up on her phone. Banks opened it and her eyes widened in slight disbelief.

'Has everyone else just received a picture message from Halloran in which he's hanging out the cab of the Kitson train wearing the driver's hat, or was this very special pleasure reserved just for me?' Banks called over.

Kitt, Grace and Evie all checked their phones in unison, and then held up their screens to Banks to confirm they too had received the photo. Banks wasn't quite standing close enough to Kitt and Grace to see their phone screens in detail, but she could just make out the outline of the image.

'I hope he gets it out of his system before we get home,'

Kitt called back. 'I cannot be doing with another night of playing referee between Halloran and Iago over a train set.'

'Banks,' DS Robinson said as she approached her from behind.

The officer's appearance hadn't escaped the notice of Kitt, and she walked over from Halloran's car to join the conversation.

'How is everything going at the station?' Banks asked. 'Is Graves happy with DuPont being pulled in?'

'Oh, yes, there was a big box of doughnuts waiting for us when we got in this morning. I've had three already so I'm expecting a sugar crash of epic proportions in T minus two hours.'

'Three doughnuts for breakfast, that's impressive even by my standards,' Banks said with a smile.

'Well, you know how it is on cases like this, you'll turn to anything to keep you going,' Robinson said, the dark circles under her eyes betraying the fact that she hadn't had much sleep the night before. 'We got the court order through for DuPont's phone a few hours ago. We managed to retrieve some deleted text messages.'

'Between him and Siobhan?' said Kitt.

Robinson nodded. 'This goes no further, mind. They were from a burner phone but they were signed by Siobhan. The gist was that she and Emily Cook were planning to expose Adam for taking advantage of them twenty years ago.'

'That's motive right there,' said Kitt. 'No matter what

unsavoury choices he made twenty years ago, he's got a family now. It's likely that he'll do anything to protect them, just as his wife tried to when we questioned her the first time round.'

'Have you talked to DuPont about the messages yet?' said Banks.

Robinson nodded. 'I spent the best part of two hours interrogating him early this morning. He denies he had anything to do with Emily's disappearance or Siobhan's murder. He also denies ever having had any inappropriate contact with either of them. But, of course, he would say that. We've had no choice but to hold him while we do further forensic tests on his house and his place of work. The text messages are pretty damning but I'd prefer to go to court with a little more than that. At present, there's only evidence that the girls threatened DuPont, not that he did anything about that threat.'

'Maybe the sash he used to strangle her will turn up during the house search?' said Banks. 'He might have held onto it rather than binning it, knowing that in a bin it might be found by somebody.'

'Here's hoping the house search turns something like that up,' said Robinson.

'Did the text messages make a demand for money or anything like that?' asked Banks.

'No,' Robinson said. 'There wasn't any mention of anything DuPont could do to stop the process. There was just a clear threat to expose him. He did try calling the number back but there was never a response. So, he didn't get a chance to try and reason with them.'

'Presumably, then, something did happen all those years ago at school and between them they'd finally drummed up the courage to name and shame DuPont,' said Kitt. 'I don't know exactly what he did, but despite his denials it sounds very much like he had relationships with those students that passed professional boundaries.'

'That's certainly the way it looks,' Robinson agreed. 'But with one person dead, and the other missing, it's going to be very difficult to prove what kind of relationship, if any, he had with Emily or Siobhan.'

'Doesn't the fact that they're missing and deceased, and thus not able to expose him, point strongly enough to the fact that he's likely to be behind what happened to them?' asked Kitt.

'That's the kind of case we're hoping to build, but the text messages are, at present, very much the cornerstone. You can't build a case on an absence of evidence. If we find the sash, that's going to be a big breakthrough, but presently we haven't got any other physical evidence tying DuPont to the crime. Still, his behaviour yesterday was shocking to say the least, so the case has that going for it. I'm very sure the truth will come out eventually, one way or another,' said Robinson.

'I'm glad,' Banks said. 'For all kinds of reasons.'

'I won't be telling my DI this, of course, who has now swanned off back to Leeds because he thinks the case is pretty much on its way to being closed, but I wouldn't have got to the truth of this situation without both your help. So, I'm really grateful. No doubt I'll get quite a few brownie points for closing this case so quickly.'

'Don't you mean doughnut points?' said Kitt.

'Even better,' Robinson said with a wink.

'I only hope you recover Emily Cook in the process,' said Banks, her smile waning at the thought of the girl they'd, as yet, had no leads on in terms of her whereabouts. 'No body has been found. I can't work out whether he's got her stashed alive somewhere as a bargaining chip, or if he did also kill Emily two weeks ago and was just able to cover his tracks better.'

'I'm hoping that something is going to come out in DuPont's interviews. It's my top priority to locate her, one way or the other,' said Robinson, the light in her eyes dimming enough for Banks to deduce she suspected the worst. And Banks couldn't blame her for that. With each passing day, Banks knew deep down that it became less and less likely that Emily would be found alive. In some ways, working a missing persons case was more emotionally gruelling than working on a murder. With a dead body, the best you could ever do for the victim and their family was make sure the right person saw justice. But with a missing person there was that hope, ever present, that you would be the one to bring them home. That the person in question was still out there, somewhere, waiting to be rescued. And that on some bright future morning you'd deliver them to the doorstep of their family, who would never know such sharp relief, before or since, as they do on seeing their loved one alive.

Sadly, that was rarely the outcome when it came to missing persons. Especially if that missing person was a young woman. Banks knew what Robinson was up against. She would do her best and prepare for the worst, just as Banks always had done in similar situations.

'I could help with the search, if you need me to,' Banks said. She had suspected the worst about her brother, and in the end those fears had been unfounded. Perhaps today was a day for hoping for the best.

'Thank you, but I genuinely think you've helped enough. It's time to close the case as far as you're concerned.'

Banks nodded. She couldn't overstep on another officer's case. Robinson had been more than generous about just how much she had shared. Banks couldn't ask any more of her. 'I'm glad we could help,' she said, shaking Robinson's hand, before sliding into the driver's seat.

It was at that moment that Robinson's phone rang.

'Robinson. What? That can't be right . . . ' Robinson's eyes widened. She turned 180 degrees and stared. Her eyes only grew wider as she looked off into the distance. 'I'm on my way,' Robinson said into the phone before hanging up.

Frowning, Banks got back out of the car and looked in the same direction Robinson had just a moment ago. Plumes of black smoke rose into the air. Somewhere a building was on fire.

'It's the industrial museum,' Robinson said. 'It's caught fire, and it sounds serious.'

'What?' Banks and Kitt said in unison as they watched the smoke curl higher and higher into the atmosphere.

'The museum is right next to the train station; Mal must already be on the scene. That's why he hasn't come back,' said Kitt, pulling out her phone and dialling Halloran's number.

There was a pause and then a collective sigh of relief as Halloran's voice said 'Hello?' at the other end of the line.

Safe in the knowledge that her partner was unharmed, Banks turned back to Robinson. 'You arrest Adam DuPont for murder, and then the building where the murder took place just happens to catch on fire?' Banks looked again at the black smoke billowing up into the blue sky. 'Sounds to me like we might have an arsonist in our midst.'

CHAPTER TWENTY-FIVE

To Banks's tired and glassy eyes, there was something immensely sad about the sight of the industrial museum burning. As if the recent murder hadn't shaken this small community enough, one of its most iconic buildings being reduced to cinders was the last thing that the people of Andaby needed. Mercifully, the fire brigade had arrived promptly but they had been battling with the flames for a couple of hours and were only now just putting out the last of the fire's spread.

Robinson had been on the phone non-stop since she'd arrived at the scene. Banks, and Halloran had done what they could to support, while Kitt, Grace and Evie had been forced to wait on the other side of the cordon line.

At the earliest opportunity, Banks and Halloran made their way over to their loved ones for a check-in. 'Any news on how quickly they'll be able to determine where the fire started?' said Kitt, who barely waited for them to be back in ear shot before she started talking.

'These things usually take a few days at the minimum,' Halloran explained. 'But the crew might be able to give us some sense of what they think once the building is secure. Often, they can use the spread of the fire to give you a good estimate before they ever write anything official on a form. But I don't know what their verdict will be on this place. There's quite a lot of wood and other flammable materials. They might not be able to give us a hunch this time.'

'What about DuPont?' said Grace. 'Do you know if he used his phone call to arrange this? It's a scary thought, but, if it is arson, there must be some reason that this particular building was targeted. Banks is always talking about how coincidences almost never happen in these kinds of cases.'

'And I stand by that sentiment here,' Banks said. 'From what Robinson said, the only person DuPont has called is his lawyer, but that's not to say his lawyer couldn't have relayed information to his family or friends. If they did, someone might have felt prompted to take matters into their own hands. Right now, that's the most logical theory I have, again assuming this is arson and not some wild coincidence.'

Banks refrained from going a step further than Halloran; from speculating on who might have been enlisted by DuPont's family and friends. As casually as she could, Banks checked her phone again. Still no word from Ewan.

'You're thinking the same thing I am, aren't you?' said

Kitt. 'That Maya Garrison might be behind this. Trying to destroy any remaining evidence that might lead to her husband's conviction.'

'She has withheld information before to protect him,' said Banks, raising her eyebrows. 'It's clear she will take the law into her own hands, if necessary. I suppose we don't quite know exactly how far she'll go to protect her family.'

'There is a big difference between not informing the police of a rumour about your husband and committing arson, though,' said Halloran.

'I know,' said Banks. 'And to be honest, I hope to God that there is some other explanation. Those little kiddies they've got didn't ask for any of this and aren't going to have anyone to look after them at this rate.'

At this point, Robinson came to join them. 'I've pulled every single CCTV stream we have that even vaguely covers this area of the town. We haven't got much, it's only a small place at the end of the day, but we've got a couple of angles and we might get lucky. The uniforms back at the nick are going through it now.'

'Have you managed to speak to the fire team?' Banks asked.

'We have spoken to them briefly,' said Robinson. 'They say they won't be able to give us an official report for days but, given the timing I'd be surprised if we weren't looking at arson here. If that's confirmed, the point of origin will likely be either the room where Siobhan was killed, or the room where her body was found. Exactly why the killer would want the place burned down, I don't know. If there was any evidence to be had in there, I'm pretty confident we would have found it.'

Banks nodded along. She looked down at her hands. They were shaking. She couldn't remember the last time her hands had shaken like this. She'd always considered herself a pretty sturdy individual but there was a feeling inside that she could not banish and to hide it any longer would be both dangerous and irresponsible.

'There's something I have to say,' said Banks. 'And, I don't really know how to say it.'

'What's going on?' said Evie, a rare frown marking her brow.

'My plan was to see Ewan this morning to say my good-byes before I headed back to York. I sent him a text message when I got up first thing and, usually, he would text me right back. But I haven't heard from him, and I can't figure out if that's because something really terrible has happened to him or because he's *done* something really terrible.'

'It's only been a few hours,' said Evie.

'I know, but Ewan goes radio silent the morning that there's a fire in the building where Siobhan died? Maybe it's nothing, but I at least want to try and find out why he's not picking up his messages.'

'Maybe you should go to your brother's flat and check on him,' said Robinson. 'There's really nothing more to be done here and if you've got a hunch that something is up it's probably best to find out what's going on.'

'I'll do that,' said Banks. 'Perhaps I'm overreacting. Maybe, after all that's happened this week, I'm just fearing the worst. But it really isn't like him not to text back. And with this fire . . . I don't know . . . '

'It makes sense, follow your instincts,' said Robinson. 'They've certainly served you well so far. Just let me know what you find, yeah?'

'Sure, no problem,' said Banks as breezily as she could while dipping under the cordon line. Evie followed her back towards the green where their car was still parked. Banks felt Evie's hand nestle into her own and squeezed it. Why did she feel that she had to hold onto Evie as tight as she could right now, or else she might lose her? And why couldn't she shake the feeling that Ewan's lack of contact was more serious than a hangover? Banks unlocked the car, climbed in and pulled the door shut behind her. As she turned the key in the ignition, she found herself praying that her brother would be at his flat alive and well and was decidedly not in any more trouble than he was yesterday.

CHAPTER TWENTY-SIX

'What's going on?' said Banks, as Robinson walked into the break room at Andaby Police Station. 'It sounded urgent on the phone. I suppose it must be if you've called me down here.'

'Have you heard anything from your brother yet?' Robinson said, plonking herself down in the chair next to where Banks was sitting.

Banks shook her head. 'Nothing, it's really not like him.' When she and Evie had visited his flat, they had banged on his door for a good twenty minutes but there had been no answer. Banks had even tried calling him a couple of times but on both occasions the call went to voicemail. They'd checked with the neighbours on either side but they had only briefly met Ewan once or twice since he'd moved in a few months back and couldn't offer any concrete information about his movements or possible whereabouts.

Since there was clearly something afoot, Evie and Banks

had informed Robinson that Ewan was currently nowhere to be found and then regrouped with the others to reformulate a new plan for the next few days in light of recent developments.

The fire breaking out, if not the sudden disappearance of Ewan, had made it clear that there was more to closing this case than anyone had anticipated just the day before. Consequently, Halloran and Evie had driven back to York together, while Banks, Kitt and Grace had relocated to a B&B in Andaby itself. In the relative comfort of their new guest house, they had spent their time mulling over the various possibilities and waiting for any concrete news on how the fire fit in to the bigger picture. Kitt wasn't due back at the library until Friday evening, so they still had two more days to tie up any loose ends of the case. Technically speaking, of course, the murder scene catching fire just as DuPont was apprehended only added more weight to the theory that he was guilty. But, over the years, Banks had learned to trust her gut. And, right now, it was telling her that this was not the time to go home. How could she anyway until she located her brother? He was the whole reason she was even involved in this case. If his involvement had become a likely prospect again, she had to see the investigation through to the bitter end.

'I called you in because Maya Garrison reported her car stolen early this morning,' Robinson explained. 'It's definitely her car on the CCTV pulling up to the industrial museum. A figure exits the car with what looks like a small canister of petroleum and hurries back some minutes later.'

Banks narrowed her eyes, digesting this new information. 'So, it was deliberate. Not that there was much doubt. Is the figure in the footage Maya, then?'

Robinson shook her head. 'It doesn't look like her even a little bit. At the time the car is seen driving down the street on the CCTV footage, Maya has an alibi anyway. A friend had come round to watch the kids so she could go into work, albeit a bit late. She didn't want to send them to school today with everything that was going on in case rumour had spread about her husband being arrested. But, of course, she still had to go in to work herself.'

'So, she didn't do any burning with her own hands. But couldn't Maya have paid this person or otherwise orchestrated them to burn down the building?' Banks said.

Robinson sighed and offered Banks a strangely sympathetic smile that under the circumstances seemed a little odd to her. 'It's a possibility, but we haven't had the time to scrutinize her bank records yet – see if there's any large withdrawals or payments to a third party. I'm sorry this wasn't wrapped up like we all thought. You really are not obliged to stay in town, you know. We probably have got the right suspect in custody given the timing of the fire.'

'I don't want to outstay my welcome, so you can tell me to sod off whenever you want and I promise I won't take offence. But it seems to me you've got a lot of strands here and not enough people to untangle them.'

'Isn't that always the challenge?' said Robinson, pausing for some time before speaking again. 'Whoever lit that fire could be the key to proving DuPont was the killer. So, we need to identify them as soon as possible.'

'What can I do to help?' said Banks.

'You could take a look at the footage. Tell me if you recognize anyone you might have spoken to during your enquiries?'

There was an edge to Robinson's voice as she said this. Something seemed to be going on here, something that Banks couldn't quite put her finger on. Was she imagining it? She had had a hard knock to the head the day before and hadn't exactly had a lot of sleep that week. Or maybe Robinson was just acting a bit funny because she was tired. She'd seen it before with other colleagues. When you're working a case like this, sometimes it can seem to everyone else like you've had a personality transplant. Sleeplessness does weird things to people's brains.

'Sure, of course I'll look at the CCTV footage,' Banks said, before following Robinson through to the main office. Within a few seconds Robinson had clicked a couple of buttons on her computer and a video flashed up on screen.

Just as Robinson had said, the footage showed the road just outside the industrial museum. After a few seconds, a yellow Nissan pulled up and a figure got out of the car. The second Banks saw the figure, a chill came over her. At once she realized why Robinson had been acting strangely. And why she had asked Banks to come in and review the footage.

It was difficult to make out any concrete details given the distance of the camera to the car and the fact that the figure was dressed all in black. But there was one detail that Banks noticed. A detail she couldn't miss due to its familiarity. A crop of chin-length black hair.

'Oh, my God,' Banks said, shaking her head and struggling to hold back tears. 'That's my brother.'

CHAPTER TWENTY-SEVEN

Taking a deep breath, Banks pushed open the door of the interrogation room and gently closed the door behind her. Would she ever get over the humiliation of seeing her brother's face on that CCTV footage? Not in a hurry. As Banks had suspected when she first glimpsed her own flesh and blood on that recording, Robinson had known all along that the person in the footage was Ewan. It had been a test of loyalty. Robinson had wanted to know who she could trust. She wanted to know if Banks would identify the man in the video as her brother? Or feign ignorance?

Perhaps Banks should have been angry with Robinson for testing her, but she wasn't. What else was she supposed to have done to ensure that she could keep Banks as an extra body on the investigation? Even if it was in a completely unofficial capacity. Robinson was smart enough to know that Banks might prove particularly useful now that a blood relative of hers had been incriminated in a related offence.

'So, this is the next ploy, is it? Sending my own family in here to try and coerce me into talking,' Ewan said, before Banks could even get a word out, let alone take a seat.

Robinson's first priority after realizing that it was Ewan in that CCTV footage was to locate him. Apparently, he'd been found trying to hitchhike on the A646 in the direction of Burnley. So, after everything he'd been through, after sticking out a twenty-year prison sentence, he'd found himself on the run within three months of getting out. And there was no denying his crimes this time. Banks had seen it with her own eyes. Her brother was either a murderer himself, or was in the employ of someone who was. How he had the audacity to make cracks at her like that, she didn't know. But she was sure of one thing. She was going to get the information she needed from him. No matter what it took.

Sitting down across the table from her brother, Banks shook her head and then slowly met his eye. 'I've told everyone to go on their tea break. Nobody is watching through the glass. I'm not here as an officer. I'm here as your sister.'

Ewan sneered and Banks couldn't blame him. Even as she said those words, she knew they weren't sincere. Almost a decade she'd been working in the service – working her way up from a community officer to DS. That was slow progress by most people's standards. But every single career move had been made with caution. Every I dotted; every T crossed.

Because of this man. Because she never felt she could step too far out. Because she thought she was destined to forever keep her head down and not hope for anything too grand when she had a murderer in the family.

With all this in mind, the job had come first for as long as she could remember. It's something Evie accepted with the kind of grace that only made Banks love her even more. So, was it even possible for her to put her brother first in this scenario? Maybe not first. Justice for the victim had to come before everything else, no matter who was involved. Still, she believed the advice she was about to impart was in his best interests, whether he wanted to hear it or not. Whether or not he would comply.

'Things are looking really shaky for you, right now,' Banks said, leading with the most honest thing she could think to say. 'And I'll admit, at this point I haven't a clue what the hell you've got yourself into or how you've managed to do it. But here's what I do know. You lied about your alibi, that alone was enough to have your probation officer come down on you like a tonne of bricks. But now you've been identified as a perpetrator in an arson case. My own brother, caught on CCTV with a can of lighter fluid in his hands. Why didn't you just take a bus back to prison and walk in willingly? Because, I'll tell you, there's no two ways about it, Ewan, you will go back to prison for this. The only question is, how long for? How many extra years of your life are you willing to sacrifice for someone else?'

She forced herself to take a breath after those words. Let them settle. Gauge his reaction. She was doing her best to make it sound as though she still believed DuPont was guilty of the murder. In truth, she had no idea whether Ewan had started that fire to burn evidence that incriminated Dupont, or himself. Her words didn't draw a reaction. He simply sat there, his face blank. As though they were engaging in a childhood game to see who of the two of them would blink first. Banks could only hope that this time she would win.

'With your newfound freedom, I don't believe for a second that you willingly entered into this mess,' she continued. 'After all you've been through, you're not daft enough to think that you would just get away with it. That much I know. And that means you've got information that could mean justice for one, possibly two, bereaved families. If you don't start talking, though, they might start looking into booking you for conspiracy to murder. That's going to be a *very* long time behind bars.'

'They've got no proof I had anything to do with that murder. You said so yourself. They have to pass a threshold.'

'It's true, but starting a fire in the building where the murder took place is a pretty incriminating thing to do. And that's just the information we have at present. Very soon, the fire chief will come back with his assessment. And, I wonder, will the fire have broken out in the very room where the murder took place . . . ?'

At this Ewan swallowed and tried to moisten his lips. In

doing so, he confirmed to Banks that this was exactly where he had started the fire. With every second that passed, her brother's protestations of innocence fell more and more flat.

'Well,' Banks continued, 'that's going to be construed by any jury as an attempt to destroy evidence. The case will be pretty much open and shut. They might not be able to ascertain exactly why you were involved. But they won't care. Not about somebody who's already taken a life. Somebody who's already proven themselves as a violent thug. They'll just send you down for it. They arrested somebody else only last night, and then this morning you magically chose to burn down the building where the murder took place? There are very few conclusions people are going to draw from that sequence of events, and all of them are going to point to your involvement in the death of Siobhan.'

'Look, Charley, I can't tell you the truth,' Ewan said, banging his fist on the table. Banks didn't flinch. Didn't move. Instead, she silently revelled in the fact that he was starting to crack. With a little more pressure, she might just get to the truth.

'If I talk, someone far more innocent than me will suffer,' said Ewan.

This statement gave Banks pause. DuPont had claimed he was innocent, true. But was there even a connection between Ewan and DuPont? Not that Banks knew of. Maybe he was talking about DuPont's family.

'Maya? And the kids?'

'Who?' Ewan said, cocking his head.

Not them then. Banks thought a little longer. A little harder. And then it dawned on her.

'You mean, Nancy, don't you?'

The way he flinched at the sound of her name assured Banks she was very much on the right track.

'You don't know anything about it,' Ewan said.

'I know more than you think,' said Banks. 'I know that Siobhan tortured Nancy for years at school. And probably since then. They live in the same small town. But the few connections Nancy's made over the years are all here. She doesn't want to move away. Be bullied out of her own town, like she was at school. And Siobhan, well Siobhan probably left Andaby for six months at some point in her early twenties, realized nobody thought she was anything special and then boomeranged back to the one place where she could be a big fish in a small pond. So, the pair were left to rub along together. Only Siobhan created a lot more friction for Nancy than Nancy ever did for Siobhan.'

'Do you think it's right? That somebody can go around the place, treating another human being like that? She made her life hell at school, for years. And it didn't stop there.'

'No, I don't think it's OK,' Banks said. 'But I don't think it's right to murder a person for it either. And if Nancy had something to do with Siobhan's death, she'll be looking at exactly the same prison term you served the first time round.'

'But it's not fair,' Ewan said. 'That woman put Nancy through hell for years. Even after they left school, she would torment her in the street.'

'Until she snapped.'

'She didn't mean to . . . that's it, I won't say any more. And I won't put any of it on record.'

Banks leaned in so her face was close to her brother's. When she spoke, she looked him dead in the eye. 'If you don't, another woman is going to die. If she's not dead already that is.'

'What are you talking about?'

'Two weeks ago, Siobhan Lange's best friend from school, Emily Cook, went missing,' said Banks. 'As yet no body has been found, which means there's still a small chance she's alive somewhere. And if that's the case, and if Nancy is behind this, I think we can safely say that she did mean to, no matter what she told you.'

Ewan frowned and shook his head. But Banks could see confusion brewing in his eyes. Perhaps her brother wasn't quite as guilty as she had first thought. Perhaps he had gone into all this with the intention of helping the underdog. He went to prison quite young after all and, yes, he would have had experiences while serving his sentence, but prison wasn't society as the rest of us knew it; perhaps in some ways Ewan was still quite naive. And perhaps Nancy had exploited that in order to finally have her revenge on Siobhan.

'This wasn't an accidental killing. That's what she's told you, isn't it?' Banks said with a sigh. 'Siobhan Lange was strangled with a school sash from her graduation day twenty years ago. I don't know about you, but that's not the kind of thing I just happen to have on me day-to-day. This was premeditated. And if Nancy coerced you into burning down that building, it's because she thinks she left something behind that points to her.'

Ewan paused for a moment, seemingly taking in everything Banks had had to say. She recognized this moment from every interrogation she'd ever conducted. This was the moment where the subject either told her everything, or stopped talking all together.

'She said they just got into an argument and she snapped.' Ewan said, slowly, cautiously. 'She'd gone to see Siobhan to finally confront her and things just . . . got out of hand. And then she didn't know what to do, and I, of course, I've been in that situation. Looking down at a body. Knowing you were the one to punch the life out of it and there's nothing you can do to take it back.'

To Banks's surprise, tears rose in her brother's eyes, but he swallowed them back.

'She said she panicked after she'd done it, so she moved the body to another room in the hope of confusing the police. She toppled the yarn tub in the hope of incriminating someone at work. It was no secret in the town that nobody who worked at the museum was a fan of Siobhan.

Nancy only told me about it all last night. She was in a real state. And she said she thought she might have left some evidence behind in that back office. Something she hadn't thought to clear up, because she was panicking.'

Banks listened to what her brother had to say carefully, waiting for him to offer every fragment of the story he knew without any interruption. As he explained, Banks wondered what on earth it was Nancy had left in the industrial museum that she thought warranted burning down the building. It seemed to Banks that something that obvious would have been picked up by the police on their very first sweep, just as Robinson had theorized when they were standing outside the burned-out museum.

There were two likely possibilities. The first was that Nancy was completely paranoid after what she had done and, even though there was no evidence at all to incriminate her, she had taken the risk of going back, or sending somebody else back, to be doubly sure there was nothing left behind that could see her sent to prison. There was, however, another much darker possibility. And that was that Nancy didn't believe there was any evidence there at all. That she had sent Ewan to start that fire, knowing that he would likely be seen, knowing that he would then become a prime suspect, especially given his history. Nancy's claim that there was evidence at the mill could have been nothing more than a ruse to make sure that blame was shifted from her to an already-known criminal.

'If everything she told you was true, the one thing that doesn't add up is that Nancy has an alibi,' said Banks. 'Robinson confirmed it.'

Ewan scratched his head. 'Yeah, I – I don't know how she worked it. How she managed to be in two places. But there's no way she'd just confess to murder like that. Unless she really had done it. Nobody would think that was a joke. Especially given my history. She knows I wouldn't see the funny side of that.'

'Yes, your history,' Banks said, almost under her breath. 'In many ways, you were the perfect boyfriend for Nancy. You'd be the first one the police asked questions of, not her. You'd be sympathetic to her story if she ever needed help, or things got too much. I don't know how she knew about your history – the local rumour mill more than likely, with a splash of Googling – but she's done her research. And by the sound of things, she's been manipulating you every step of the way. What you did all those years ago, it was a terrible accident. But with Nancy, there have been no accidents, Ewan. Not one. And if you don't go on record and tell DS Robinson what you know, you might yet have Emily Cook's blood on your hands. Do you really want to be responsible for another person's death?'

CHAPTER TWENTY-EIGHT

'Here you go, not exactly the best cup of tea you'll ever have but it's something to keep you going,' Kitt said, handing Banks a cup full of steaming liquid from the machine in the waiting room at Andaby Police Station.

'Thanks,' Banks said. 'I appreciate it. Breakfast feels a long time ago now, I can tell you.'

Banks tried not to think about how hopefully she had wolfed down poached eggs on toast at the guest house that morning. Smiling over at Evie and daring to dream that her brother was truly innocent after all. That this ordeal was well and truly over. That the pair of them could start to build a life together without any secrets. She should have known better. Looking back, alarming head injury aside, it was just a bit too easy. Someone had handed DuPont to them on a silver platter. And, right now, Banks's money was on that someone being Nancy.

'How did it go? With your brother, I mean?' Kitt said. 'You

can tell me to mind my own business if you want, by the way. I don't mean to pry. I just want to know where we're at, and that you're OK.'

'After all you've done for me, you're well within your rights to ask,' Banks said. 'I'm relieved to say he's giving his statement to Robinson now. From everything he said, it looks like Nancy might be behind it. Uniforms are picking her up now. He insists he committed only the arson and that he had nothing to do with the murder, or possibly the murders – plural. I told him to underline the fact that he pulled the fire alarm as he left the industrial museum in an attempt to preserve life. That he had no intent to harm anybody. Why the hell I'm telling him anything that's going to help him at this stage, I don't know. A sense of sisterly obligation, I suppose. And a vague hope that he has been manipulated by Nancy, just as we all have.'

'Regardless of how our loved ones hurt us, part of us knows that hurting them back won't make us feel any better,' said Kitt. 'At least not in the long-term. You did the right thing. Both for your brother and for your own peace of mind. I should think that aspect, about him pulling the fire alarm, will be particularly important if, or rather when, this goes to court. Especially given his criminal record.'

Banks nodded. 'Arson so often turns into manslaughter or murder because people are in the building at the time the fire is lit, sometimes without the arsonist realizing. Obviously, sometimes arson is designed to target a particular individual. Burn down a person's home with them in it. But a lot of the time, it's about making a statement, or giving a warning, and nobody is ever supposed to get hurt. Ewan's going to need to make it really clear that he didn't intend to cause physical harm when he lit that fire if he wants to see daylight again before he dies.'

'How did he even get in that back office to light the fire in the first place? Or know where it was?' said Kitt.

'This is one of the elements that makes his story a bit more plausible,' said Banks. 'Apparently, Nancy coached him. He says she told him she'd been to the museum a few times before and knew where the staff areas were.'

'A few times . . . ' Kitt mused. 'Or had she been deliberately stalking Siobhan? Perhaps going so far as to vary the days and times of her visit to stay inconspicuous. Making notes about the locations of all the staff areas. Essentially drawing herself a little map of the place.'

'If she did go that far,' Banks said, 'she'd have been able to observe and record the movements of all the employees, including Siobhan.' Listen in to the casual conversations of the staff and learn all kinds of things about the building. It's security strengths and weaknesses, for example.'

'Like the cameras not working?' said Kitt.

'Exactly,' said Banks.

'But, even if she varied the timings, didn't anyone notice how regularly a local was visiting the museum? To say that it's odd behaviour is perhaps a bit of a stretch. But most of us never get around to doing what's on our doorstep, if you know what I mean?' said Kitt.

'I agree, it's surprising nobody noticed,' said Banks. 'But perhaps she fed them a story, like she was working on a local history project or something. Or maybe, people really just didn't notice her. Ever.'

'I suppose it's quite likely that the people around here have spent their whole lives not really noticing Nancy,' said Kitt.

'I think so,' said Banks. 'At school, the only reason anyone noticed her was because they wanted to pick on her. That was the only kind of attention she ever got. But as she grew older, probably fewer people noticed her. Adults aren't quite as prone to picking on each other as kids are,' said Banks.

'Depends on the adults,' Kitt said, 'but yes.'

'So, she's probably spent a large portion of her life being ignored. This time, it just happened to work to her advantage. Apparently, she overheard the staff joking about the cameras not working on a semi-regular basis. From what she told Ewan, or allegedly told Ewan, she hid in a small gap behind those yarn tubs when the industrial museum closed one night. And waited. Waited until there was nobody else left in the building, except Siobhan. She told him she didn't plan to kill Siobhan at that stage. She insisted that part had been an accident. But she wanted to be alone with Siobhan, to confront her about her behaviour, and didn't think she'd agree to such a meeting willingly.'

Banks did her best to focus on this theory and not the underlying sense of dread that had returned ever since Nancy's alibi had been confirmed. She wanted to believe Ewan was telling the truth. That he had had no part in Siobhan's death. But he had already lied about where he was the night the crime took place, and at present had no alibi for the murder window. On this basis, particularly given his history, there was still no ruling him out.

'I understand why you're saying "allegedly" when it comes to Ewan's account,' said Kitt. 'There is the small issue of Nancy having an alibi. Something that doesn't add up at all.'

'I know, that's my question mark, or one of them, too. She was never a formal suspect before but, as we know, a member of Robinson's team gave the head of the knitting circle a ring. They confirmed that she was there that night, no doubt about it.'

'It is a bit of a mystery, that one,' Kitt said. 'But, thinking about another thread in the case, if Nancy was really calculating enough to make notes and observe the workings of the museum to execute her plan, then she would definitely be cunning enough to buy a burner phone, get hold of DuPont's number and send him text messages to incriminate him.'

'Yes, that bit tracks,' said Banks. 'According to Ewan, she did topple those yarn tubs to focus the police's attention on the victim's work colleagues too.'

'But the question remains, if she was acting alone how did she manage to murder Siobhan and create an alibi for herself at her knitting group? The more likely scenario is that she wasn't acting alone.'

'I know,' Banks said, running her fingers through her hair. 'And Ewan doesn't have an alibi for the evening. You tell me what that suggests.'

'Charley, Ewan has only known Nancy for a couple of months, remember that. He was in jail for twenty years. Is he really going to risk going back for someone he's only just met? No matter what sob story she fed him about how she was bullied at school?'

'I don't know,' said Banks. 'Maybe consorting with the criminal element for twenty years has only hardened him against cooperating with law enforcement figures. Or maybe he saw a chance to commit murder, and took it, and is now sending his partner down the river because, as you say, they've only known each other a short time. The only thing I know for sure is that he is denying it hard in there. But all other signs are pointing to his involvement. Either way, he's looking at jail time for the arson. But there's still a small chance Emily Cook might be alive. We need to find her. And I want the truth. I want to know if . . . '

Banks trailed off then and Kitt turned to see what she was looking at. She quickly turned back round to face her friend so as not to appear too conspicuous.

Nancy Murphy had just walked in through the doors, her head bowed as the officer guided her towards the main desk and checked her in.

She wore very similar clothing to the first time Banks had met her back in the grocers. The oversized cardigan, a high-necked buttoned-up shirt. She didn't look like the kind of person who would ever hurt anyone. But then again, maybe that was part of her plan too. Almost everyone Banks had spoken to had underlined that they didn't believe Nancy was likely to do any harm and, looking at her, Banks could understand why they were so sure of themselves. But had any of them stopped to wonder how authentic that image was? After her conversation with Ewan, Banks certainly couldn't look at Nancy Murphy the same way she had before.

On the whole, Banks liked to think she was a pretty good judge of just how much someone was telling the truth. Nancy Murphy may well have pulled the wool over her eyes once. If that turned out to be the case, she wasn't about to let her do it again.

CHAPTER TWENTY-NINE

Banks watched through the two-way mirror as DS Robinson laid out a series of images from the crime scene, depicting Siobhan Lange in her deceased state. This was a common tactic amongst investigators of violent crimes. A suspect's reaction to such imagery could often tell you a great deal about their levels of guilt.

In certain circumstances, being confronted with a clear visual of their crimes was enough to make some people crack.

It seemed Robinson would have no such luck in this case.

Nancy sat in silence, her eyes flitting over the images before she looked up at Robinson.

This considered reaction didn't much surprise Banks. If Nancy really had gone to the lengths of dating her brother so that he might be incriminated in her place, listening into conversations at the mill for months on end and somehow creating a false alibi for herself, then she wasn't going to crack at the first sign of pressure. If everything Ewan said had been true – and at this stage that was a big if – then maybe Banks had finally figured out why Nancy had acted now rather than ten years ago, or fifteen years ago, when the pain of the bullying she'd endured at school might have been fresher, more searing.

If the information Ewan had conveyed was accurate, then he and his arrival in Andaby may have been the reason that Nancy had decided to strike now. After all, what better opportunity could there be to ensure somebody else takes the fall for a murder you committed than having another murderer newly moved to town? All you have to do is make sure you leave behind no physical evidence and commit the murder shortly after that person arrives in the area. Under these circumstances, the new arrival is almost guaranteed to be a suspect. Certainly, Ewan's door was the first one Robinson knocked on, and, in her position, Banks would have done exactly the same.

How had Nancy known about Ewan's past in order to frame him for the murder? Banks had had to think hard about this one. But finally, one possibility had reared its head. Though finding work was difficult for somebody who has served any kind of prison term, Ewan had, Banks understood, applied for one or two jobs as they'd come up locally. Just a bit of shop work or whatever was being offered. He had been declined every time, more than likely because of his criminal record. But what had those potential employees done with that information? Had they kept it to themselves that there was a new arrival in town with a criminal record? Or had their chins started wagging? Even if the person who started the gossip had no idea what Ewan had gone to jail for, the Chinese whispers effect would ensure that before long most residents of the town would have suspected him of murder, without actually realizing that this was the crime he'd done time for.

Of course, this was just speculation on Banks's part. She had no idea if there was some other twisted reason Nancy had struck when she did. But from the picture that was building, it was clear that Ewan was instrumental in this murder, whether he realized it at the time or not.

'How do you know this woman?' Robinson asked, taking a seat on the other side of the table from Nancy. Her tone was completely neutral, as though she were ticking off a list of questions she might ask anyone about these pictures. Another common tactic. Be led by the emotions of the suspect. Play into their reaction. Start with small easy questions. Don't say anything incriminating until a clear picture builds.

'I didn't know her very well at all, actually,' Nancy said. 'I went to school with her a long time ago. She didn't like me very much and made no secret of it.'

'What about since school? Any interactions?'

Nancy shrugged, shaking her head. 'Not really. She sometimes comes in to where I work – the grocers' shop, you know, in town – because she needs to pick something up.'

'And how was she, when she came into the shop? What was her manner with you, I mean?'

'Same as she was at school, to be honest,' said Nancy. 'She would be quite rude to me. I think she knew if I tried to talk back to her that she could tell the owner and have me fired for being nasty with a customer, like. But I wouldn't have bothered biting back. There was no point with the likes of Siobhan. If she didn't like yer, that wore that. Pointless arguing with her.'

Robinson waited a moment. Allowing a little time to pass before she spoke again. This was a good way of leaving suspects wondering if you believed what they were telling you. Sometimes you'd even get lucky and they'd leap in to fill the silence.

'What about this woman?' Robinson said at last, placing another photograph down on the table.

Nancy leaned in, looking closely at the photograph. 'That's . . . Emily Cook, isn't it? She was friends with Siobhan. Well, I think they were still friends, mind. They did have a big argument at graduation. Rumour has it they both fancied the same teacher but I don't like to get involved in gossip.'

This sentence gave Banks pause. She pulled out her notebook and sifted back to the notes she made directly after their first interview with Nancy. Yes. Nancy had explicitly told them she didn't know what Emily and Siobhan had argued about. But she just told Robinson that she knew they fancied the same teacher. Nancy would only argue that she forgot what had caused the fight when she had talked to Banks and Kitt, of course, but it was a chink in her story. If she knew why Emily and Siobhan fought, then she could have been behind those text messages sent to Adam DuPont. They were sent from a burner phone after all. They may have been signed from Emily and Siobhan but anyone can type that into a text message.

Whilst she was thinking about text messages, Banks pulled out her own phone and sent one to Kitt.

Nancy just made her first slip in interview. She did know why Emily and Siobhan fought. She is probably behind the messages sent to DuPont. Will hang on here and see if she knows anything about Emily's whereabouts.

'We've been speaking to Ewan, Nancy,' said Robinson, 'and he's told us everything he knows.'

'He has?' Nancy said.

Robinson nodded.

'Oh, thank goodness. Honestly, I wasn't sure how much longer I could go on defending him. Not if it means I'm going to be getting into trouble for it. I told him not to do it. I begged him not to. I said after all these years it's not worth it. I've let it go. It's of the past. But he did it anyway.'

'Did what, exactly?' said Robinson.

'Well, killed Siobhan, of course, you said he'd told you,' said Nancy. 'He said he did it for me. Because of how she treated me. How they all treated me at school, because she encouraged them to bully me. I didn't ask him to. And he didn't tell me until after. But now Siobhan is dead. And probably Emily too, and there's nothing I can do about it.'

There was something familiar about the way Nancy responded to this news about Ewan's confession. It took Banks a moment to realize exactly what it was. But then she remembered how Nancy had behaved when they told her Ewan had admitted he'd given a false alibi. She had seemed relieved then too. And talked about how little she had wanted to go along with what Ewan had done. But claimed it had been out of a protective nature.

She was using precisely the same tactic now. Even her facial expressions looked identical to the ones she'd shown to her and Kitt. And, now that she was looking at them from a distance, they seemed more practised. More contrived.

Banks's phone buzzed with a text message from Kitt.

The only thing propping up that girl now is her alibi. Me and Grace will find out where her knitting group takes place. If it takes place every Wednesday, we could go tonight for ourselves. Talk to her fellow knitters in person.

'The thing is, Nancy,' said Robinson. 'According to the statement we've had off Ewan, it's you who committed the murders. Not him.'

'What?' Nancy said, frowning. 'No, no, no, that can't be right. Ewan wouldn't do something like that, would he? He wouldn't try to frame me for something he had done?'

For all she was starting to consider that Nancy might be

playing some kind of part, these words stopped Banks in her tracks. She should have been able to answer Nancy's questions without reservation. She should have been able to say, Ewan would never do something like that to somebody who was truly innocent. She should have been able to say what happened twenty years ago in Glasgow was nothing more than a terrible accident and there was no way that Ewan would deliberately take a life or frame someone else for his wrongdoing.

But during their meeting in the square on the little bridge, he had taken pains to impress on her how hard prison had been for him. How he couldn't have survived it any longer if he'd had to. How he never wanted to go back. Nancy was up to something, that much was obvious to Banks. But that doesn't mean that Ewan wasn't up to something too. If he had got himself into trouble, Banks found herself unable to honestly say just how far Ewan might go to keep hold of the freedom that had been denied to him for so long.

CHAPTER THIRTY

'Am I to understand that you're denying killing Siobhan Lange?' said Robinson.

'Of course, I'm denying it. I didn't kill Siobhan,' said Nancy. 'I would never do something like that. Even if I ever wanted to, I wouldn't stand a chance. Look at the size of me, I couldn't overpower somebody like that.'

Robinson raised an eyebrow. 'You could have done, if you'd knocked them unconscious first.'

There was something about the way Nancy blinked at this statement that told Banks that Nancy was definitely hiding something. Of course, that didn't mean that Nancy had actually been the one to murder Siobhan. Maybe Ewan had been the one to do the killing. Maybe she knew nothing about it until it was too late. But she knew something she wasn't letting on. Maybe the truth about whether Emily Cook was still alive or, if she was no longer with us, where her body was.

Robinson laid another photo down on the table and pointed to a particular spot in the image Banks couldn't quite see from her angle behind the two-way glass. 'The medical examiner concluded that before she was strangled, and crushed, Siobhan received a knock to the back of the head hard enough to leave her unconscious. Marks on her wrists and ankles suggest she was bound – likely to an office chair – for some time. Whoever did this to the victim was not acting spontaneously. The situation was no accident. It was meticulously planned and premeditated.'

Banks frowned. Robinson had never relayed any of this to her. Had she held back because she had genuinely suspected Ewan all along, or possibly Banks herself? She did what she could to squash that idea. In cases like this, information had to be compartmentalized. Robinson had given them everything she could, and more than she should have, if the truth be told. By rights, Banks shouldn't even be standing behind the mirror right now, watching the interrogation. No, she didn't resent Robinson's need to keep certain aspects of the case under wraps on a personal level.

It's just that being apprised of such crucial pieces of information could have meant catching the real killer quicker. In Banks's mind, she had been likely looking for someone who was either strong or who had an accomplice based on the description of the crime. Now, as it transpired, neither of those things might be true. A lot of thinking power had gone to waste on that one. But then again, technically speaking, Banks shouldn't have been thinking about the case at all. Perhaps she'd just have to accept the hit on that one.

'So, you see,' Robinson said. 'It's perfectly plausible that with the proper planning, you might have committed this crime. Even with your stature. Taking somebody off guard and knocking them out is not a difficult thing to do if you've got something heavy to hit them with. It's a sneaky, manipulative thing to do, yes. But it doesn't take quite the physical strength you're suggesting. So, I'm asking you again if you're denying committing the murder of Siobhan Lange.'

Nancy raised both her eyebrows and looked down at her hands, resting on the table. 'I think I can see what kind of story you've spun. It's quite plausible after all.'

'What story is that?' asked Robinson.

'The one about a small-town, downtrodden woman who was mercilessly bullied day after day at school by the people who were supposed to have been her friends.'

Nancy paused then, but Robinson knew better than to leap to fill the silence.

'After all those lonely nights of crying in her bedroom with nobody to turn to,' Nancy continued. 'After deciding to lead a small, humble little life so that nobody would notice her enough to bully her any more. After countless humiliations in the street from the same person who made her life miserable at school, who'd got a job at a local museum. After seeing that woman flirting in the pub with her new boyfriend. Not because the woman in question wanted that particular man but because she knew that he belonged to the poor little creature she'd tormented all those years, and this was just another way of winding her up. After all that, you could understand why that downtrodden, small-town girl would snap and decide enough was enough.'

Though she was speaking in the third person, it was obvious to anyone that Nancy was making a confession. And now that she thought about it, Robinson had said that Ewan had admitted to flirting with Siobhan once in his early days of living in Andaby. Had Nancy seen Siobhan flirting with her boyfriend? Is that really what had been the final straw? When they spoke to Nancy in the grocers, she talked about how long it had been since something as good as Ewan had come into her life. There was no doubt in Banks's mind that Nancy would have had to plan everything she'd done in meticulous detail before she committed a murder, including taking on an ex-con as a boyfriend. Somebody she could pin the blame on or claim had pushed her into it. But maybe, once they started their relationship, she discovered she quite liked having him in her life. Maybe that part was genuine.

'Nancy,' Robinson said. 'Is Emily Cook still alive?'

Nancy, who had drifted off into a kind of trance, started then. 'I have no idea if she's alive. Strap me up to a polygraph and ask me that question. You'll see, I'm telling the truth. That story that you've created about the downtrodden small-town mouse, it's plausible, I'll agree with you that far. But it's not about me. I suppose there's a chance that Ewan is keeping Emily Cook alive, somewhere. But I have no idea where she is, or, if she is alive, how much longer she'll last.'

Banks took a moment to really analyse what Nancy was saying. The way she was behaving. Why had Siobhan picked on her? Yes, she was a bit shy and awkward, but most people are at that age. Thinking back to her own time on the playground, Banks remembered that kids at school were usually teased for being smart by people less smart than them. For some reason people become teenagers and then it becomes some kind of heinous crime to try hard at anything. All of a sudden Banks found herself wondering what Nancy's average grade had been during her time at Andaby Comprehensive. And if she had been a straight A grade student, whether she was wily enough to put on an act. To lie low all these years waiting for the perfect revenge on the people who had made her life hell for what must have seemed an eternity.

And then there were Nancy's words. She said she didn't know how much longer Emily would last. A rather odd thing if you're trying to convince someone you don't know if a person is still alive. And then there was the crack about the polygraph test. She seemed to be very concerned with proving that she didn't know whether Emily was dead or alive.

'You're only going to make things worse by denying it, Nancy,' Robinson said.

Nancy looked at Robinson with the same wide eyes that had fooled Banks the first time she'd questioned her. 'You don't seem to understand DS Robinson,' she said. 'I couldn't have committed the murder of Siobhan Lange. I have an alibi.'

CHAPTER THIRTY-ONE

Banks strode into the small community hall that stood just across from the railway viaduct on the outskirts of Andaby. It was the kind of venue with dark brown polished floorboards and a stage with curtains made from remaindered fabric. The spotlights only ever turned on for the local Christmas nativity and possibly an am-dram performance of *Macbeth* once a year. It smelled of rice pudding and stale bread, and the remnants of the hundreds of events that had likely been held here over the decades the hall had been standing.

It was just after seven o'clock on a Wednesday evening. A week precisely since Siobhan had breathed her last. And just like last Wednesday, the Andaby Knitting Circle had met in this small function room and chatted together while working on various woolly works in progress. Or so Banks imagined.

After relaying all that Nancy had said in the interrogation room to Kitt and Grace, they had made plans to visit Nancy's knitting group and talk to the members themselves about Nancy's behaviour on the night of Siobhan's murder. Robinson had made it clear that at this stage she was convinced that Ewan and Nancy were working together and were feeding the police conflicting stories to prevent her from getting to the truth. Either that, or they had been working together and were turning on each other. With this in mind, her team was busy conducting searches of their properties and following up on the fire at the industrial museum.

If Banks couldn't find something that didn't fit with Nancy's alibi, then she would have to face the fact that more likely than not her brother was now a double murderer. If they didn't find Emily Cook alive, potentially a serial murderer. Her brother's future and the future of their relationship rested upon whether Nancy really was where she said she was at the time of Siobhan's death.

'I'm sorry to interrupt ladies,' said Banks, causing the five women already seated in fold-up chairs to start and turn their heads.

'Is there something I can help with?' said a white-haired lady in a rainbow-striped cardigan that Banks imagined the woman might have knitted herself. She stood up from her chair and walked over to where Banks, Kitt and Grace were standing. 'I'm Lorraine, and I lead the knitting circle here if you wanted to join in. New people are always welcome and we've got spare needles and wool just in case. I like to say it's a tight-knit group, pun intended.' With this Lorraine gave them a little wink, which the trio responded to with a smile.

'Thank you, but no,' Banks said, before Grace could accept. Her eyes had lit up at the prospect of giving knitting a go and, although Banks would never willingly stand in the way of someone following their passions, they really didn't have time to be learning how to purl stitch right now. 'I'm afraid I'm here because we've been investigating the recent death of Siobhan Lange, and I need to talk to you about Nancy Murphy.'

'She hasn't turned up tonight, and it was her duty to sort the wool balls out!' said another woman. She looked up at Banks as she spoke but continued to knit without missing a stitch. 'We don't like it when people miss a week. It throws the whole dynamic off, it really does.'

'I'm afraid she's otherwise engaged,' said Banks. 'We are trying to ascertain whether or not she did attend the meeting here on Wednesday the sixteenth of May?'

Lorraine folded her arms and almost all of the warmth and cheer she'd displayed previously disappeared in a flash. 'I already told the police that she was here. What do they need it confirming a second time for, eh? Should I chisel it in stone? Will that be enough for them? I don't know, you take the time to explain things to people. Do they listen? No! They never listen. And I do hate repeating myself. Worst thing in the world, it really is.'

'When a crime is so serious, there's no harm in double

checking things. I'm sure you understand,' said Banks, being careful not to correct Lorraine's assumption – that they were re-checking these facts on behalf of the police. She had done her best to behave as a civilian investigator while working this case, but the way Nancy had talked about Emily in that interrogation room, the fact that she wouldn't say whether or not she was alive or dead – not to mention her offer to be hooked up to a polygraph test – had left Banks wondering if she'd stashed the woman somewhere and really was unsure about her status. If there was even a vague chance that Emily Cook might be alive, she had a duty to use every asset at her disposal to find her. Even if that meant using other people's assumptions against them.

'Well, she was here that night . . . and she was not here,' another woman sitting in the circle piped up.

'Ooh, would you hush up!' said Lorraine. 'Always causing trouble you are.'

'Sorry, can I take your name?' Banks said, ignoring Lorraine's protests. Banks did, however, take a notebook and pencil out of her pocket to signal to the woman who had spoken that what she was about to say would be documented. She had to record all conversations for her official investigations anyway but she found it served as a strong visual cue to the person she was talking to. A reminder that what they said might be used as evidence and they should thus choose their words carefully.

'Er, it's Lucy, Lucy Carrington.'

'What did you mean by that comment, Lucy?' said Kitt. 'That Nancy was both here and not here?'

'The others said they didn't notice anything, so I wasn't to say nothing about it in case I got Nancy in trouble,' said Lucy. 'But I thought she was behaving proper strange last week. Really off her game, she was. I can't believe I was the only one who noticed but, apparently, I was.'

Lorraine sighed her disapproval at Lucy raising the topic and shook her head.

'Any observations might be useful, Lucy, so we never discount anything,' said Banks. 'It's best that we know everything people saw or heard, and then we can put it all together and come to a sound judgement about the situation.'

'When you say Nancy was acting strange, how do you mean, exactly?' said Grace.

Lucy looked around the other women in the circle who had all put their heads down and seemed, to Banks's eyes, to be knitting twice as fast as they had been before.

'Well, for starters, she was a few minutes late, which isn't like her at all,' said Lucy. 'She looked quite red in the face, you know. All puffed out. As if she'd been for a run or something. But she only lives round the corner and I thought then, that wasn't much of a workout by anyone's standards.'

No, Banks thought to herself. Walking around the corner was not much of a workout. But knocking another woman unconscious and binding her securely to a chair would take considerable effort. Not to mention hurrying out of the building in case anybody saw you. The industrial museum wasn't that far from here. At a guess, only a few minutes' walk. Had Nancy killed Siobhan right at the beginning of that murder window and then hustled herself to her knitting circle so she'd have an alibi?

'Anything else we should know?' Banks pushed. 'Any detail at all might be relevant so don't leave anything out.'

This was already sounding promising. It was clear from Lorraine's behaviour that there was no way she would have told Robinson's team this over the phone. Indeed, if Lucy hadn't been in attendance, they may not have learned anything at all. Thank goodness someone in this room had noticed something suspicious that night, despite Nancy's protests that nothing was out of the ordinary and that she just attended her usual knitting meeting without any hitches. The question was, would whatever Lucy told them be enough to poke a real hole in Nancy's alibi? They would need a little bit more than an appearance of mild agitation.

'She made some excuse about popping home for a spare needle halfway through, around the eight o'clock mark. We tried to tell her that we had spare needles here but she wouldn't have it. She said she wanted her own spares and would be back in a few minutes. I've never known her be so fussy about that. It seemed bananas to me. Why would you bother going out and coming back again when there were already spares here? Eats into your knitting time, it really does.'

'And was she? Back in a few minutes, I mean,' said Banks.

'Yes, she was,' said Lorraine. 'She was only gone a few minutes, Lucy. You're making a big fuss over nothing. I can't believe you're doing this to poor old Nancy.'

'It was nearly quarter past when she got back 'ere and she only lives a couple of minutes away,' Lucy protested. 'Then, she left really sharpish at the end. She was out like a rocket. I've never seen her move so fast. Not even that time when Lorraine brought chocolate-coated Hobnobs instead of regular Hobnobs and she was worried that she'd miss out if she didn't grab one quickly.'

'Well, you know she's been seeing that Ewan lad,' said Lorraine, 'she might have been off to see him. Did you ever think about that?'

'Maybe, but if you ask me, she was on another planet that night. Didn't join in the conversation. Just sat there, staring at her knitting, barely working the needles at all,' said Lucy.

'When you say she left sharpish, what exactly did you mean by that?' said Grace.

'Well, she actually left a bit early. No more than ten minutes, like. But it were a bit weird. She usually hangs around to help us clean up. We were all left to do it ourselves last week.'

'I don't think that she could have committed a murder in the space of three or four minutes,' Lorraine said, shaking her head. 'She was here for most of the meeting. Certainly, she didn't have a chance to hurt anybody and she wouldn't anyway, not our Nancy. They're just going after her because she's timid and won't fight back. She's done nothing wrong.'

'Thank you so much,' Banks said, smiling and flipping her notebook shut. 'That's been very helpful indeed. We won't interrupt you any longer. We'll see ourselves out.'

With that, Banks turned on her heel and strode out of the hall into the cool night air. As she did so, she looked up and down the road in either direction.

'I don't mean to be rude but are those women all blind, or what?' said Grace. 'That's the most suspicious behaviour I've ever heard. And they're all carrying on as though Nancy is the picture of innocence. "Oh, not our Nancy,"' Grace started to impersonate Lorraine. '"She's a member of our tight-knit group that never does anything wrong. Except knit sweaters for Satan every Wednesday."'

'Grace, please calm yourself,' said Kitt, although even she was chuckling at Grace's antics.

'They're in denial, pure and simple,' said Banks. 'It's a powerful force. It's much easier to believe that the police have it wrong than it is to accept you may have been sitting in the same room as a potential murderer for weeks on end.

'Are you thinking what I'm thinking when it comes to Nancy's timeline that night?' asked Kitt.

'Like Ewan said, she hid in the museum until everyone except Siobhan went home. And then she knocked Siobhan unconscious and secured her to the chair in her office,' said Banks.

'But she knew she needed to secure an alibi,' said Kitt. 'So, she left Siobhan unconscious in her office and hurried to the meeting a few minutes late.'

'But not without grabbing Siobhan's set of manager's keys first,' said Banks. She'll have locked Siobhan's office door. Anyone who tried to open it would just think Siobhan had gone home for the night, and it would also mean that Nancy could lock the main doors to the building too.'

'That makes sense,' said Grace. 'If anyone had passed by and seen the main doors hadn't been locked up, they might have phoned the police or gone to investigate. Particularly since quite a few of the employees live in the local area. They might have been walking past and spotted something weren't right. So, it makes sense that Nancy would've taken Siobhan's keys to give the impression that it was situation normal.'

'So, Nancy's sitting in her knitting circle knowing that Siobhan is tied up unconscious in her office and there's no going back,' said Kitt.

'Lucy said that Nancy wasn't paying attention to the conversation, because she was likely contemplating the next steps. Or steeling herself to carry out a plan she'd already concocted,' said Banks. 'Imagining something like this is one thing but carrying it out is quite another. It doesn't matter how much the perpetrator thinks they want to carry out the task, unless they are a psychopath, the odds are the murderer is going to feel *something* once the process is in motion. And those feelings can often be unexpected and overwhelming.'

'So, starting to panic now, Nancy makes an excuse to leave the knitting circle, and that's when she does it,' said Kitt. 'That's when she strangles Siobhan using the sash they were all given at graduation. She'd had Siobhan tied to a chair in her office for an hour at that point. Whatever happened next there was going to be serious consequences. So she went ahead and murdered Siobhan. She missed the fibres on the body because she was probably not thinking quite as straight as she could have been. But perhaps she also wagered that the graduation was so long ago nobody would put two and two together about where those fibres had come from.'

Banks nodded. 'She knows times of deaths are estimated within a couple of hours and wants to make sure she has a firm alibi for the full time frame. So, she kills Siobhan right in the middle of her knitting circle meeting. Knowing that she can lock up again and come back later, when there are fewer people about, to arrange the body and incriminate Siobhan's co-workers.'

'If this is the case, Nancy really was manipulating your brother. Not the other way around,' said Kitt.

After the shock of seeing Ewan on that CCTV footage earlier that day, Kitt's words made Banks catch her breath.

Was it too optimistic to hope that this meant Ewan was off the hook as far as the murders went? That, yes, he may have been taken in, like a bit of a sap, and committed arson, which was no small-fry offence, but that he hadn't hurt anyone. And he never meant to hurt anyone. Was it too soon to hope for that? Against her better judgement, Banks found herself hoping for it anyway.

'It does seem more likely now that Ewan's arrival in Andaby is what prompted her to take the chance, finally, with this plan. And she probably isn't just behind the murder, but also Emily Cook's disappearance and the text messages to Adam DuPont, just as you suspected after listening in to her interrogation,' said Grace. 'She masterminded the whole thing for revenge. The intricacy of it would be almost admirable, if it wasn't completely sick and twisted in a way that made you want to go and buy ten extra door locks on the way home.'

'It's usually the window where they get in,' Banks said, flashing Grace a wry smile.

'Noted,' Grace replied.

'It is amazing what people choose to pour their energies into,' said Kitt. 'As you say, this wasn't cooked up overnight. The level of planning is off the chart.'

'It's also amazing just how people can throw you off the scent,' said Banks. 'Talk to anyone in this town and they'll tell you there's no way Nancy is capable of something like this. And, if I'm honest, the first time I met her I might have been one of them. She's unassuming, she's quietly spoken, she's the picture of low key and low confidence. And that's how she's managed to evade suspicion or notice.'

'She's made sure people expect so little of her that the idea of her committing murder is beyond the comprehension of anybody and everybody who knows her,' said Kitt.

'I'll call Robinson and let her know what our bit of prodding has uncovered,' said Banks. 'Maybe it will help her to put pressure on Nancy to fold. But I've also been thinking. When Nancy said in her interview that she didn't know whether Emily Cook was dead or alive, she was obviously telling the truth as we've discussed. Otherwise, she wouldn't have been so bold as to suggest she should be hooked up to a polygraph. In fact, that sentence might be the one truth that fell out of her mouth across the whole interview. Emily Cook might be alive somewhere and we've just got to hope that crushing her alibi is enough to make Nancy talk.'

CHAPTER THIRTY-TWO

Banks hung up the phone after talking to Robinson and turned to Kitt and Grace. They were gathered around a small table in The Oak Tree – one of three pubs overlooking the small square in the centre of town. They had decided to congregate there and plan their next move as it didn't have loud music blasting over the stereo system, unlike the other two pubs. Banks had no particular gripe against pubs playing music but just then they needed a place where they could hear each other talk and have the necessary quiet to think. Besides, most of the pubs round here seemed to specialize in playing nineties pop hits and it was difficult to think strategically with 'Barbie Girl' by Aqua worm-holing through your ears.

'Robinson is going to lean on Nancy about her alibi, see if she can get her to admit what was going on that night,' Banks said. 'The investigative team are still working on processing all the evidence from the searches and interviews.

And DI Graves is back in the office to oversee what's happening with Nancy and my brother, so we probably shouldn't show our faces at the station unless it's absolutely necessary. Anyone high on the suspect list is already in custody, so in the meantime we're going to search for Emily Cook. It may be a long shot, but finding her alive would mean there was at least one silver lining on this case.'

'So, where do we start looking for her?' asked Grace with a frown. 'I must admit my first instinct is to panic and run around town looking anywhere and everywhere for her. But, of course, I know that's not really going to achieve anything, and, if she really has been held captive all this time we need to think strategically. Otherwise, we run the risk of being too late. I can't think that Nancy has been feeding her much of anything. And what if she's been kept somewhere without heating? It's probably not quite cold enough to freeze to death but it can't be good for you'

'There's a chance she'll develop hypothermia ... and I feel just the same with cases like these, even with all the experience I have,' Banks said with a sigh at the thought of Emily gradually getting colder and weaker. 'But, as you say, it's important to be strategic about this. Robinson is doing a search on Nancy's property holdings and those of anyone in her family. We'll need a warrant before we can access any of them, but there's a fair chance that the reason she's confident that the police won't find her is that Emily is being held on private property. Somewhere the police wouldn't automatically have access to. Somewhere like a garage or a basement.'

'Would Nancy really do something so bold as to keep Emily – dead or alive – on a property that she or a family member owned?' said Kitt, who was sitting opposite Banks on a bar stool, staring into her glass of lemonade. Slowly, she raised her eyes to meet the others at the table. 'There would be no way of palming off blame in that case.'

'I don't know. Given all we suspect she's done so far, including possibly stalking the victim in broad daylight at her place of work, I'd say boldness isn't really something she's lacking,' said Banks.

'True, on that point I hear you,' said Kitt. 'But, so far, she's made sure there's been plausible deniability in every action she's taken. Nancy may not quite be a psychopath but so far she seems to have taken self-preservation to extreme levels while planning this murder. By the standards of any case I've worked in the past, she's gone to some pretty outlandish lengths to keep herself out of prison.'

'You're right,' said Grace. 'When you add up absolutely everything: the burner phone and the messages she sent to DuPont; the alibi she tried to create; going out with someone with a criminal record. She has made sure in each case that somebody else could take the fall for her.'

'Maybe this was the reason she had to take so many precautions,' said Banks. 'Because she was hiding Emily in a property that had her name on it. Or somebody in the family. If a person is found on your property and you've taken enough precautions to misdirect the investigation, you might still be able to claim that you knew nothing about that person's presence there. You might try to claim that somebody else had been keeping that person on your property without your consent or knowledge.'

There was a pause as the group digested this idea. Somewhere, in the periphery, money rattled out of a one-armed bandit machine one of the drinkers was playing at. Banks took a moment to reflect on how wonderful it must be to have nothing more pressing to concentrate on than strategically shoving coins into a slot.

'After what I know of this Nancy lass so far, I wouldn't put it past her to pin it on her own mother,' said Grace. 'Pretend she knew nothing about it and that her mother had committed the murder because of how badly her daughter was treated. I can see it now.'

'That's the kind of theory we're working to when it comes to the property search under her name,' said Banks. 'Nancy actually doesn't seem to care who goes down for Siobhan's murder, as long as it's not her.'

When this all started, Banks had been convinced that Ewan was trying to set her up in that very same manner. Whatever tangled mess was playing out at Andaby police station, though, Banks was at least ninety per cent certain that nothing like that was afoot any more. The sheer amount of manipulation from Nancy to make sure her plan went as she imagined it would was quite unbelievable. It wasn't just that Banks no longer believed her brother wouldn't send her down the river like that, she also wasn't convinced he'd ever been that organized in his life.

'I want to find Emily alive just as much as the rest of you,' said Grace, tucking a curl of brown hair behind her ears as she spoke. 'But why would Nancy keep Emily alive when she killed Siobhan? I still don't get it. To me, it seems like a completely unnecessary risk.'

'I don't know the why when it comes to that aspect of the case,' Banks admitted. 'We discussed the possibility of someone using Emily as a scapegoat. Maybe that's Nancy's plan. Find some way of framing Emily for Siobhan's murder. Or maybe she thought she could use Emily's life as a bargaining chip. Who can say? There's no guarantee at all Emily's still with us but finding out what happened to her is really the only way we can constructively help with the case right now.'

'Then I guess we need to start thinking about possible other places Nancy could be holding Emily,' said Grace.

'Any warrants to search a property won't come through till tomorrow at the earliest now, so if you have any other ideas about where Nancy might have stashed Emily, yes, I'd be more than happy to hear them,' said Banks, before taking a sip of her orange juice.

'I don't know that I have anything so helpful as an

alternative suggestion,' Kitt said with an apologetic smile. 'You said she seemed confident in the interview that Emily wasn't going to be found?'

'That's the sense I got from the way she spoke, yeah,' said Banks.

'So, as you say, the private property of a relative, especially a distant relative, is the best bet because a warrant is needed to search them and, even if one is acquired, there's still plausible deniability.'

'Or maybe Nancy just figured out there was somewhere else she could hold Emily?' said Grace. 'Somewhere the police would never think to look.'

'Somewhere nobody has any cause to go,' said Banks, looking around the dark wood interior of the pub as though Nancy might have stashed Emily behind the bar. 'In a town as small as this one there's not going to be many places like that. Most of the buildings are in use, either for personal or business purposes. Even if they aren't in use, they'll be accessed on a regular basis and Emily has been missing for two weeks now. It has to be somewhere that nobody will have accessed in that time.'

'I think there are quite a few mills in the vicinity that aren't in use,' said Kitt. 'Maybe Nancy found one that isn't accessed very often and decided to hold Emily there?'

'Maybe,' said Banks. 'It might be worth drawing up a list of any that haven't been repurposed. Unless you're working on refurbishing a building like that, there's not much reason to go out to it. I suppose there's also the possibility that some of the repurposed ones are used as holiday homes and the owners might not use them that often. Although, it is a bit of a risk if it's not your property. The owners could come along to access their property at any time. If Emily's alive, she probably has a good idea who her captor is. So, Nancy would have to be completely sure that nobody would access the building in her absence. I'm not sure an old mill – repurposed or not – provides that kind of assurance?'

'No, you're probably right,' said Kitt with a dismissive wave. 'Nancy hasn't left any other part of her scheme to chance. There's no reason to think she would have done that with something so crucial as this.'

'What if she's not holding Emily in a building? Maybe she's holding her in a car somewhere. Like a car boot maybe?' said Grace.

'That would definitely offer the control factor. But the odds of somebody surviving in a car boot for two weeks are not high,' said Banks. 'It's warm enough during the day but even in a garage, temperatures will drop low at night. Their body temperature would never properly recover from day to day. They'd essentially die of hypothermia.'

'So, it would have to be somewhere that was sheltered enough for Emily to survive,' said Kitt. 'Somewhere nobody has any reason to go any more.'

'Wait a minute ... ' said Grace, her eyes widening and

grabbing Kitt's arm. 'Didn't Maya Garrison tell you in her interview that the school moved all its students and all its records over to a new campus?'

'Oh, good God,' said Kitt, her eyes now just as wide as Grace's. 'Yes, she did. That's right.'

'What happened to the old building? Was it demolished?' said Grace.

'No,' said Banks, kicking herself for not thinking about this sooner. 'She said it was derelict. If Nancy really did do all this because of what happened at school then what better place to hold one of your tormentors than the very building where they committed all their wrongs against you?'

Banks downed the rest of her drink. 'Come on, we can't sit on this. If Nancy's the only person who knows Emily's there, and we assume she's restrained her, just how Siobhan was restrained before she was murdered, then she'd be reliant on Nancy for food and water.'

'Emily might also be able to tell us things Nancy has done,' Kitt said, pulling on a red fleece jacket. 'Testify against her. Maybe Nancy is relying on the police not finding Emily until it's too late.'

'I know we're in a rush but we'd better pick up some small supplies on the way,' said Grace. 'A couple of bottles of water at least. If we do find Emily there, she's likely to be dehydrated.'

Banks stood from her bar stool. She nodded and pulled

her car keys out of her pocket. 'All right, one stop. But then we've got to get to that old school right away. Maybe there's nothing there. But at this point, we can't leave anything to chance.'

CHAPTER THIRTY-THREE

'Yep,' said Grace as she looked in at the old, stone school building in the near darkness, which was almost completely overgrown with vines and ivy. 'This looks like the kind of place that nobody gets out of alive.'

'Would you give over?' said Kitt. 'If you didn't watch so many ridiculous horror films you wouldn't say such stupid things.'

'Come on,' said Banks, pushing open the old iron entrance gates which creaked in their own dilapidated agony as the three women squeezed into the courtyard.

As Banks approached the entrance, she was careful to slowly ease open the main door, though it did take quite a bit of rattling to get the damn thing to cooperate. A padlock dangled off a chain from one of the handles. It looked like it had been cut. By Nancy? Or had a rough sleeper found a way to break in?

Chunks of crumbled stone lay all around and the smell

of stagnant water from the abandoned drains filled the air. You didn't have to be an architect to know that this structure wasn't sound. The last thing Banks needed was to explain to Halloran how Kitt had suffered a life-threatening injury – or worse – from falling masonry, so she would have to be on full alert during their search for Emily. At least they knew that Nancy would not be joining them here for some big showdown. She was in the interrogation room and could do nothing to stop them. Exactly what they would uncover in this place, she couldn't say. Given Nancy's choice of murder weapon, however, and the victims she selected for her revenge, the old campus of Andaby Comprehensive seemed almost inevitably the place where the truth would come out.

'Torches on,' said Banks. She and Grace switched on the torch settings on their phones, while Kitt, ever prepared, pulled out an actual torch from her satchel.

'Follow me, step where I step,' said Banks. 'I don't need any blood on my conscience, if you don't mind.'

Kitt and Grace for once nodded their agreement without further comment.

Carefully stepping around chunks of rubble, and piles of leaves that had blown in from the broken window, Banks made slow but steady progress down what she assumed was the old atrium and main corridor of the school. Beneath all of the dust you could just make out the black and white tiling that had no doubt once been brand new and gleaming.

It seemed as though the school had been mostly cleaned out before it had been left to rot. There were very few objects left behind. One locker, that looked as though the door had been smashed in, stood in the corner. An old chair, which was missing a leg, lay upturned on the floor, but otherwise the building was empty.

'What was that scuttling sound?' Grace asked, a concerned note in her voice.

Banks smiled. 'We're in the country here, I imagine all manner of little beasties have made this place their home now that the humans have moved out.'

'Oh, great,' said Grace. 'The one field trip I actually get to go on and it has to involve vermin. Couldn't we catch a case on a luxury cruise again? That was much more my style. Or maybe on an exotic island somewhere in the Bahamas that has only twenty inhabitants, so you know the murderer is one of them and can very easily narrow the field. Can we try and make sure our next case is like that?'

Under ordinary circumstances Kitt would have tried to silence her assistant, but it was obvious from the way Grace was wittering that she was scared. Understandably so. Nobody would have chosen to enter this abandoned school unless they absolutely had to. There are many words that could be used to describe Kitt Hartley. Some of them less flattering than others. But cruel was not one of them.

'Grace, you get to do plenty of field work that doesn't

involve vermin, so please just do your best to focus on the task in hand, will you?' said Kitt, her voice gentle.

'All right. But I'd really rather not spend any longer than necessary in here, so let's start thinking creatively. Where do you think Nancy might be holding Emily?' said Grace. 'The sooner we figure that out, the sooner we can be . . . anywhere else.'

'It won't be somewhere easy to get to,' said Banks, shining her torch up at the classroom windows as she passed to make sure there were no obvious signs of life inside. 'I'm sure the odd vagrant must use this place as somewhere to rest their head. Nancy will have figured that out, and, if she's hiding anyone here, they'll be somewhere a bit out of the way like . . . ' Banks shone her torch up at a door that had a small sign on it. The lettering had almost faded away but it was just readable.

'Oh, no,' said Grace. 'The boiler room? Nothing good happens in there.'

'Exactly,' said Banks, opening the door. Cobwebs hung over the door frame. Banks took a breath and strode through them, working her way down a set of concrete steps that at first glance seemed to go on forever. Kitt and Grace followed closely behind. Grace asked every three seconds or so if there were any spiders on her, while Kitt reassured her that there weren't.

At last, they reached the bottom of the stairs. Banks flashed her torch over the labyrinth of pipes and gate valves.

At first, she saw nothing but then her light flitted over something. She shot the torch beam back a few inches. It was a human head, sagging forward, the long, bleached hair hanging over the face. Emily had had hair like that, in the picture they'd seen of her.

'Look,' Banks said, barely able to breathe as she approached the body, which she could see from just a few paces away was zip tied to nearby pipes. The body looked thin. Nancy had been starving her, dehydrating her. Was she alive? It was impossible to say just by looking at her. She wasn't moving, that was for sure.

'Emily?' Banks said, and reached out a hand to brush some of the hair out of the body's face. 'Emily?' she tried again. And this time the face stirred. Jumped almost.

Emily's eyes widened as she realized there were people in the room with her and then a tear slid down her cheek. 'Help me,' she croaked out. It may have been the most heart-breaking sound Banks had ever heard. 'Please, help me,' she croaked a second time. And that's when the hysterics began.

'Nancy!' Emily screamed, though her throat must have been raw from dehydration. 'She's crazy! She's going to kill me! Help me! Please!'

'It's OK,' Banks said with tears in her eyes as she pulled out her penknife and cut the zip ties. The second Emily's hands were free, Grace supported her. She was so weak she could barely stand. Kitt passed her a bottle of water they'd picked up from a small garage in the centre of town. She tipped her head back and drank without stopping until the bottle was empty. Kitt presented her with another one and she did the same again.

'Please,' Emily whimpered. 'Help me. Nancy. She's going to kill me.'

'I won't let her,' said Banks, as Emily buried her face into Grace's neck and sobbed.

CHAPTER THIRTY-FOUR

The following morning, the passenger side door to Charley's car opened and Robinson slid inside. Banks had parked on the crest of a hill overlooking Andaby, but the rain was making it difficult to admire the view, fogging up the windscreen and obscuring the scenery with sheets of water streaming against the glass.

'I haven't seen rain like this in a long time,' Banks said to Robinson.

'Lucky you,' Robinson replied. 'I'm half-woman, half-duck living out here.'

Banks chuckled and let out a big sigh. 'Thanks for offering a bit of a debrief of the case. I know you didn't have to do that, but after everything it would be nice to have some closure. Though, I must admit, I don't want to be too long. The doctors don't expect Emily to wake up anytime soon but I would like to be there when she at last opens her eyes.

Just so someone who found her can offer a little context in case she doesn't remember.'

'You're a very caring person Charley,' Robinson said. 'You should let that part of you shine a little more, you know?'

Banks smiled but at first didn't quite know what to say to that comment. Would Banks like to let her caring side show a little more? Yes, that would be preferable to hiding her softer side away all the time. But when you were in a line of work where you dealt with people like Nancy, that was difficult. Vulnerability was beautiful but it could also be exploited. Was it wise to risk that kind of exploitation when you were brushing up against the region's most hardened hearts every day?

'I promise I'll try,' Banks said. That was the best promise she could make in light of recent events. 'Now come on, you can't keep me in suspense any longer. Has Nancy caved and confessed?'

'No such luck,' said Robinson. 'Though I wish you could have seen her face when she found out Emily had been recovered alive. That clearly wasn't part of her plan. I've never seen skin turn grey before, she looked like a member of the undead.'

'Which probably means Emily knows everything about what she did,' said Banks. 'I don't know exactly what her plan was with the kidnapping of Emily but the few words the poor woman blurted out when we found her made it clear that Nancy was at some point going to kill her.

If Nancy still views Emily as her school tormenter, she might have tried to torture Emily by making her believe she was going to kill her and then putting it off until a later date. That's definitely some of the behaviour you'd expect to see from someone with serious control issues.'

'Which, I think we can safely say, Nancy has,' said Robinson. 'And that's putting it politely. The moment she found out that Emily had been found alive she refused to say another thing and asked for her lawyer, so I'm not holding my breath on a fully signed confession.'

'Surely, it's only a matter of time before you uncover something at her property that incriminates her?' said Banks. 'Nobody that obsessive is getting rid of everything that relates to their revenge fantasy. You'll find something, somewhere. You mark my words. It'll just be a matter of figuring out exactly where she's hiding it.'

'I know, you're right,' said Robinson. 'We've already recovered a burner phone from the bins outside her property. We think it might be the phone she used to send the messages to DuPont. Tech are getting the data off that now.'

'That's a really big win,' said Banks.

'Yeah, it is,' said Robinson, 'but I must admit, I've got these strange mixed feelings about the whole thing. Nancy's conviction is going to hit Andaby hard. She was known by everyone as a very quiet, kind person. I think this case might actually have the capacity to affect how neighbourly everyone is to each other around here. When someone who is seemingly that much of a sweetheart turns out to be a murderer, well, people aren't going to know who to trust. Mind you, I'm amazed I haven't had the Andaby Knitting Circle braying on my door protesting her release.'

'After my experience with them, I have to say I'm a little surprised by that too,' said Banks. 'They were definitely covering for Nancy, although I don't think it was a conscious effort to pervert justice. They just couldn't get their heads around the idea that their little Nancy would do something so heinous.'

'To be honest, I'm the one who booked her for it and even I'm taking some getting used to the idea,' said Robinson. 'I'm not sure if she really planned on carrying out the murder all along. I have a suspicion that it might have been this little fantasy she played out in her head from time to time. And each time she revisited it, the fantasy got more detailed, and then the need to make it real overtook her. I don't think this is something she truly planned on doing since she was eighteen years old, although maybe that's me trying to comfort myself.'

'I'd say that theory is the most likely,' said Banks. 'If she just wanted to commit murder, I think she would have done so before now, even with the risk of getting caught. This felt very specific, and, as you say, was probably a fantasy that she at last decided to make real.'

'I try not to dwell on the fact that something like that can be considered by some a fantasy,' said Robinson.

'I know what you mean. I'm not sure if it's OK to ask this but what about Ewan?' said Banks. 'I assume he'll be headed back to the clink at the first opportunity?'

'No way around that, I'm afraid,' said Robinson. 'But I have made sure to underline just how instrumental your brother's cooperation was in the apprehension of Siobhan's killer. If he keeps his head down, he should be out again in a few years on good behaviour.'

'I really appreciate that. I know you didn't have to do it. He's lucky that you're willing to. Maybe after a second stint in prison, he'll learn to make more sensible life choices,' said Banks, trying not to think about what her brother had said about not being able to make it another day in prison. Perhaps she'd given him enough to hope for. A reconciliation between the two of them when he got out. She would have to check in with him as regularly as possible to make sure he remembered there was a world outside. One that he could be a part of again if he just hung on. 'I sort of understand why he was manipulated by Nancy. I suppose we all were to a certain extent. But arson is a pretty serious offence to get mixed up in for a woman you've only been dating a few months.'

Robinson shrugged. 'She did use his personal history against him though. She essentially told him she was in the same position he was in twenty years ago. All he'll have been thinking is how he wished somebody had stuck their neck out for *him*.'

'I suppose that should have been me, in the absence of anyone else,' said Banks.

'I'm sorry, I didn't mean—' Robinson began, but Banks waved to cut her off.

'You don't owe me any apologies, for anything.' Banks made eye contact with Robinson at this point to make sure she knew exactly what she meant by this. It was clear from the fact that she had withheld information, and from the fact that she'd seen fit to test Banks's loyalty, that Robinson had secretly been in conflict about how far she could really trust Banks when it came to the issue of her brother. As far as Banks was concerned, these reactions were completely reasonable under the circumstances and she didn't want to do a post-mortem. The main thing was, Nancy would serve time for what she had done. Emily was safely at the hospital getting the care she needed, and Ewan would get a second chance at freedom, if he just held on long enough. All things considered, the whole situation couldn't have turned out much better than that.

'I suppose I better ask the big question before I get off to the hospital to see Emily,' said Banks. 'Does DI Graves know anything about my involvement in closing the case?'

'No,' said Robinson. 'I did tell him that you had been one of the people who found Emily, but I emphasized that Kitt was a private investigator who happened to be in the area, and you were just one of her companions. I'm not sure if he bought it but, to be honest, I think so long as Nancy goes down for what happened, that's all he cares about. I shouldn't need your testimony to send Nancy down. Not between Ewan's testimony and Emily's testimony, so I think you can rest easy in the knowledge that this time you've managed to fly under the radar.'

'How nice it will be to have a job to go back to once my honeymoon is over,' said Banks.

'Well, just for the record, if you do ever go for a DI job in Bradford, I for one would be very happy to work with you again. And next time, I might even let you take some credit for the work you do.'

CHAPTER THIRTY-FIVE

After her conversation with Robinson, Banks had checked in on Emily at the hospital every day. It had been three days since she'd recovered her in that old boiler room at the now disintegrating original campus of Andaby Comprehensive. The nurses had told her that Emily had had odd bouts of consciousness but that she hadn't been particularly lucid during them. She was suffering from exhaustion and thus understandably spent most of the time resting. Hardly surprising after the ordeal she'd been through.

While Emily had been sleeping, Banks had not been idle. The wedding was now just a week away. With this in mind, much of her time had been spent making the final arrangements with Evie. Never one to miss the opportunity to make an entrance – especially an entrance with a vintage twist – Evie had begged Banks to keep the tradition of her walking down the aisle to be given away. It meant a lot to Evie's parents who, considering they were divorced, were definitely more conservative than most of the people she and Evie spent time with. Of course, although she deemed it a deeply old-fashioned sentiment indeed, Banks wasn't really in the habit of denying the woman she loved the things she wanted most. Thus, she had agreed.

On top of this, Banks had made regular phone calls to Robinson so she was informed about any leaps forward in closing the case. At some point between now and the big day Banks made a note to visit Kitt at the agency. Not just for a debrief on the case but to thank her for all she did. Banks was fairly convinced she would have gone out of her mind trying to figure out her brother's involvement in all of this if it hadn't been for Kitt and Grace.

During her visits to the hospital, Banks spent most of her time mesmerized by the digital blips of Emily's vitals beeping and lighting up the machine she was attached to, and this moment was no different.

Except for one tiny factor.

Emily's eyes flickered open.

They focused on the room.

They filled with tears.

And Banks knew that Emily had remembered in an instant all that had happened to her over the last two weeks. Based on some of the things the nurses had said about Emily's condition, it's not a period in one's life anybody would want to remember. Nancy had essentially left her there to starve in the dark. Banks had deliberately kept the lights in the room low but still Emily squinted from weeks of light deprivation. Some people had endured wartime torment and received better treatment than Emily had at the hands of her captor.

'It's OK, said Banks. 'You don't have to talk or anything. You might not remember because you were very sick, but I was one of the women who found you. The first thing I want you to know is that you are safe. The person we believe did this to you is in police custody, and cannot hurt you any more.'

Emily nodded and raised her hand slowly to reach for a glass of water. Banks was out of her chair in a split second and brought a straw to Emily's lips. The doctors had been rehydrating her body with tubes for the past seventy-two hours but still her throat must be parched.

'I remember you,' Emily managed to croak out. 'After what you did, I'll never forget you.'

Banks smiled. 'I was just doing my job. But I don't mind telling you that finding you alive was one of the biggest reliefs in living memory. I'm going to need to let some people know that you're awake. When you're all healed, we can see to making sure that the person who did this to you gets the justice they deserve and can never do anything like it to anyone else.'

Emily tried to form the 'n' sound with her mouth but hesitated and shook as the name passed over her lips. 'Nancy,' she said.

'There will be time for the full story later. You can rest. You don't have to tell me now.'

'I do,' Emily said. 'I do have to tell you now. Because I don't want it to live inside me any more. I need to let it go. I need to let it go.'

Banks wanted more than anything to squeeze Emily's arm to reassure her that she had nothing to fear. That she didn't have to worry about anything. But it was not prudent to touch a trauma victim uninvited. When she was ready for physical contact again Emily would make it clear. Until then, Banks would just have to do what she could verbally.

That desire, though, to essentially spit the story out straight away was something Banks had seen on many an occasion when somebody had been through the unthinkable. It was as if the act of saying it out loud vaporized it in some unquantifiable way. Not everyone was able to speak about their trauma, but those that could never wanted to wait any longer than necessary to get it out of their system. To such people, the act seemed to be almost like throwing up. The worst thing in the world while it was happening but then afterwards everything felt that little bit better, that little bit more settled.

'You'll be able to do that, I promise. Maybe not absolutely right away, but soon. And the second we have all the information we need you won't have to talk about it any more. You'll be able to put everything behind you.'

Emily took in a deep breath and slowly let it out.

'She knocked me unconscious, you know. I was walking home and . . . and . . . when I woke up, I was . . .'

'In the boiler room,' Banks finished for her. There was little point in allowing Emily to struggle over words. Anything she told her now wasn't going to be taken in evidence. That would need to be done officially. If Emily wanted to tell her story right now, Banks would make sure that she helped her anyway she could.

Emily nodded and tears started to flow down her cheeks. 'She said she was going to kill me. Said she was going to write a note, just tell everyone I killed Siobhan. Said she would make it look like a suicide, like I'd gone crazy, and they would think I haven't eaten or drunk anything because I was crazy.'

Emily paused then, as though she was trying to rearrange all the pieces of the story into an order that made sense. After a few moments, she was able to speak again.

'I couldn't ask her why she was doing it. If I talked, she would put tape over my mouth. In the end I gave up. Trying to scream. Trying to talk. But I knew the answer anyway. She was doing it because of the way Siobhan and me treated her, all those years ago. It was a punishment.'

'It wasn't Nancy's place to punish you, not like that,' said Banks.

'You must think I deserved all this,' Emily said, as more tears flowed down her cheeks.

'I don't think that at all. I think when we're eighteen

we all do some things that we will later wish we hadn't. If we were all judged on the people we were at eighteen we would have no chance. It takes time in this world, to figure out who you are and what you want to stand for. We can't have it all figured out at that age.'

As she spoke, Banks felt something strange happen. She thought about her brother. Not in the resentful, dismissive light she had done for as long as she could remember. Instead, she thought about her twenty-four-year-old brother and the mistake he made. Banks had been quick to judge him, and she had never let him forget that grave error. Maybe, given somebody had died by his hand, that was the right thing. But she had spent the last twenty years treating him as though what he had done was premeditated. That he meant to do wrong. But unlike Nancy, he hadn't set out to kill somebody in cold blood. And shouldn't intention count for something in this world? He had been a young man. He didn't have it all figured out yet, and he had paid a heavy price for that. They all had.

'I know it will sound like I'm trying to wriggle out of what I did all those years ago,' Emily half whispered. 'And I don't mean to speak badly of the dead. But the best thing that ever happened to me was the fight I had with Siobhan. It was only after I got some space from her, made new friends, I realized how scared I'd been of her. That's why I'd always do what she said. No matter how cruel or unforgivable it was. Nancy didn't know that I was bullied by Siobhan too. She didn't know that when she kidnapped me.'

At this, Emily broke down into uncontrollable sobs.

'I really can't imagine what you've been through,' said Banks.

'I don't want to imagine it ever again,' Emily said through her tears. 'How am I going to move forward? Be in the house by myself? Walk home from work? Forget it all?'

'My first bit of advice would be not to try and tackle all of that in one go. That's a lot for anyone,' Banks said, a warm smile on her lips. 'But if there's one thing I've learned about human beings being a police officer, we are all more resilient than we know. Not because we want to be. Who wants to be resilient? Nobody wants that, not really. We're resilient because we need to be. Because that's the world we live in, and sometimes just living through the next moment is the biggest challenge. But after what you've been through, I know you can meet it. I know you can keep going and I believe you will do good in this world.'

'What's your name?'

'Officially, Detective Sergeant Charlotte Banks, but my friends call me Charley, and, in case it wasn't obvious, you can call me Charley.'

'Thank you, Charley, for not giving up on me.'

'I think not giving up is going to be my new specialty, and I think I've got you to thank for it.'

Banks felt suddenly very fortunate that she wasn't at work at that moment and so had the luxury to be here and support Emily. If she'd been on her usual shift pattern, she would have already rolled onto the next case. She may have had the odd update from the hospital about when she could go in to question Emily but there wouldn't have been time for the kind of follow-up she wanted to do. It wasn't just the fact that she had been glad to find Emily alive. It was what Emily represented. Ewan could have just kept quiet. He could have refused to cooperate, even if it had meant more jail time. But instead he chose to help Banks and Robinson understand the full details of Siobhan's murder which in turn revealed that Nancy was behind Emily's disappearance too. When Banks thought of Emily, she would think of how glad she was to find her still breathing, still with hope left in her lungs. But she would also think of the life Ewan saved. It didn't erase the life he had taken but it was one step closer in the direction of atonement.

CHAPTER THIRTY-SIX

Banks flipped down the hatch on one of the holding cell doors at Andaby Police Station and looked through to her brother. She wasn't really ready for this. To see Ewan go back to the slammer. After everything that had transpired, however, neither of them had a choice in that matter. It was still quite surprising to Banks that after a twenty-year sentence he would have done anything to risk going back to an environment that, by his own admission, he didn't know if he could survive. The difference was that last time Banks had never wanted to see Ewan again, whereas, now, the thought that this might be the last time they spoke left her petrified. He had hinted that he might not be able to endure even another week inside a prison cell. Banks didn't know what lay in store for the future of their relationship; she only knew she wanted to find out.

Robinson had agreed to explain how helpful and cooperative Ewan had been when he realized Nancy was a murderer.

How his testimony had led to them being able to acquire a warrant to search Nancy's property and recover concrete evidence that she was the one who had ended Siobhan Lange's life that night. On this basis, she thought Ewan was looking at around four years back in prison, possibly three years if he got out on good behaviour. Banks could only hope that, despite his concerns that returning to incarceration would be the end of him, regular visits from her might offer enough hope for him to keep going.

When she lifted the hatch, he had been sitting on the small wooden bench attached to the wall, but when he realized it was his sister looking through the small square of light he stood up and walked over to greet her.

'I've just been given a few minutes to say my goodbyes,' said Banks. 'But I thought you'd want to know that we found Emily – alive.'

Ewan scrunched his eyes shut and a single tear fell down his cheek. Banks could count on one hand the number of times she'd seen her brother shed a tear over anything, even his own conviction. To her surprise, she was quite choked up by his reaction, but did what she could to keep her tone steady as she spoke. 'She's told us that Nancy was the one who kidnapped her. That Nancy planned to fake Emily's suicide and pin Siobhan's murder on her if the plan to place blame on Adam DuPont or Siobhan's co-workers failed. She told us a lot more too. Her testimony should mean that you avoid murder charges.'

What Banks couldn't tell Ewan was that even though Nancy had refused to comment any further after Emily was recovered, the police had found one vital piece of evidence hidden under a floorboard in Nancy's home. A blue graduation sash that had Siobhan Lange's touch DNA all over it. Sentimentality was so often the tragic flaw of a murderer. This discovery would prevent Nancy Murphy from spinning any more of her stories in the courtroom. There was no more denying what she did.

'But no matter how good your intentions,' Banks continued, 'you've broken the conditions of your parole and you will be going back to prison for a few years.'

Ewan nodded. 'I know. Robinson explained the likely terms. I'm . . . I'm sorry Charley. Nancy's not my usual type, you might have noticed. But I thought when I got on with her, she would be a good influence, you know? I wanted to stay away from trouble. Trouble found me, and somehow I – I suppose I just didn't make the right choices. Story of my life really.'

'It's not the whole story though, is it?' said Banks. 'You had a choice, when you were sitting in the interrogation room with me a few days back. You had a choice about whether or not to talk, and confess to the arson, go back to prison and potentially save a girl's life or stay quiet, possibly save your skin and potentially let another person die. It took courage to do what you did, Ewan.'

'You really think so?' he said, his eyes glassy.

Banks nodded. 'I do. When you made that choice. When we found Emily alive because of what you did and what you told us. It made me proud to be your sister again. Not because you are perfect but because you are imperfect and still found the strength to do the right thing.'

'I don't know what to say,' Ewan said. 'Knowing you were proud to be my sister, even for a minute there, it's all I've wanted for the past twenty years. To not feel like an utter disgrace to my family.'

'Well, I can't say that you're there yet, but you're certainly on your way,' Banks said, a grudging grin forming on her lips.

'I hope I see that smile again,' said Ewan.

Banks swallowed, trying to keep her cool. 'Serve your time. Stay the distance and try again. When you get out, I'll be waiting for you.'

'That doesn't sound very comforting,' Ewan said, managing to offer her half a smile.

'It's a promise, not a threat, honest it is,' Banks said. 'I feel like we've come a long way together in the last few days. Further than we have in the last twenty years. I will want to see you when you come out so hang in there, if not for yourself, then for me.'

'I know I wasn't invited anyway; I didn't deserve to be. But I really wish I could have seen you get married, Charley. I'll be thinking about you on that day. Hoping that one day I'll be able to sit down with you and your wife not just as people with blood ties, but as a proper family.'

Banks took a deep breath. Could that really ever happen? After everything her brother had put her through? She had no idea. But for the first time in a very long time, it's what she wanted. More than anything. 'I'm going to hope for that too,' was all she could think to say in response. With that she smiled at her brother and held on even tighter to the tears that were threatening to fall.

Slowly, she began to close the hatch.

'I love you, Charley,' Ewan whispered, just before the hatch shut completely.

Banks pulled the hatch down once again and looked at her brother. He may have been older than her but she could see the fear in his eyes at the thought of going back to prison. 'I love you, Ewan,' she said. Of all the words she had expected to say to her brother in this situation, somehow those ones hadn't featured in any of the scenarios she'd imagined in her head. But despite Ewan's past, despite all that he'd put her through in the last week, and before, those words were true. Strange, that no amount of distance or time or disappointment had changed that.

Slowly, she closed the hatch on the door and walked down the corridor towards the entrance of the police station. As she did so, she could not think of her brother back in that cell. Or what the prison environment might do this time round to the boy who used to be her hero.

CHAPTER THIRTY-SEVEN

Banks walked through the door of Hartley and Edwards Investigations on Walmgate. The second she had opened the door, however, she wished that there was some kind of magic mechanism to close it again. For sitting in a chair in front of Kitt's desk was none other than Ruby Barnett. Today, her unique fashion sense saw her dressed in a tie-dye cloak that stretched from her neck to her toes. Banks had absolutely no idea what could possibly be underneath that much linen, and, frankly, she was happy not to find out. When it came to Ruby, all bets were off.

The agency itself was just a small office unit. One of several along this row of shops, but Banks was immediately struck by just how many books there were in the room. Halloran was always talking about the way in which Kitt turned any available space into a mini library. And, indeed, Banks had seen Kitt's living room, which also greatly resembled the library she worked in – as did this office space. It seemed a bit odd for a PI, a job title that Banks had always associated with technology and gadgets. Instead, this room was essentially a specialist book section in criminal profiling and investigative method. Actually, when Banks looked at it that way, she wouldn't mind spending a bit of time here. So long as she had some noise-cancelling headphones to block out Grace's distracting antics.

'So, you see,' Ruby said to Kitt, an expression of great anguish painted across her face, I lost my third eye in the ether somewhere, and I thought I could hire you to track it down.'

'Yes, well although I always appreciate new business opportunities, that's not really our thing, Ruby,' said Kitt. 'The supernatural is more your arena.'

'I know,' said Ruby, 'but I've already said a prayer to Saint Anthony. I don't know what else I'm supposed to do.'

'Yes ... well perhaps ... perhaps this was meant to happen,' said Kitt, with a triumphant note in her voice.

'You what?' said Ruby, her eyes narrowing at Kitt's words.

'Think about it!' said Kitt. 'You're always telling me how everything is meant to be and that the fates decide every single grand choice in our life, so maybe the universe wants you to try getting by without a third eye for a while. Maybe it will be returned to you when that time has passed and you have learned whatever lesson it is that you're meant to learn.'

'I hadn't thought about that,' said Ruby. 'I'm not sure, you know. I need to get home and consult me runes about it.'

'Yes, why don't you do that? I would say that the runes are going to be more help than me in this instance.'

'All right, love, I'll see you tomorrow,' said Ruby.

'I have no doubt,' said Kitt as Ruby hobbled out of the room, nodding at Banks as she left.

'Hi, Charley, sorry about that, but I don't like to just turf her out, you know.'

'No, I know. The case of the missing third eye doesn't quite have the right ring to it though, does it?' Banks said with a chuckle.

Kitt shook her head, 'Drink?'

'Tea?'

'Actually,' said Kitt, 'after that I think I could do with something a little bit stronger. Kitt produced a small bottle of sherry from her drawer and pulled two glasses off the shelf from behind her.

'I can safely pour us a measure apiece because I know you're not on duty,' said Kitt.

'That's right, I am making the most of that I can tell you,' said Banks.

'Is everything OK?'

'Yes, everything is fine, I just wanted to let you know that Robinson has got a court date for prosecuting Nancy. So, it looks as though that's going to finally be put to rest in the next couple of months.'

'I'm glad to hear it,' Kitt said, handing Charley a glass of sherry.

'It looks as though her lawyers are going to play the sympathy card. The expectation is that Nancy will plead guilty and explain all the bullying she was subjected to. They may even go for a plea of diminished responsibility, claim that what happened affected Nancy's mental health.'

Kitt nodded. 'It is difficult, isn't it? Nothing justifies murder, but there are so many things that aren't against the law – but are most definitely crimes – that people are never held accountable for. Like bullying at school.'

'We do not live in a black and white world. If I didn't know that when I started this case, I'm certainly more than aware of it now,' said Banks, taking a sip of her sherry.

'I take it life in Andaby has pretty much got back to normal and DuPont was released without charge?'

'Yeah, Robinson wanted to know if I was going to press charges for GBH against the guy but I decided it wasn't worth it. My head has healed well, and he was in a pretty desperate situation. Emily verified that there was no truth to the rumours Siobhan had spread about her and DuPont. She also said that they weren't fighting over him at the graduation at all. Emily had worn a new shade of lipstick and Siobhan had kindly told her she looked like a prostitute.'

'What? That's what the big fight was over?'

'I think it was the last straw after years of living in Siobhan's shadow, to be honest,' said Banks.

'At least Siobhan didn't succeed in sullying DuPont's

reputation, though I don't know if we can say the same,' said Kitt.

'I don't think word of his arrest got out to be honest,' said Banks. 'The police weren't allowed to name him because he hadn't been officially charged. There might be the odd rumble but I think, in spite of some very bad choices, the DuPonts will move on from the experience without too much trouble.'

'Did Robinson ever explain why she withheld information from us about how Siobhan was murdered?' said Kitt. 'Was it just about keeping the important case information under wraps, do you think?'

'Aye, pretty much,' said Banks. 'Although I get the impression she didn't know quite how far she could trust me at the time. The thing with a murder investigation is, as you've seen, you can't really afford to trust anyone. Even someone who protests that they're only there to help you.'

'It's not a guarantee that they're telling the truth, I know,' said Kitt.

'So, I think she just had to keep her cards close to her chest and see what shook out as each step in the investigation unfolded. There're certainly no hard feelings between us,' said Banks. 'I understand that nothing, not even loyalty to your fellow officer, can come before justice.'

'Of course it can't,' said Kitt. 'It was a very difficult position for Robinson to find herself in. But what about our Emily, how is she doing?'

'Better each day if the text messages are anything to go by. She wanted me to say thank you to you again, and I also wanted to say thank you,' said Banks.

'I think you already have, haven't you?' said Kitt.

'Not really. I haven't seen you since we found Emily, and I've been busy helping her back on her feet and making sure all her statements got taken; that she wasn't just left to fall through the cracks in the system, you know.'

'Well, that's much more important than coming to say thank you to me,' said Kitt.

'Yes and no,' said Banks. 'One of the reasons that I knew Evie was the right person for me was that I felt like I could open up to her straight away. Yes, I can still be a bit guarded from time to time but if she asks me a straight question, I'll give her a straight answer and she knows that.'

'Good old Evie. As strong a listener as she is a talker, and that is a rare find I can tell you. Just ask Grace.'

Banks grinned at Kitt's comment. 'What I'm trying to say is that I don't relate to people that well. It's my own doing, of course. Nothing to do with anyone else. But I never forget when somebody goes out of their way to help me like you did. I may not have made the biggest effort to get to know you in the last six years or so but I'd really like that to change. I think it could be good for me. I think it could be good for you, and I definitely think it will be good for Evie.'

'If it's good for Evie, you can always count me in . . . Er, except to one of those ridiculous crash diets she's prone to going on. Please, no more of those. I don't suppose you could put in your vows that she's no longer to try anything like that, could you?'

'Sadly, I think that might be slightly infringing on her free will.'

'Yes, tricky isn't it, that slippery slope with free will. But,' Kitt said, 'I suppose it's a good thing when it comes down to it. It gives people the chance to choose to be better, like your brother did.'

'Yeah,' said Banks. 'In our line of work, it's easy to forget that sometimes people do choose that.'

'I think that's the biggest challenge of the work. Looking into the darkness and searching for the one candle that is burning. Oh, good grief, I'm sorry. I'm starting to sound like Ruby. I think she's starting to rub off on me.'

'You can get arrested for doing that in public, you know.'

'Oh, give over, you're as bad as Mal, though admittedly still more restrained than Evie,' said Kitt.

'Well, here's to both of them,' said Banks. 'And to both of us too.'

'Cheers,' said Kitt.

CHAPTER THIRTY-EIGHT

'I've worked with you for some years now, Banks, and I think this might be the first time I've ever seen you look nervous,' Halloran said, a twinkle in his eye. The pair were standing at the front of the old Tudor hall Banks and Evie had decided to get married in. It was just a stone's throw from the Minster and was the perfect historical venue for a woman like Evie who loved all things from the past.

Banks was particularly pleased with her wedding attire, as she was wearing a kilt. She loved to wear one on special occasions to reconnect with the country she left behind when she moved to Yorkshire. Though it was only a couple of hundred miles to the border, sometimes it felt like it might as well be two thousand miles due to how busy work kept her. It was rare that she got back to visit her mother, and like so much else in Banks's life from here forward, she very much intended to change that.

'Well, I wish I could say the same to you, sir,' Banks said, responding to Halloran's quip. Halloran had also scrubbed up nicely in the vintage suit Evie had picked out for him, and had apparently decided that his job for the day was to provide light comic relief.

'Banks, it's your wedding day, don't call me "sir".'

'What am I supposed to call you?' said Banks.

'Mal.'

'I can't call you Mal . . . it's like meeting the Queen and calling her Betty.'

'I'll pretend you didn't just compare me to the Queen, if you don't mind,' said Halloran.

Banks grinned. 'Anyway, you're still calling me Banks. Practise what you preach if it's that important to you . . . or is this just a distraction to take my mind off my nerves?'

'Charley,' said Halloran. 'Yes, this is absolutely a ploy to take your mind off your wedding day jitters.'

Banks offered Halloran a grudging smile. 'It's not so much jitters, I've never been surer about anything than I am about marrying Evie.'

'Let me guess,' Halloran said. 'Absent friends?'

Banks nodded.

If she was being honest with herself, she would perhaps have preferred a few more days between the wrapping up of the Calderdale murder and her wedding day. Once Emily was back on her feet there was barely any time at all to make the final arrangements. And somehow, marriage and murder seemed like two sentiments that should be separated by a lot more than that.

Slowly, however, Banks was starting to unwind from the experience. By the time they were on their honeymoon, Banks might even be in a frame of mind where she could relax and enjoy herself. Perhaps that was yet another reason she loved Evie so much: she made sure Banks lightened up once in a while. No easy task given the kind of workload and subject matter she was used to dealing with.

'You probably haven't noticed, but I keep myself at a bit of a distance,' Banks said to Halloran.

'No. You? Really?'

'If you wouldn't mind laying off the sarcasm a little bit, I'm trying to actually open myself up here.'

'Sorry,' said Halloran. 'Yes, I've noticed.'

'Part of it has always been shame, you know, about my family and what certain members have done. But after I marry Evie today, I won't be able to withdraw like that any more. I'll have to let her share in my problems. In my shame. It just feels like a big thing to ask of somebody else. I also can't help but notice that trusting people doesn't get any easier when you do a job like ours. I suppose, what I'm saying is, I really don't want my job title to screw this one up for me.'

Halloran paused. 'Can I speak now?'

'If you must.'

'What you're describing, that's true of any meaningful

relationship. Married or not. But I think marriage is going to be very good for you, Banks, especially marriage to Evie who obviously loves you for who you are. Your brother's actions are his own. You have no control over them. You are not responsible for them. You've no need to feel shame over them. I think you'll wake up on your honeymoon in some exotic locale and realize you've already got a family you can be proud of – the woman lying next to you.'

Banks narrowed her eyes and looked Halloran up and down. 'Have you and Kitt been frequenting that Chinese restaurant on Micklegate again, because you sound like a fortune cookie.'

'For that affrontery, I will not dispense my philosophical nuggets about trust,' said Halloran.

'Oh, come on, sir, don't deny me that special pleasure. It is my wedding day after all.'

'I know you're being sarcastic but I think you could stand to hear what I think. Trust is always the rub. Trust is in some ways more powerful than love. But trust *me* when I say, you and Evie have got it. All you have to do is hold onto it.'

'That almost makes sense, sir. Are you feeling well?'

'Very funny.'

Just then, the music started and Banks turned to see Evie floating down the aisle in a vintage lace tea dress. Her blonde curls bounced as she walked, while a small net veil covered the worst of the facial scars she was still so self-conscious about. She needn't have been. She looked an absolute dream. And Banks would never forget the sight of her slowly, step-by-step making her way to her side. As her bride walked ever closer in time to 'Moon River' sung by Audrey Hepburn, Banks began to ponder what Halloran had said a little more closely.

After what had happened with her brother at that early age, she'd thought the easiest thing was to disconnect. Cut family ties. Never let anybody in. But maybe, rather than not have a family, the smarter choice was to build a new one. Evie was her family now. And they could decide what their future looked like, and how to deal with the old baggage one inevitably carried from the past, together. When both people were sharing the weight, it didn't feel so heavy anyway. Tears rose to Banks's eyes at the thought of no longer having to carry that burden by herself any more. How tiring it had been. How ready she was to feel the lift of someone else bearing some of what she carried. She had believed that carrying it alone was the noble thing to do. But sharing it was actually the brave thing to do. She may not be able to trust her own flesh and blood quite yet, but from this day forward there'd always be at least one person she could turn to.

Ewan wasn't sitting in the congregation today but the symbol of what he had done was. Emily waved at Charley and smiled. She was seated between Grace and Kitt who had made a complete fuss of her since the moment she arrived. She wasn't looking quite so thin. And when she smiled it seemed to Banks that she really meant it. She had only been out of the hospital for a day so it was, quite frankly, something of a miracle that she had managed to make it to the wedding at all. There was still a long way to go but wasn't that true of everyone? Wherever they are at. Whatever they're grappling with.

Banks had always been one of those people who felt they had to figure things out. Perhaps that's why she was so drawn to solving crimes. It was an intellectual challenge – there were elements to figure out and when you did everything made sense, at least for a while. And you were able to restore some order to a world which otherwise felt very chaotic.

What Banks had eventually learned is that not everything can be worked out in your head. You had to feel your way through some experiences, and you might not always get it right first time. The main thing was to accept that just because you don't have all the answers today, doesn't mean you never will. That was the kind of logic she was good at connecting with when it came to her work, less so when it came to emotional relationships. When it came to those, Banks realized, she wanted all of the answers today. She wanted to know that she would be loved. That she wouldn't be betrayed. That everything would work out well. When the truth was that emotional relationships were about saying yes, even when there was a risk that you might never know all that.

Perhaps it was time for Banks to get more comfortable with not knowing. With taking a leap and seeing what happened. She couldn't think of a better way to start than getting married. Than saying yes to a lifetime of uncertainty.

Banks had thought that she already knew the ending of the story between her and Ewan. But as it turned out there was always more to tell. She could only hope that would remain the case, both for herself and Ewan and for her and Evie. She didn't expect marriage to be some magical happily ever after. She just wanted the story to continue, whatever that looked like.

ACKNOWLEDGEMENTS

For every Kitt Hartley adventure that makes it to the page, I remain immensely grateful to my publisher Quercus Books, specifically Stef Bierwerth and Kat Burdon for their continued support of both myself and the series. Heartfelt thanks also go to my agent Joanna Swainson for all her encouragement and excitement over these stories, set in a part of the world we both hold dear.

Dean Cummings and Ann Leander, you are my writing partners and the writing process would be much more lonely without you. No amount of thanks will ever be enough to acknowledge all that you do.

I'm grateful also to Hazel Nicholson for her invaluable advice on police procedure and to Andy Basford for using his time in the mill trade to offer insight into exactly what kinds of industrial machinery and equipment might plausibly kill a person.

To our Dad, I am grateful for you sharing your unbeatable

train knowledge so that the fictional *Frederick William Kitson* train could make its maiden journey.

To my darling Jo – thank you for not nagging me about all the papers on the dining-room table, and all the other slack you cut me. Books wouldn't get written without such undying tolerance and leniency.

Discover where it all began . . .

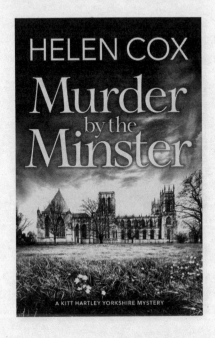

**Meet Kitt Hartley: librarian,
no-nonsense Yorkshirewoman . . . detective?**

Out now in paperback, eBook and audio

**The second page-turning instalment of
the Kitt Hartley Mysteries**

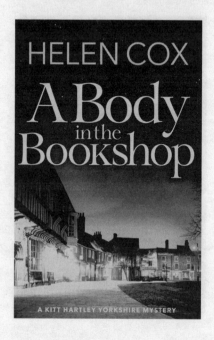

In which Kitt Hartley discovers that some books
are worth dying for . . .

Out now in paperback, eBook and audio

The third Kitt Hartley mystery starring
everyone's favourite librarian-turned-sleuth

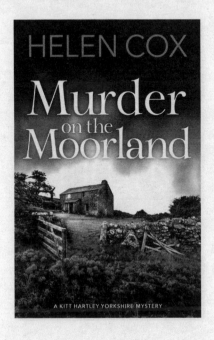

'Brilliantly funny and charming'
Northern Life

Out now in paperback, eBook and audio

QUERCUS

Kitt Hartley is back in the beautiful town of Durham
where not all is as it seems . . .

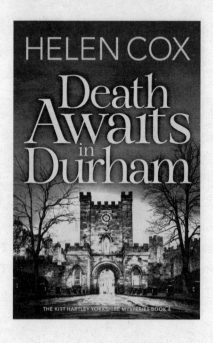

How can you solve a murder when there's no body?

Out now in paperback, eBook and audio